Lily Graham

Christmas at Hope Cottage

ID0708657

Bookouture

Published by Bookouture in 2017
An imprint of StoryFire Ltd.
Carmelite House, 50 Victoria Embankment, London EC4Y 0DZ
www.bookouture.com

ISBN: 978-1-78681-301-5
eBook ISBN: 978-1-78681-300-8

To my family, wild, nutty and wonderful all.

'Nothing can cure the soul but the senses,
just as nothing can cure the senses but the soul.'

Oscar Wilde

ONE

They say that bad things happen in threes.

Emma Halloway, who made a point of *not* believing this sort of thing, found herself, nonetheless, wondering if there wasn't a grain of truth to the superstition after all, on that particular, soggy, Tuesday afternoon, while she lay in a pool of her own blood on the ice-cold concrete, the ambulance sirens getting steadily closer.

She supposed, looking back, that the break-up Post-it left on her morning cup of tea had been the first.

I just can't do this any more.
Pete.
P.S. Might not be the best time to mention it, but just so you know, you're out of washing powder.

The postscript was typical Pete. He was breaking up with you, yes, but heaven forbid you might run out of clean underwear.

It's what had attracted her to him in the first place. His practicality, his evenness, the fact that he was the polar opposite of everything she'd ever known growing up in Whistling, Yorkshire, where time stood still, families passed down centuries-old feuds like genetic maladies and people believed that the food the women in her family made could heal anything, even broken hearts.

Pete had been her ticket *up* the rabbit hole, away from all those Mad Hatters and March Hares. Her ticket away from Jack Allen most of all. The boy she'd given her heart away to at the age of six, who she'd spent the past four years trying to forget.

For a long time after she found Pete's message, while she sat on the kitchen floor surrounded by the shards of the mug she'd thrown onto the linoleum, her eyes filled with hot, unshed tears, she'd tried to work up some blame that didn't point inward. Some anger towards *Pete*. Breaking up with someone on a Post-it note was a fairly shitty way to end a four-year relationship, after all.

When she tried to phone him, it went straight to voicemail. Ten minutes later he texted back a response.

You know I love you. But the only one who seems oblivious to the fact that you don't feel the same way – is you. I can't do this any more. Please, Em, don't reply.

But, of course, she did. Letting sleeping dogs lie wasn't part of her make-up. *Pete! I do love you, don't be silly.*

He didn't respond, so she sent another.

I'll try harder, okay? I'll do anything, please don't do this. We can work this out, can't we?

But he didn't reply. Not even then. Which was when the tears really came.

Emma supposed – lying on the concrete, the pain starting to build, the flashing lights approaching – that the second bad thing was really a result of the first.

She'd decided, once she got up from the kitchen floor, her eyes puffy and swollen, a painful, barbed knot in the space where her heart used to be, that her weekly food column for the *Mail & Ledger*, and this week's topic a cheery look into the history of Christmas food, could wait until the urge to throw herself off her building passed. To help it along, she'd decided to get some fresh air, and some vodka. She took her bicycle, the one Pete had bought her as a surprise in a rare display of spontaneity when she'd mentioned a longing for an old-fashioned bike, complete with wicker basket and floral-print panniers. It was a painful, sunlit memory that she tried to ignore. As she pedalled for the off-licence a few blocks away, she couldn't help noting, somewhat wryly, that the basket, which had enjoyed an innocent life till then, filled with baguettes and flowers and Emma's overflowing research bag, was now about to experience a significant fall from grace as a large bucket for an obscene amount of booze.

Which just goes to show that someone upstairs was having a bit of a laugh, because instead of getting a respite from her awful day, she'd just cycled into the little street round the corner when she was hit by the postal van.

With the bicycle wheels whirring above her head, her blood blooming on the concrete and the sharp, searing pain burgeoning in her skull, Emma might have expected that the day couldn't possibly get any worse, but when the driver asked for her name, Emma realised, suddenly, that actually *it could*.

The driver, whose hands were shaking, looked dismayed when she told him who she was. Eyes wide with horror, he explained, 'I had this package on the passenger seat and it fell off. I took me eye off the road for just a second to put it right, it was just a second mind, but then I hit you. It was like you came out of nowhere. But what's really bizarre,' he said, his large, grey eyes almost popping, 'was – I was on my way to drop this off at your house! Crazy, innit?' he asked, hefting a monstrous package from the car and bringing it down to where she could see. 'Huge fing too,' he muttered.

Which was when Emma started to laugh, the type of laugh when, really, you're about to cry; when you realise how cruel fate can be. A type of laugh she was all too familiar with, being born a Halloway. Emma realised, judging from the size and shape of the package, that her grandmother had sent her the stupid family recipe book. The one she believed would change Emma's life, and get her to admit that her life in London had been nothing but pain and heartache, and now as a result of The Book, everything would get better. Only it had done the opposite, as usual.

Sometime after that she must have passed out.

She woke up in hospital, feeling as if she were being buried alive beneath a slab of cement, and gave a cry of pain and fear. Close to the bed, a nurse with large brown eyes blinked in surprise, backing away from the bed in shock. The next thing she knew, there were a half dozen people in the room, though she couldn't make any of them out clearly. Behind them were strange glittering colours, seeming to flash before her eyes. She blinked, trying to make sense of any of it, but couldn't.

Everyone began speaking at once, creating a cacophony of voices, painful and overwhelming, as if fishhooks were repeatedly pricking her ears. Emma clapped a hand over an ear, and felt another jolting stab of pain, noting through her strained vision that the other hand looked as if it had been pieced together like something for Frankenstein's monster. Protruding from it were scary-looking pins, surrounded by a heavy white cast.

Her throat turned dry in fear. Something had gone horribly wrong. The noises were coming from the people around her and the sounds were unfathomable. At last, she saw a pair of lips move and registered the word 'blanket'. It was the nurse from earlier. She looked down and could see, rather hazily, what looked like a thin blue covering over her legs.

'Take it off!' she hissed. With hesitant, shaking fingers, the nurse lifted it off, and just like that the pain stopped and so did her screams. She blinked back her tears. Struggling to understand. What had they put on her? Why had it hurt so much?

People crowded closer, and her head began to spin, her heart to race. Were they speaking another language?

No. It wasn't that. The sounds were simply incomprehensible, the objects around her a blur; only when she focused hard on their lips did the babble change, miraculously, into words.

Then someone in a white lab coat mouthed three of the scariest words imaginable: *possible brain damage.*

It took a few days before they knew for sure, though Emma didn't need the tests, or the scans, or the people who came into the room with clipboards who kept asking questions, to know it was true; she could feel it. Everything felt wrong.

It had taken some time before her vision registered that the flashing lights weren't coming from her own head but a somewhat garish display of Christmas lights, despite the fact it was only October.

'We start Christmas early here,' explained a brown-haired nurse with gold tinsel threaded in her ponytail, with a small, slightly embarrassed giggle. Emma felt lost, disorientated. In another life she would have shared a grin, understood, as a fellow Christmas lover, appreciated the sentiment and the need for some cheer in a place such as this. Now, all she felt was gratitude when the nurse switched off the lights, providing immediate relief to Emma's overwhelmed senses.

Sounds didn't make sense: she could confuse the sound of the television with the telephone, and the click-clack of heels with the opening of a drawer. She couldn't taste any of the food they brought and it didn't seem to have a scent. When the giggly nurse told her that she'd be taking the flowers some thoughtful friend had sent into the nurses' station due to their powerful perfume, she realised she hadn't been able to smell them either; or anything else, for that matter.

She saw everything in double, which caused splitting headaches and nausea as she felt off balance too. Perhaps worst of all was the way that nothing felt the way it should: a breeze could feel like a flame, while someone's touch might feel like ice, or nothing at all.

After a few days, a doctor explained, sitting on the edge of her bed and making sure that she could read his lips. He'd brought along a small whiteboard with a black marker just in case she couldn't understand him, though she found that impossible to read, as the letters scrambled so much when she tried to focus on them. Luckily, if she concentrated on his mouth the words made sense, though they were hard to face nonetheless: 'As well as your left leg and arm, which were broken, it appears your accident has caused some damage to your olfactory nerve – which has affected your senses. From what we've gathered, the best way to explain it is to picture your senses as if they were sets of wires, and some of these have moved slightly out of place, while others appear to have crossed or been cut off for the moment.'

She nodded. The word she would have used was scrambled, like an egg. The definition wasn't her real interest though, not at this stage; what she wanted was a prognosis, if she could only find the right words. But speech was tricky; she had to think hard those first few days, choose words carefully, hunt for them.

She swallowed, tried to focus on the doctor's face, saw, as if through a fog, blue eyes and a stubbled jaw, several times over like a row of negatives. 'How long will I be like this?' she asked, finally.

'It's hard to say. It may well be temporary; we have every reason to hope that is the case. However…'

Emma looked away. It was funny how just one word could undermine all the ones before it. Yet. But. Nonetheless. However.

With difficulty, she tuned in to the rest of his words, focusing on his lips to match the sounds, but she found little comfort in them.

'I have personally never encountered an injury like this before, and from the literature available, it's unclear – it could be months or…' His voice trailed off and she realised that it was possible she could be like this for a long time, perhaps even permanently.

'Our main concern, however, was that with an injury of this kind you would need care. Or that you may need to be moved to a treatment centre. But luckily, that isn't something you need to worry about.' He permitted himself a small chuckle. 'I dare say you are in rather good – if a little eccentric – hands.'

While Emma was still wearing a puzzled frown, the door opened and an attractive, older woman paused before the entrance. She was tall, slim and wiry. She had wide blue Halloway eyes, the blue of lobelias and Cape starlings and secret springs. Her wild hair perched on her shoulders like a living thing, in a salt and pepper mix that was tending more to salt nowadays. She wore faded blue denim dungarees, a collared shirt printed with springing hares and an expression that always made those around her sit up just that little straighter, like she could tell just by looking at you what you were thinking.

'Don't worry our lass,' said her grandmother, with a wry smile, taking a seat next to her, and patting her hand. 'I'll be taking you to Hope Cottage in the morning. The girls and me are working on a recipe, you'll see, you'll be right as rain soon enough,' she went on with a wink.

Other people had nans, or grans; Emma had Evie. It had never occurred to Emma that it might be strange to call her grandmother by her first name, till it was too late and the habit had stuck. It suited her though. Evie had always been something of an original.

'That's the spirit,' said the doctor, giving her grandmother the look people often gave Evie Halloway, which was part admiration, part bewilderment.

Emma closed her eyes, stifling a groan. This was the third thing, she realised. It wasn't bad *exactly*, she did love Evie – and her crazy aunts, even if she was sure the whole lot of them needed medication – but in its own way this was the worst of the three, as it was everything she'd being trying to avoid: going back to Whistling, back to her ex Jack Allen and back to Hope Cottage.

TWO

In the small village of Whistling in rural Yorkshire, with its rolling green hills, purple moors and butterscotch cottages, some things never change. October marks the start of the frost, it always snows at Christmas and whenever anyone's in trouble they visit Hope Cottage, where remedies come on plates.

Emma was in trouble all right, as she stood outside the familiar cottage with its faded blue door, the colour of a duck's egg. Leaning on her crutch, she looked up at the odd, cat-shaped knocker with its somewhat cantankerous expression and, despite the place's picturesque beauty, she wished with all her might that she was anywhere but here. Wished that she was still with Pete and that her whole life and everything she'd so carefully built hadn't turned to ashes in the space of a few days.

Since her accident, Evie had packed up her clothes from her flat in London and let her editor at the *Mail & Ledger* know what had happened so that they could plan what to do with her weekly food column, 'The Historical Cook'. They had put up a notice on the column's accompanying blog that she would be temporarily (at least, so Emma hoped) out of service. What had been worse had been telling her freelance clients what had happened. While they were incredibly supportive and sympathetic, the trouble was this small, prized collection of contacts from newspapers, magazines and blogs provided the bulk of her income, which paid for the rent in her tiny, hard-won flat in London, and without it she was afraid she might have to give the place up. It didn't bear thinking about. The only thing worse than losing her flat in Catford was the idea of going back to living with weird flatmates. Somehow, she'd always had the worst luck with them. The last had tipped her over the edge, making her work harder than ever to get her own place: Bernard, who'd kept his toenail clippings in a jar on the shelf in the shared kitchen and sung all his responses to her attempts at conversation, had done a lot for Emma's professional drive. Going back to another version of that just didn't bear thinking about.

'We'll make the Mending Soup when you've settled in,' said Evie, who had materialised by Emma's side while she was lost in thought, her fingers coming up to touch a copper brooch she'd pinned onto the collar of her shirt, absently.

Emma shook her head. 'It would be a waste; besides it's not like I can taste it or anything.'

Of all her affected senses, it was taste she missed the most; the world seemed so flat without it. She would have given anything to taste something, anything.

'You don't have to be able to taste it for it to work,' Evie pointed out, unlocking the door.

Emma sighed, 'And you don't need to give up every nice thing you own just for me.'

'It's my choice. Besides, you know it doesn't work unless there's some form of sacrifice.'

Emma didn't want to get sucked back into her family's mad beliefs about the recipes they made, so she just gritted her teeth, fighting a wave of fatigue and vertigo in the process. Mercifully, Evie said no more as she wheeled Emma's bag across the threshold. Emma and her crutch followed slowly.

Inside, the cottage was as it had always been although it was all in duplicate due to her unfocused vision, she could see the familiar whitewashed stone, the same nooks and crannies in the walls, filled with dried flowers and sleeping cats named after herbs, a Halloway tradition. There was Marjoram, Parsley and Tansy. And if she were able to smell, she was sure the air would be thick with the scent of heather, wood fires and something that always seemed to hold that first whisper of Christmas. Cinnamon and nutmeg and ginger-snap biscuits.

She paused before the stone stairs, but Evie shook her head, leading her into the kitchen instead. It was a large room with an enormous navy blue range dominating one wall; next to this was a pale blue Welsh dresser, adorned with herbs and spices in clear jars with blue and white striped lids. Opposite was a large scrubbed wooden table with cream and indigo mismatching chairs. In the centre of the table usually sat the old family recipe book, the size of a concrete slab, which generations of Halloway women had filled over the years. Evie put it back in its place now, then gave Emma a smile as she indicated the small alcove towards the left, near the back door. 'We've made a spot for you here,' she said, showing her behind a large blue screen painted with wispy pink cherry blossoms. Behind this was a single bed, with a forest green, iron frame that had once sat in her childhood bedroom. Next to this was an old wooden wardrobe, with clawed feet and a three-legged stool, on top of which was a jam jar filled with dried bell heather, picked, no doubt, on one of Evie's many foraging heathland walks. The effect was charming, old-fashioned and slightly quirky – like Evie herself.

'I thought it would be easier for you to be down here rather than having to face the stairs,' she said, putting Emma's case down on top of a pale lilac quilt.

Emma nodded. It made sense. Stairs wouldn't be easy with her crutch.

A noise from behind made her turn, and what she saw made her smile in sudden delight. An old bulldog named Pennywort snuffled forward, his bottom waggling, his face split in a wide, doggy grin.

'Penny!' she cried, bending down to touch his soft, dappled brown and white fur. She took a seat on the edge of the bed, and Pennywort jumped up to settle his considerable bulk in her lap.

'He's missed you,' said Evie, giving the old dog an eye-roll for his soppiness. 'I'm no substitute, apparently,' she added with a grunt. Then she grinned. 'But Sandro's a firm favourite now. I dare say you've finally got a bit of competition at last.'

Emma patted the dog, and then frowned. Before she could ask who Sandro was, Evie touched her arm and said, 'I'm sorry about Pete.'

'Me too.'

Evie didn't say what Emma knew she was thinking – that he'd never been right for her. None of them had ever really got her decision to date Pete.

'It's not just that's he's about as exciting as a can of PVC paint,' her great aunt, Aggie had said a few months before, when they'd all come for a visit not long after she moved into her flat in Catford. They had pulled faces at the tiny space that smelt a bit like the kebab shop below, a factor that she couldn't help any more than she could mask the sounds of her neighbour's naughty films creaking through the parchment-thin walls. Right then they could hear a gruff, American voice drawling, 'You like that, huh? You like that?'

He kept asking, so Emma thought that perhaps she didn't.

'It's, erm, lovely,' said Dot, glancing around at the place with wide eyes, her handbag clutched beneath her armpit.

Plump, with a kind face and flyaway silver hair, and nail polish that was always chipping, her great-aunt, Dot Halloway, was a terrible liar.

It was the first time Emma had seen them in several months. They'd decided to take matters into their own hands and come down to see her after she'd excused herself too many times from visiting Hope Cottage.

'No, it's awful, but that's not what's concerning me,' said her other aunt, Aggie, who always told things as they were. She was tall and stout with short black hair and the family's piercing blue eyes. She gave Emma her customary hard stare now. 'I mean, look at you,' she said, concerned.

'What?' she'd said, looking down at her pale chinos and smart white shirt with a puzzled frown.

Dot, Evie and Aggie shared similar looks of worry.

'It's like you're starting to fade away, like you're trying so hard to be just like him – or what you think you're meant to be like, really – that you've started to rub yourself out.'

'I… what?' she'd spluttered, outraged, turning to Dot and Evie for support. 'I'm not trying to be somebody else – this is who I am!'

Evie shook her head, sadly. 'No, 'tisn't, love. Trust me, when you try to let go of who you are well – that's the result,' she said turning Emma around to face the mirror in the hallway.

Dot frowned. 'When was the last time you even cooked something?'

As if that solved anything.

Still. Staring at herself, Emma had no choice but to see her wan face, her lank, once bright hair now the colour of pale rust, and her listless, dull blue eyes staring back at her. She shook her head. 'I eat, trust me,' she said, though she knew that wasn't what Dot meant; but she wasn't about to admit how much she missed cooking. They'd simply read too much into it.

'I've just been busy that's all – it's the column, my freelance work. I've given a few lectures at the university on Victorian baking as well, so that's meant some late nights lately, I don't get time for much else, really, none of this has anything to do with Pete. I mean, I know, he's not exciting, but—'

There was a snort from Aggie, who muttered, 'You can say that again,' beneath her breath, though Emma heard her nonetheless.

Emma crossed her arms. 'But he's very sweet and kind, which is all that matters to me.'

'Of course he is,' said Evie, in placating tones. 'And you're right,' she added.

'About what?' asked Emma.

'That it has nothing to do with Pete.'

Emma turned to her with a look of suspicion on her face, waiting for the 'but'. Evie shrugged. 'It has everything to do with you – and what you need to face.'

'What I need to face?' she echoed with a frown.

'Yes. Why you've run away.'

Evie, Dot and Aggie all nodded.

She looked at them all and shook her head in exasperation. 'I haven't run *away*. I live in London now, where I have made a life – a good life – for the last four years! I'm – I'm happy.'

Aggie snorted. 'Yeah. You look it. About as happy as someone facing the noose, love.'

She'd been upset with them for ages after that. They simply didn't get the pace of life in London – didn't understand that her Catford flat, despite its less than savoury appeal, was a mark of her independence. Besides, it wasn't called a rat race for nothing, and she'd been working really hard lately just to keep on top of things. Her part-time lecturer post had helped; it would mean that she could just about manage her rent for the next few months. The extra work had meant juggling a crazy schedule, working sixteen-hour days, but it had helped to bring her head above water, as there had been times when she had seemed to simply live on credit before. And things with Pete had been good – they'd been talking of finally moving in together in the New Year, looking for a nicer flat, somewhere far away from a kebab shop and pervy neighbours – till he ended it. Really, looking back, things had gone downhill since she'd run into Suze while she and Pete were having coffee, a few weeks before. Suze was a colleague from the *Mail & Ledger*.

Suze had done a double-take when Emma introduced Pete as her boyfriend.

'My God, Em, you dark horse, the way you always spoke about him – I just thought he was your brother!' She laughed, flicking back her long blonde hair, eyeing him with an admiring smile.

When Suze left, Emma had dismissed the comment as silly and thought no more of it – but clearly, Pete hadn't. He'd chewed on it for hours, in his quiet, contemplative way, mulling it over and over. She'd found him sitting in the dark in the early hours of the morning and when she asked him what was wrong, he'd just said, 'That's not normal, Em, people thinking that, that I'm your brother.'

She'd scoffed – a mistake, she realised later. 'You aren't upset about that still?'

He'd looked at her with hurt eyes.

'She's a twit, honestly, I hardly know her. I've spoken about you, of course, but not that much, I don't know why she got that impression, but please don't take it seriously.'

But he did. After that it was like he looked at their whole relationship differently and what he saw seemed to prove Suze right, no matter how strongly she argued against it. The trouble was that theirs had never been a passionate relationship, but it was based on something much better, or so she had thought – friendship. He might not have been exciting, but then, after a lifetime of excitement provided by her crazy family and previous relationship with Jack, that had been a relief.

'He was very upset when I phoned him,' said Evie now. Emma did a double-take as she snapped back to the present. 'You phoned Pete? When?'

'It was the day I arrived at the hospital, a week ago, just wanted to let him know what happened. He felt terrible when he heard, felt responsible I suppose.'

Emma sighed. 'The accident wasn't his fault. Well, not technically.' If it was the fault of any one thing, as far as Emma was concerned, it was The Book – though she knew, logically, that didn't really make sense, and she would never say it out loud, not because Evie wouldn't believe her but because there was every chance that she *would*.

At Evie's frown, she explained how she'd decided to get out of the flat after she'd found the break-up Post-it, which was when the postal van knocked her down. 'It was just bad luck, really.'

Evie, however, had really only heard one thing. She was looking at her incredulously, her blue eyes amused.

'He broke up with you on a Post-it note?' Her lips started to twitch.

'Don't. It was actually very sad,' Emma said, though she felt a sudden mad urge to laugh as well.

'Oh? I'm sure it was very heartfelt. What did it say? Let me guess – something like this: "To do: Pop into Tesco for gluten-free bread – no more gyppy tummy for me. Buy some exciting new slacks, think maybe – gasp – brown, do I chance it? Yes Pete, yes you can! Also. Break up with Emma?"'

Emma laughed. 'No, but he did add a postscript that said I was out of washing powder.'

Evie pressed her knuckles to her lips, her shoulders shaking as she tried, and failed, to suppress a giggle. 'Sorry!' she gasped as her raspy laugh echoed against the stone walls. There were tears leaking out of her eyes.

Emma bit her lip, trying not to giggle too. 'No, don't, he's – well, he's really nice when he's not breaking up with someone on Post-it notes.'

'Yeah, especially on laundry day, that's for sure.'

'Stop it,' Emma giggled, and then frowned. 'When you told him, didn't he want to come see me?' She couldn't help feeling hurt by that.

'Course he did, love. But I told him it would probably be for the best not to as I was taking you home – and well, seeing you like this might have meant…'

'That we'd get back together.' Emma couldn't help wishing that he had decided to take that risk. Her shoulders slumped. The worst part was that he didn't even want to speak to her, even now.

'He said that I wasn't in love with him.' Emma hadn't meant to tell Evie that, it simply slipped out.

Evie looked at her, didn't say anything for a while, then, 'Maybe it's for the best, love?'

Emma looked away. Best for who? Not her, surely? 'It isn't true, you know. I *do* love him.'

Evie touched her shoulder. 'Aye love, we all know you *care* for him.'

At Emma's sharp look, she added, 'A lot, but – but it's not the same as real love, is it?'

Emma closed her eyes. A tear tracked down her cheek. What she knew about 'real love' was that it ripped you in two, made you give up everything, including the only home you'd ever known, just to get away from it. This, the version she'd had with Pete, at least as far as she was concerned, had been so much better.

'You look exhausted,' said Evie, smoothing back her hair.

'I feel it,' she said, with a sigh. Exhaustion had become her constant companion since the accident.

'Why don't you have a lie-down?'

Emma nodded. A lie-down sounded like exactly what she needed.

Three days later, and all Emma had done really since she arrived at Hope Cottage was sleep. She felt like a puzzle that had been put together wrong, the pieces jammed together at odd angles to create an odd, almost cubist version of the person who was once Emma Halloway.

The girl who once got around by cycling all over London and stayed up all night inspired to finish an article now got overwhelmed by the idea of leaving the house, and had to take a nap every few hours just so that she could form coherent sentences.

The girl who'd bought most of her clothes at trendy vintage shops (beige slacks that Pete had bought her notwithstanding) now wore pyjamas like a uniform.

Nothing felt right. Her scrambled senses could muddle the touch of water with the prick of needles, or the sound of Elvis's crooning with chainsaws. She had to rely on Evie for everything. Her hazy vision meant that even opening up the right pill bottle or making herself a cup of tea was a challenge because she couldn't rely on her other senses to help guide her.

The smallest thing could feel like a battle, like early the next morning when she tried to put on socks and it felt like she had applied a heat rod to her soles. Evie found her sobbing on the edge of the bed.

'That's the worst of it,' she said, as Evie stroked her back, tried to calm her wails. 'I feel so overwhelmed all the time. I just want my old life back! I just want things to make sense – literally.'

'It will, love, just give it time.'

Time was all she had now, great bucketloads of it. Her world had turned small, constricted to the alcove around her bed and the wider surrounds of the kitchen and the downstairs bathroom.

She couldn't escape into a novel as the letters scrambled across the page like moving ants, and even if she could watch television, Evie had never owned one, though she suspected that the moving images and sounds would have simply worn her out anyway. The same was to be said of social media; it was all just too hazy and there was a real danger of her typing something that didn't make sense at all.

'You're home now love, you'll see, things will get better soon,' said Evie, getting up to put the copper kettle on the range for tea.

Home. One of the things that she did look forward to about being back – one of the only things really – was seeing her oldest friends, Maggie and Jenny, who, along with Gretchen (who, sadly, lived in Scotland now) had been a constant in her life since her first year at school. Who needed social media when you could have the real thing, she thought with a grin.

Emma lay back against the cushions and thought: home. When she pictured it, it was this. The large, whitewashed kitchen with its navy blue range, the same behemoth that generations of Halloway women had used since Grace Halloway swept into the village of Whistling some two hundred years before, with dust lining her coffers and only her family recipes to her name. The flagstone floors and pale weathered beams were the same too. Cats asleep in shadowy corners – though always just outside the kitchen, which was, as ever, Pennywort's domain. Dust-mote rainbows in the lemon-coloured sunshine. Herbs drying on the windowsills. Pennywort himself, seated on a chair, his old head resting on the large scrubbed kitchen table, keeping an eye on what they made. Miraculously still going strong after all these years (the aunts insisted that it was due to one of their recipes for longevity; Emma thought they'd just got lucky). Evie.

But it was also this: the sound of anxious knocking on the door. The reason why, in many ways, she'd been happy to see the back of Hope Cottage.

Shooting Emma an apprehensive glance, Evie opened the door to find Mary Galway standing in wait. Her pale eyes darted nervously around the room, widening in alarm when they took in Emma lying in bed in her fluffy pink pyjamas. Emma cursed herself for having moved the blue silk screen that blocked the alcove from the rest of the kitchen, en route to the bathroom the night before. She fought the urge to hide beneath the covers.

Mary dithered, with one foot on the threshold like a startled rabbit, ready to flee at the slightest provocation. Her mousy hair hung in lank strings down her face and she had that deflated look of someone who had become recently thin, like a soufflé that had popped in the oven.

'Cup of tea?' Evie asked.

Mary nodded, and Evie asked, 'For you as well, love?'

Emma stifled a groan. What she really wanted was for Evie to put the silk screen back in place, so that she could pretend for just a second that she hadn't re-entered the twilight zone.

'No thanks,' she said instead.

Evie shrugged, beckoning Mary inside where she took a tentative seat next to Pennywort, who eyed her solemnly for a moment then jumped down as if he would offer the two some privacy.

'What seems to be the problem, Mary?' asked Evie.

Some things never changed. No one came to Hope Cottage at dawn, not unless they had a problem they couldn't solve any other way, because what the Halloways offered always came with a price, a sacrifice.

It was the tradition, as old as the cottage itself. If you needed the Halloways you came at sunup. Being a Halloway and having a lie-in were not things that often went together.

Mary swallowed and darted Emma a nervous look, hesitant to say what it was in front of her, no doubt. Emma hid a grin. She half suspected that that was Evie's plan, why she'd put her bed in the kitchen and not the living room – so that she could be drawn back in to the life of the cottage.

Not today, thought Emma, getting up with some difficulty. She shrugged into her fluffy pink robe, which clashed rather magnificently with her badly-in-need-of-a-brush red hair, and hobbled away with her crutch. 'I'll leave you two to talk,' she said pointedly, Pennywort following at her heels.

'No, stay,' said Evie, patting the chair next to her.

Emma snorted. 'That's okay, thanks,' she said, shuffling into the living room where she closed the door and leaned against it, fighting the sudden wave of nausea from her hazy vision as well as something else, a feeling that always came whenever she was here: the urge to get involved despite her better judgement; but she wasn't going to get sucked back in to the family madness – not if she could help it.

She made her way to the sofa and closed her eyes. Waking up only to need a nap seemed like a bad sort of joke, but that's what her life had turned into lately.

Emma woke up a few hours later when Pennywort started to scratch at the door to be let outside. Emma got off the sofa with some difficulty, crossing the flagstone floor into the now mercifully empty kitchen. When Emma opened the back door though, the breath caught in her throat; there across the low wall of their garden, next to a lolloping black Newfoundland dog, who looked almost as big as a baby bear, stood Jack Allen. Despite her hazy vision, she'd recognise him anywhere.

She felt her throat turn dry. Her knees turn weak. It had been four years since she'd seen him last, since she'd left Whistling in a storm of hurt and pain, with the vow that she would do whatever it took to get over him.

She'd almost succeeded – or so she'd thought. It was most unfortunate, she realised, standing there in her fluffy pink, dog-hair-covered robe, with one arm and leg in a cast, hair a wild, rust-coloured mess, to discover that somehow, despite everything, she still felt exactly the same way about him as she always had.

THREE

Jack was gaping at her from across the garden wall, where he'd come to a complete stop, his dog barking at his heels.

Emma closed her eyes, fought for calm and lost. She'd been thinking of this moment for years, and what she'd do when she saw him again. Somehow it had never included standing in her fluffy robe, looking like an extra from *The Walking Dead*, wincing in sudden pain as her broken foot started to throb when she put pressure on it as she shifted on her crutch.

She'd hoped to get back inside the cottage before he saw her but it was too late. He'd already opened the low garden gate in a rush, his mouth forming her name in shock.

It didn't help that, despite her fuzzy vision that still showed her most things in repeat, he looked, if possible, even better than she remembered. It wasn't fair that age did that to men. As he neared she saw that his face was leaner, his features more defined. But it was the familiarity that made the ache in her chest bloom, an ache that was separate from her injuries. He was still the same, same trim, athletic build, same dark blond hair that he used to twirl with his fingers whenever he was thinking of something, same hazel eyes that crinkled around the corners and made her feel like the only girl who'd ever existed; a dangerous trait, because, as she knew, that wasn't always true, was it?

Jack's beautiful eyes were wide with concern now as they trailed over the purple bruises on her face, the scabs from where her face had grazed the road and the casts on her arm and leg. His hand reached out as if to touch her, then stopped, as if he remembered himself. 'Emma! I heard you'd been in an accident but I had no idea it was this bad. What happened?'

She cursed Pennywort for needing to go outside at this exact moment. What was Jack Allen doing here now? This was not how she had wanted him to see her. If she had pictured seeing him again it was with her looking happy, dressed in something glamorous and in the arms of Pete, not in her pyjamas, with a face full of bruises, unwashed hair and a head full of scrambled senses.

She explained about the postal van, though she didn't go into detail about her other injuries. There just wasn't a casual way to bring up brain damage.

'I'm so sorry,' he said, staring at her.

She felt her stomach flip, wishing he wouldn't look at her that way.

She bit her lip, looked away.

'Thanks.'

There was an awkward silence, in which neither of them knew what to say to the other after how they'd left things four years before.

'Look—' he started but was interrupted by his dog, who was trying his best to mount Penny, to the old bulldog's utter horror.

'Sorry – he's a bit too friendly,' he said with a laugh, breaking the tension and pulling the bear-like dog away from Pennywort, who looked deeply affronted. Emma couldn't help snorting at the bulldog's outraged expression.

'Well, I should probably go…' said Jack hesitantly, his eyes darting past her to the door, which stood open behind them. 'Don't want Evie to come out and curse me,' he joked.

She couldn't help the furrow that appeared between her eyes. 'You think she would?'

He looked embarrassed, his mouth opening, perhaps for some wry comeback that never materialised.

'I thought the Allens didn't believe in any of that.'

He laughed. 'Yeah, well—'

There was a sound from behind and they both started.

'Emma!' said a voice she didn't recognise.

She blinked, looking for the source. With the usual confusion of sounds and senses since her accident, she pictured stretches of long sandy beach, sunshine and cocktail umbrellas and tequila sipped out of short glasses. Then a tall handsome man, with an unruly mop of dark curly hair and large, laughing brown eyes, stepped out in front of her. He seemed to have been drawn in bold black lines; despite her patchy double vision, he, unlike everyone else so far, appeared in sharp relief. He was wearing black, from his long-sleeved V-neck sweater to his jeans and low, leather boots, yet somehow it was like he was in technicolour.

He came forward and squeezed her shoulder, as if they were lifelong friends. She blinked, trying to find speech, but her mouth just hung open somewhat stupidly.

The stranger winked at her. 'I heard a lot about you,' he said. His accent was mild and lyrical, Spanish, she realised. He gave her a knowing sort of grin as if they were sharing a grand old joke. 'Looks like The Book did its magic after all, eh? They – what's the word – oh yes, dithered!' He laughed, throwing his head back, as he slapped a knee. A dimple appeared in his tanned cheek, making him handsomer still. 'They dithered for a long time before they finally sent it.'

'What?' she breathed, shooting a nervous glance at Jack, who seemed to have taken an unconscious step backwards. The stranger didn't appear to notice. He just kept staring at her in utter delight.

'What are you taking about?' she asked, blinking.

He grinned, showing off very white, even teeth. Making the dimple grow deeper. 'It worked. I mean, you're here now, eh?'

'I'll see you soon Emma, I better take Gus away,' said Jack, indicating his dog. 'Come on,' he said, separating Gus from Pennywort again. 'I – er, hope you get better soon,' he said, then turned and left.

Emma opened and closed her mouth, stopping herself, just in time, from asking him to stay. The strange man regarded her with an amused look for a little longer, and then he winked and headed inside the cottage, Pennywort following, devotedly, at his heels.

Emma blinked, watching Jack leave, feeling torn for a moment, then turned to follow the stranger inside, too. She crossed an arm over her cast, hoping that she looked a little more intimidating than she felt. 'I'm sorry – not to be rude, but who the bloody hell are you?'

The stranger stopped in his tracks. 'I'm Sandro,' he said, a slightly confused look on his face, as if that name should have meant something to her.

'Sandro,' she repeated, recalling, distantly, something that Evie had said about someone named Sandro... though she couldn't remember what, exactly. 'Okay? And what exactly are you doing here?'

His brown eyes widened. 'I live here.' He smiled, and the dimple appeared in his cheek.

She blinked, wondering if her ears had played tricks on her again. They were wont to do that sort of thing since her accident. Music could sound like lawnmowers and people's voices could sound like swarms of insects.

'You live here?' she repeated.

He cocked his head to the side, frowned. 'Didn't Evie tell you?'

Slowly, she shook her head.

He smiled at her sadly, his dark eyes trailing over her injuries, clucking sympathetically while he muttered something in Spanish. Something that sounded a little like 'Pajarita', as he shook his head.

Emma ignored this. 'Where exactly?'

'Scuse?'

'Where do you sleep?' she asked, shuffling to the kitchen table, where she took a seat, balancing her crutch against the table edge, her unhurt leg shaking. She could feel a headache coming on.

'In the annexe.'

It was just off the kitchen, a small one-room studio with a view of the garden.

She stared at him. None of this made any sense. Why hadn't Evie told her? Part of her couldn't help being annoyed that he'd chosen that moment to come home, just when she'd seen Jack again, though she knew this was ridiculous; she hadn't wanted to see Jack anyway, right? And she certainly hadn't wanted him to see her, not like this.

There was a swarm of excited babbling, and Emma heard three familiar voices bickering slightly as they made their way into the kitchen.

'I told you she's resting,' came Evie's voice.

'Excuse me,' huffed a throaty voice, 'my niece was hit by a bloody *van*, the least I can do is come and see if she's okay—'

'Exactly, Evie, we're her family too, if you don't mind. It's just like when she first came to live here all over again, how you tried to keep her for yourself…,' came a voice like runny honey.

'Keep her to myself?' huffed Evie. 'She'd just *lost* her parents you bubble-head. I was trying to ease her in and you barged in then too, overwhelming her with talk of the recipes and—'

'Barged in? Barged in!?'

Sandro looked at her. 'I'd offer to hide you, but I don't think we'd make it,' he said, indicating the path to the front door.

Despite everything, she found herself grinning with him as her aunts, followed by Evie, came tearing inside. Dot's plump, cheerful face paled. She clutched her chest when she saw her. Aggie's eyes looked like they were about to pop.

'Hi,' said Emma. 'It's not as bad as it looks.'

They blinked. Dot's glasses grew foggy as tears pricked her eyes. It obviously looked pretty bad.

Ten minutes later, after Sandro had retreated with a mild 'adios' and a sandwich, Aggie looked at her, across from her cup of cold tea. She'd tried to escape to the sofa three times, but no such luck. They wanted details. All of them.

'So, we heard, you've *literally* lost your senses?'

'I didn't say it like that—,' began Evie at the same time that Dot protested 'Aggie!' at her sister's bluntness, then looked at Emma, her eyes magnified enormously behind their thick lenses. 'Is she right? Evie said they were a jumble?'

Emma nodded, though it was painful to nod.

'But how can you hear or see us, then?' she asked with a frown.

Looking from one to the other was making her eyes strain even more; she massaged her temples, and closed her eyes.

'They're not all lost, exactly; essentially they're just a mess. I can see, just not clearly, things go in and out of focus,' she said thinking of Sandro and how, strangely, he'd seemed as clear as glass, whereas everything else looked like it was shrouded in a fine mist. 'I can hear, but it can get confusing when people talk at once. I've got rather good at reading lips. But, I can't smell or taste anything,' she said glumly. This last was the worst.

'Nothing?'

She shook her head.

'And touch?'

'Things don't always feel right – it's like a muddle at times… Things that are usually soft can feel hard, like, say, the wind on my skin, which can sometimes feel like a burn, or I may feel nothing at all when really, I should,' she said, thinking of the blood tests that had been taken before she left the hospital and how surprised she'd been to see a needle sticking out of her arm. Perhaps what made it worse was that things weren't always muddled – but that was also a concern, because there was always the surprise, sometimes painful, when they were.

'Do they know how long before you recover?'

'No, all we can do is wait and hope,' answered Evie. 'And make sure she gets plenty of rest,' she said pointedly, though of course they both ignored her and made no move to leave.

'It's okay,' she told Evie with a small smile. 'Honestly, it's like I'm tired either way – when I sleep or when I don't, I feel about the same really.'

Dot clucked sympathetically. Then she gave her a wink, jerking her head in the direction of the annexe. Her eyes, behind their jam-jar lenses, wide. 'That should make you feel a bit better though, I mean you can still see *him*, right?'

'Imagine all of that, on your doorstep,' agreed Aggie, her eyes going slightly misty.

Emma narrowed her eyes, and then looked from Dot to Evie, pointedly. 'Actually, I want to have a word with you about that.'

'Oh yes?' said Evie, her tone mild, as if they were discussing the weather and not some relative stranger living in their home.

'*Yes*,' said Emma. 'Who the hell is he? How come you never said anything about him?'

'Oh!' said Evie, her eyes widening in surprise. 'Haven't you met before?'

Emma blinked. 'No.'

'Didn't I mention him before?'

'You did *not*.'

Dot and Aggie were watching the proceedings with amused shock on their faces. 'Who could fail to mention Sandro?' Dot asked Aggie, who shook her head and said, 'Caramba.'

Then they dissolved into what Emma could only think of as unhelpful giggles.

Evie rolled her eyes at them. 'Well, there's not much to say really. He's Sandro, and he's my tenant, for a little while anyway.'

Emma thought of how odd he seemed – how familiar he'd been, and how at ease he seemed with the cottage and their mad recipes, how he'd spoken of The Book, so ready to believe that it worked.

'You just let some crazy guy come live here without telling me about it?'

Evie tutted. 'He isn't crazy, love, he's *Spanish*.'

Then, as if the conversation were now closed, she looked at her sisters and said, 'So I suppose we should start thinking about the plans for Christmas. If it's anything like last year we'll need to start planning a lot sooner, particularly when it comes to ordering ingredients, you know how we always get three times as many people coming by for a recipe during the holidays. Ann Brimble said we should think of doubling our flour order, we don't want to run out halfway through the month like we did last year. And we should probably look into some new pie cutters too – the Appeasement Pie was a popular recipe last year. Oh, and Sandro asked if we wouldn't mind helping him cater for Christmas dinner down at the Tapas Hut this year. He said that last year it was about thirty people and I said we could manage, I mean God knows we've done it informally for years, what difference does it make if we're a little more formal about it?'

Christmas at Hope Cottage was always a busy, festive and welcoming affair, the table laden with food, from Dot's famous glazed ham to Evie's Yorkshire pudding and fluffy rice drowning in gravy, and Aggie's laughter booming off the walls. It was always a non-stop party, and everyone was invited. They were always good that way, making sure there wasn't anyone who was spending the day alone, not if they could help it.

Emma, though, wasn't really paying attention. All she'd heard was something about Sandro…

They all nodded. Dot took out a small notebook and started jotting down ideas. 'I agree, tapas just isn't really Christmassy, sorry to say—'

'Why is he here?' interrupted Emma, who wasn't about to let go the fact that Evie had let a stranger come to live at Hope Cottage; not without some explanation at least.

Evie turned to her with a frown. 'Sandro? Well, he needed a place to stay while his house is being renovated. He's bought an old farmhouse see, and it didn't make sense for him to waste his money at a B&B.'

Emma frowned. 'But it made sense to come here?'

'Yes, when we have a perfectly good annexe. He's paying me a bit of rent if that's what you're worried about; I told him not to, but he insisted, and it's only temporary – just a few months really.'

'What's he doing in Whistling, though – it seems a strange place for him to end up, doesn't it?'

Evie and her aunts shared a look. 'Was a girl, wasn't it? Though I'm not sure if she lived here or London really. He said something about getting on a train and finding the Dales, and himself…'

'What happened with the girl?'

'Didn't work out, never really got the details.'

Evie turned back to her sisters. 'I've been meaning to tell you, Mr Grigson came round this morning, can you believe it?'

'No,' breathed Dot in shocked tones. Everyone knew that Whistling's resident curmudgeon, Mr Grigson, who ran the local hardware store just outside the village, near to her Uncle Joe's auto dealership, had always been a little wary about Hope Cottage, especially the rumours that always accompanied it, giving any Halloway he saw a wide berth on the street.

'No heart is braver than the one in love,' Evie said sagely.

'He's eighty now if he's a day!' said Aggie.

'Still in love, his old high-school sweetheart, Moira, apparently. He's hoping they can rekindle the flame now that she's single again – well, if only she'll forgive an old transgression from their youth. It's why he came, feels like he might need a little help.'

'Oh, he might do – old Moira Bates is a bit of a stickler,' said Dot. 'I handed a book in late at the library, when it was still open,' she went on, and then pulled a face. 'Could have sworn I'd killed her old cat the way she looked at me afterwards, mean thing too, that little monster – do you remember that time—'

'When did Mr Grigson come?' asked Emma.

'While you were sleeping on the sofa, after Mary Galway left.'

Emma marvelled that so much had happened while she was sleeping, but she was still trying to process what Evie had said about Sandro. Besides, she wanted to steer the conversation away from their mad recipes as much as she could.

'Back to Sandro, sorry, I'm confused – why would you offer him the annexe in the first place? Wasn't there anywhere else he could go?'

Evie shrugged. 'I suppose he could have.'

'But he's a stranger, why would you even offer?'

Emma worried that perhaps Evie was struggling financially. It had never been easy keeping Hope Cottage; aside from Aggie, who was a semi well-known artist, the sisters had always made the recipes and the cottage a strictly non-profit affair, so perhaps there was something Evie hadn't been telling her. Why else would she open her home to a strange man?

'He isn't a stranger, you've chuffing lived in London too long – we've known him for a couple of years now,' said Aggie.

Emma was shocked. 'You have?'

'He's a good friend,' agreed Evie.

'He is?'

'You'd know this if you'd been home more often,' Aggie pointed out.

Emma ignored this. Suddenly a new thought occurred to her. She widened her eyes, snapped them back at Evie, a slow grin spreading on her face. 'Are you and he…?'

Evie snorted. She wasn't the only one. 'Are you serious – he's young enough to be my grandson!'

Emma shrugged. 'So, like you said, I've been living in London, it's not that uncommon, trust me.'

Evie shook her head. 'He's not my type, all right?'

Dot shrugged. 'Well, I don't know about that… I mean, he's the type you'd make an exception for, am I right?' she said, eyebrows waggling.

Aggie hooted with laughter. 'Oh yes, I could have those boots under my bed,' and they all dissolved into giggles, only laughing harder when they saw Emma's slightly shocked expression. 'Your generation,' said Dot. 'Such prudes.'

'I am not a prude,' said Emma, somewhat prudishly. 'What does he do?'

'He runs the Tapas Hut,' said Evie pulling The Book towards her. She began flipping the page, then stopped at a recipe titled Wind-change Wine.

Evie tapped her chin, reading out the instructions, which included allowing several months of fermentation. 'Not sure Mr Grigson has that sort of time on his hands at his age, but it's his best chance really.'

'A tapas *hut?*' asked Emma, resolutely trying her best to ignore being sucked back into the family pastime of meddling in other people's lives via food.

'You haven't heard of it?' said Dot in surprise.

Emma shook her head.

'Oh, it's wonderful,' she said, going misty-eyed. 'The best tapas I've ever had. Authentic, well, I suppose it would be, *he's* the real thing.' She laughed. 'But it's something else, rather special. It's down by the moors with these really gorgeous views. In summer when the heather is in bloom it's such a treat, a purple carpet, next to these long wooden tables that overlook the heath. It's even better at night with all the fairy lights, and the stars... And if you ply him with enough wine and encouragement, he plays his guitar. It's... bliss,' she sighed, obviously a little smitten.

All three of them nodded.

Emma blinked. It was hard to picture this happening here. Very few things changed in Whistling, where the Brimbles had always run the local store, the Leas had always run the vicarage and there had always been a Halloway in Hope Cottage. As far as she knew, no one had ever run a tapas hut...

Evie shrugged. 'Stranger things have happened.'

Emma doubted it.

When she went to bed that night, she thought of Jack. She hadn't seen him since she'd moved to London, since she'd tried to put him and the family legacy behind her, relegate it to where she believed it deserved a place – in her past. She thought of how quickly he'd left when Sandro had mentioned The Book, the expression on his face, of disbelief, mixed with something that almost looked like fear. Some things, she thought a little sadly, fluffing the pillow beneath her head, never changed.

FOUR

Since she was a little girl, Emma had been taught that there was an art to cooking. A science too. Some things add texture and flavour. If you add cream to eggs it will go thick and rich. Some things though, when you add them, curdle and separate. Like oil and water. Or Sandro's presence in Hope Cottage; at least as far as Emma was concerned, him being there was just making life even harder than it needed to be. He was just too damn loud, for one thing.

He was forever barging into the kitchen and disturbing her peace, chatting loudly on the phone, turning up the radio, his body jangling to some tune in his head, so that he would look at you while beating a drum on his knee, his whole being thrumming to its own secret music.

When he wasn't making a noise, he was invading her space, moving aside the screen and trying to engage her in conversation.

'Hola, Pajarita,' he said the first morning after they met, his dark eyes taking in her bruises with a sad frown. Making her aware, suddenly, of the tangle of her sheets and the state of her unwashed hair.

'What does that mean?' she asked. 'Pajarita?'

He gave her his mellow smile, a dimple appearing in his cheek. 'Well, it's like you, like a little bird with a broken wing.' He mimed it, his arm making a flapping motion.

Her eyes popped in outrage. 'I am *not*.'

Still, her grumpiness did nothing to dissuade him; if anything it seemed to fuel him even more. As the days passed, he was always there, strumming his guitar, to the delight of her aunts, helping himself to food, listening as Evie, Dot and Aggie worked on a recipe, his dark eyes wide as he turned to her in amazed delight. 'Marvellous. Really marvellous, eh, Pajarita? Imagine curing arthritis like this, eh?'

She'd just roll her eyes, then head out for the sofa, trying to escape. That's all she needed: more recruits for the family madness. Shoulders slumping when she'd realise that Pennywort, like Evie and her aunts, would stay with him. They seemed to bask in his attention. Making him endless cups of espresso and feeding him biscuits that they made just for him. Ginger snaps, peanut butter cookies, chocolate chip – nothing was too much trouble for him. Hearing his sighs of pleasure as he ate them made her grit her teeth, partly because she would have given anything just to taste one herself.

He was always around, or at least so it seemed, oddly for someone who owned his own business. Though to be fair, as she napped so often he might well be leaving and returning; she couldn't always be sure.

Every morning of the first week that she was back, his dark, curly head would appear next to the silk screen and he'd offer her a cup of coffee, or suggest that she come to the window to see something 'interesting', or to 'take a short walk in the garden' or go with him while he picked up some groceries.

He didn't get offended when she told him to simply 'Bugger off.'

He would just leave, chuckling. 'Maybe next time, Pajarita, eh? Adios.'

She had to swallow the urge to shout, 'I am not a bloody little bird!' Not because doing so would be mean, though partly it was that, and she didn't like that that was who she'd become, but more because shouting would hurt like hell.

When he was gone there was quiet and stillness, and the blue calm of the kitchen. Quiet was one of the few pleasures she had left and she savoured it when it came, the way she had once savoured the first delicious bite of chocolate.

The second week she was back, shuffling into the kitchen in her robe, she looked around and sniffed, though it wasn't like she could smell anything. Signs of his presence were everywhere. The different types of tapas in the fridge, neatly stored in glass containers. The shiny, new coffee machine that was constantly on, the Halloways providing him with a steady supply of espresso – she saw now that he'd left one behind, stone cold, half full and forgotten, while he dealt with some crisis at the Tapas Hut.

She picked the little cup up, but with her hazy vision, misjudged the distance and knocked it over, cursing as it oozed inky liquid onto the table that seeped into The Book. She grabbed a dishcloth and quickly mopped it up, pressing hard to make sure it didn't soak into the pages. She flipped a page to dab on the other side, then paused with a frown as her fingers traced over the stubby ends of what looked like a set of pages that had been torn out.

She frowned. It had been years since she'd looked at The Book properly, but despite this, she knew the pages by heart – or at least, so she'd thought. The torn pages were between a recipe for mending fences and another for overcoming heartache. These recipes had always been there though, which meant that the torn pages must have always been there too, and she'd simply never noticed them before. It was strange. Not all the recipes worked. Even Evie admitted that. But they were kept all the same – they were lessons, or at least that's what Evie had always maintained; they'd simply add an annotation in pen or pencil to explain what had gone wrong. But if that was the case, why then had this one been torn out?

'Package for you,' said Evie coming to her bed and handing her a small red cardboard box in the shape of a dog bone. Stuck on the front was a small white envelope, addressed simply to 'Emma'.

She frowned. 'Who's it from?'

Evie shrugged. 'Open it,' she said, making her way back into the kitchen to get started on a recipe for another dawn caller.

Emma opened the envelope, curious. Then laughed.

> *Flowers for Pennywort. Gus is sorry for his ungentlemanly behaviour. He has realised that despite how fetching Master Pennywort is, he shouldn't have got so carried away.*
> *Jack.*
> *P.S. Glad you're back.*

Inside the box were heart-shaped dog biscuits. She gave one to Pennywort, who seemed less than charmed – he was a bit too spoiled by Evie and her aunts, a factor that she was sure had resulted in his commendable longevity.

She was smiling when Evie came back into her alcove. 'So, who is it from?' she asked.

'Oh – um, a friend,' Emma hedged; she wasn't up for a discussion about Jack Allen, not today.

Noting the biscuits, Evie frowned. 'Dog biscuits?'

'Bit of a joke.'

'A good one, I hope,' said Evie as she went back into the kitchen, ready to tackle Mr Grigson's recipe so that Moira Bates might be persuaded to give him a second chance at love.

You look better than I imagined,' said Maggie, her oldest friend, pushing up her glasses and taking a seat on the edge of Emma's bed. She cocked her head to the side. 'The hair though?'

Emma's godchild Mikey, a fetching two-year-old who had fallen instantly in love with Pennywort, was now asleep on the bed, his thumb in his mouth, his curly blond hair catching the last of the autumnal light as they caught up.

'Shut up.' Emma snorted. 'You try washing your hair with pins in your fingers and a cast on your wrist.'

Maggie laughed, her green eyes dancing. 'Yeah, okay, you may have a slight excuse… try motherhood, Jase had to deal with bun hair for the first *year*.'

'Jase' was Maggie's husband, Jason Foster, a sweet-natured footie fanatic, who'd made the move from Manchester to come live with Maggie after they met at a match a few years ago, falling in love over a shared passion for the boys in red. He had his own business building websites, which did fairly well, and he'd offered her the chance to give up work, but Maggie loved her job as a route planner for a trucking company – she said it allowed her to speak to adults during the day, though for the first few months she was back at work she had spent most of her time mooning over pictures of Mikey and becoming her own worst idea of a soppy mum. She'd told Emma all this once over the phone. 'It's nuts, isn't it? I've become one of those women I used to laugh at,' she said, sobbing, from the ladies' loo. 'I mean I spent months looking forward to going back, I found one of his stupid socks in my bag today, when I was looking for a tissue for my nose, and my eyes started leaking – it was in the middle of a meeting and I was sitting there all gormless and soppy staring at his sock. *Me*.'

Emma had tried to soothe her, tried not to laugh, picturing no-nonsense Maggie, who worked in a male-dominated field and had a reputation for being a bit of an iron fist, crying over a sock.

'Things will get easier, Mags. It's hormones or something, you'll get used to it, I'm sure no one noticed,' she lied.

'Oh, they noticed. Luckily, Bob, he's the general manager, he said he was just the same when he and Jim adopted their baby girl, so that's good.'

Maggie looked at her now, her eyes taking in Emma's hair with a pained expression. 'But I mean – I'm not really sure how you have that situation going on though,' she said waving a hand at Emma's rather ratty, in-need-of-a-wash hair. 'When you've got *Alessandro* living under your roof.'

Emma winced, quickly taking off the cardigan she was wearing; it suddenly felt like someone was scratching her lightly all over with long fingernails. In her confusion as she tried to pull a sleeve over the arm with the cast, Maggie getting up to help, she frowned and asked, 'Who?'

She sighed in pleasure as her skin went back to normal. Making a mental tally. Cotton good. Wool, not so much.

Maggie raised a brow. 'You're joking, right? The crazy hot Spanish guy living in your house – ring any bells?'

Emma's eyes widened. 'That's his full name – *Alessandro*?'

'Yeah, Alessandro Sandoz,' said Maggie with a schoolgirl sort of smile.

Emma pursed her lips. Of course it was.

'You're welcome to him – honestly, I wish Evie hadn't let him the annexe, he's just always in the way…'

'What do you mean?'

Emma sighed. 'It's not a big house, and he's just always around. He helps himself to the things in the fridge, he's always trying to chat, coming into my room… He drives me mad.'

Maggie raised a brow again. 'He wants to chat to the invalid girl. Eats things from the fridge in the house where he lives. Gosh, you're right, what a dreadful human being.'

Emma's lips twitched. She closed her eyes, groaned. 'I'm a cow.'

Maggie gave her a look of pity mixed with amusement. 'A little, but, well, you're in pain, it can make anyone grumpy.'

Emma sighed. 'I suppose, but it's not a great excuse, I don't like that I'm like this. I think it's just that he invades my space. I know he's trying to be nice… But that just makes it worse.'

'I can get that. Also, I mean, it's always just been you and Evie here, well, and your crazy aunts too, but now it's *A Man in Hope Cottage*,' she said, a little theatrically, her hands making a rainbow across the air as if her words were on a movie poster. 'What will Emma Halloway do? Find out, this Saturday on Film Four…'

Emma laughed. 'You're crackers. God, I missed you.'

'Me too. I'm sorry it took being knocked over by a van to bring you home, but I'm glad you're here, for a while at least.'

'Yeah… it'll be a while too,' Emma said darkly.

'They still don't know how long the recovery might take?'

Emma shook her head. 'Or if I will completely recover.' Admitting what she hadn't had the strength to say to her aunts.

'Oh, you will. I'm sure of it. I mean, they're probably working on it already,' Maggie said, her eyebrows dancing meaningfully as she made a vague gesture towards the empty kitchen beyond the screen.

Emma rolled her eyes. 'Don't get me started. I've told them not to bother.'

'Why not? Surely every little bit helps, and if you don't believe in it, what's the harm?'

'There's other reasons.'

Like the fact that she was in this situation because they'd sent The Book, and the postal worker who'd tried to deliver it knocked her down. She knew, logically, an inanimate object hadn't been the cause, but it was hard to forgive it all the same.

As if she could read her mind, Maggie glanced at the table and said, 'Is that it? The Book,' she added in reverential tones.

Emma shrugged. 'Yes, in all its two-hundred-year-old glory.'

'C-could I –' she cleared her throat, 'Would you mind if I had a look? I didn't dare ask when I was a kid… and there was always someone around so I couldn't really sneak a peek.' She winked.

'Knock yourself out,' said Emma, easing herself back on her pillows next to Mikey, who was still fast asleep. Maggie crept forward eagerly, flipping through the pages. 'Some of these are ancient!' she said, turning to one that dated back to 1818, her mouth flopping open. 'This newsprint on some of them – it's amazing, it's like a bite out of history!'

'Yeah,' said Emma, 'I think it's partly why I became a food writer, I mean, moving aside all the folklore and stuff attached to this book and us. The recipes offer a real sense of history – from the early recipes before the introduction of spices, times when meat was in short supply, and before sugar was a staple.'

Maggie nodded eagerly, still flipping the pages, 'Like this – "Peasebread"?'

'Yeah, that was popular in these parts back in the day. Some of the recipes call for these forgotten foods, like peasemeal. Evie's good that way though – I mean, in the garden she grows lots of old-fashioned herbs like tansy and rue, and she kept almond milk long before it became fashionable to do so.'

'Incredible,' remarked Maggie. 'Oh, my goodness, these names!'

'I know,' said Emma, giving her a wry grin. The names, frankly, were a little mad. 'Evie told me once that they say what they mean, not what they are.'

Maggie frowned. 'I suppose that makes sense.' She leaned forward to read. 'The instructions are wild,' she said with a laugh. She read one aloud: 'The herbs should be picked during the light of the harvest moon, and added before twilight on the second day.' She made a noise of surprise. 'It even comes with a warning – *A volatile recipe, to be made only with a calm temperament. Clear your emotions before you begin the layers, so as to avoid any unintended consequences, or be prepared to deal with the aftermath.*'

'Do they really do all this?' she asked, meaning Evie and her aunts. She didn't ask, 'Do you?' – she knew the answer was no, or at least, not any more.

Emma shrugged. 'Yeah, they do.'

Maggie shook her head. 'You know, I was always a bit envious of you growing up… I mean, I never told you this but I used to wish that Evie would adopt me, or maybe it would turn out that actually I had some family connection too. My nan said that one of the first Halloways married a Gilbert, so it seemed possible,' she said, with a wry smile, shaking her head at herself.

Maggie's family, the Gilberts, like the Allens, Halloways and Leas, were one of the oldest families in the village. Maggie had told Emma that herself the year she first came to live at Hope Cottage, after Emma's parents had passed away. It was the same occasion as when she had told Emma rather matter-of-factly at the school gates that they could be friends if Emma liked. Emma, who'd been feeling lost and alone, had been really touched.

Emma sat up now in surprise. 'I didn't know that! Or that you felt that way.'

'I never said anything. Didn't want to be "that guy".'

They both laughed.

'You could never be "that guy". Still, trust me, you're better off – that book, the whole "Halloway legacy" it's made things harder than they had to be.'

Maggie nodded. 'Yeah, I'm sure.' Between them Jack Allen's presence was thick, though unspoken.

After Maggie left, she couldn't help thinking of the past, when she'd first come to Hope Cottage, when everything changed for evermore.

FIVE

Hope Cottage, 1995

Evie Halloway's life changed for ever the day the eight magpies flew over the village, making their strange cries. There were few who didn't stop to cross themselves and rattle off the old rhyme, wondering what it had brought that day.

One for sorrow, two for joy, three for a girl,
four for a boy, five for silver, six for gold,
Seven for a secret never to be told.

Eight though. What could it mean? Old Ann Brimble, who ran the Whistle-In Store with her husband, said it meant change and that it had something to do with the Halloways. She could tell by the lingering scent in the air of burnt vanilla and new beginnings, the way some people know a storm is brewing from the ache in their knees.

Had Mrs Brimble peered inside Hope Cottage, her suspicions may well have been confirmed. It was the first time in fifty years that the old range had been cold to the touch, and the first time the old door, aged the colour of a duck's egg, had failed to open at the first, desperate, knock from those anxious enough to seek hope from a Halloway edible prescription.

As all villagers knew, food made in the kitchen at Hope Cottage, using the same tempestuous range that all the Halloway women had used since Grace Halloway's day, appeared to change lives, though no one really knew why.

It was said that when a Halloway woman kneaded dough, long-held quarrels ironed themselves out, and when she sieved flour, things fell smoothly back into place.

Need is what shaped the relationships of most of the villagers with the women of Hope Cottage. Few lifted that old brass knocker, shaped like a curmudgeon of a cat, when they wanted a simple Christmas cake or to learn how to perfect their Yorkshire puddings; people generally knocked only when they were at their wits' end, when they were prepared to pay the price, though it wasn't one that was metered by coin.

Evie Halloway, however, could hardly be blamed for not opening the door that particular day. News of the accident reached most people's ears via the six o' clock news on The Whistle Blower, the local radio station, but for Evie it had arrived much earlier, shortly after dawn, with the discovery of the tiny egg the colour of an old bruise nestling among the six brown, speckled shells she'd collected from beneath the hens. A shiver ran down her spine, as if someone had whispered something in her ear. The phone began to ring as she crossed over the threshold, and it was with a leaden heart that she lifted the receiver.

'Mrs Halloway?' enquired a prim-sounding voice.

'Just Evie – no missus,' corrected Evie, automatically, in her distinct Yorkshire brogue.

'Oh,' said the voice, with a polite hesitation. 'I-I'm afraid I have some rather bad news. I'm dreadfully sorry to have to tell you this over the phone, but it appears your daughter…' the voice faltered for a second, '…and your son-in-law have been in a car accident. I'm afraid… they didn't make it.'

There was a pause, long enough for Evie to feel her heart crack in two.

The voice continued, as if from a great distance, while Evie slumped against the kitchen wall, forgetting to breathe. One word, however, brought the voice back into sharp relief.

'I beg your pardon?' asked Evie.

'Your granddaughter? Thankfully, she's fine – a few bruises and scratches. Physically, she'll be okay, I mean emotionally, well, there are already a few effects as you can imagine – she hasn't said a word since the accident—'

'My g-granddaughter?' stammered Evie, blinking against the hazy fog of tears. Trying and failing to comprehend.

'Emma is fine,' reassured the voice. 'We'll be sending her on to you as soon as possible, as you are the only next of kin, we believe, for both of the deceased… it falls to you, unfortunately, to make the necessary arrangements.'

Necessary arrangements? The air left her lungs when she realised that the woman was referring to the funeral arrangements.

When the phone clicked in her ear, Evie's eye fell on The Book, open on the scrubbed wooden table, the same large tome that Halloway women had swollen with recipes over the past two hundred years – the same book that her daughter had attempted to burn before she slammed the door on Hope Cottage forever.

'Oh Margaret,' she whispered. 'How can I find out I've got a granddaughter on the same day I lose you?'

It was the shortest day of the year, and the longest night, when Emma, at the age of six, saw Hope Cottage for the first time.

It was a day when the cold wind skipped along the cobble-stones, trailing stiff fingers along the walls of thousand-year-old stone cottages, whispering inside the drainpipes and making that low whistle that some said had given the town its name.

It blew Emma's long red hair across her face and rattled the old brass knocker against the pale blue door, announcing their arrival before they could.

Emma shivered in her thin London coat, wondering what was waiting for her on the other side, hoping that it was better than the foster home she'd been placed in while they tracked down her 'grandmother' using records that had taken more than a week to find; someone she'd never met, or even knew existed until the day before, when she was told that's where she'd be going to live from now on. In her grief and despair, the idea of a granny had been like a light in a world turned dark. The foster home had peeling paint and dirty floors, and was filled with screaming children and a tired, overworked woman who smelt perpetually of cooking grease, and whose only words of comfort had been a suggestion for her to 'Make yourself scarce' and 'Be quiet, stop that crying, you're not the only one who has lost their parents,' when her howls woke up the household. Perhaps Emma had taken this advice a little too much to heart, as she hadn't been able to find her voice to make a sound since.

The social worker, Mrs Roberts, who would have been horrified if she knew about the rather callous nature of the temporary family she'd placed Emma with, gave her a nervous smile as the door opened with sudden speed. Then warmth as delicious as the first soak in a tub after a long, cold day spread across Emma, setting to work on easing the chill from her fingers and toes. It was followed closely by the scent of heather, wood fires, cinnamon and something that whispered to her, somehow, of Christmas.

It would always be the scent that brought Hope Cottage to Emma's mind from then on. That and the image of Evie.

Her first thought upon seeing Evie Halloway for the first time was that she didn't look like a granny. Grannies were plump. They wore half-moon spectacles and shawls round their shoulders and they always seemed to be cradling balls of yarn between their fingers. At least, they did in the books Emma had been allowed to read. Books that were more educational than anything else, and which had helped to give her a rather advanced reading age.

The woman across from her was tall and wiry. She had the type of hair that broke brushes and caused hairdressers to roll up their sleeves; it perched on her shoulders like a shaggy grey animal wearing its thickest wintry coat, appearing to pulse with life. Her eyes were large, and blue, and her skin was smooth and tanned. She wore faded denim dungarees and brown leather boots that laced up to the knee, and the sort of stare that made Mrs Roberts feel the need to swallow, and pat down her neat bun, as she made their introductions.

Evie, though, only had eyes for Emma. She noted the child's skin – how it was the type that was prone to freckle without provocation. The eyes, which were large and sad and seemed to say everything her frozen tongue could not. They were scared and hopeful and she noted with some satisfaction that they also appeared a little relieved. She noted the colour, the Halloway blue. The blue of lobelias and Cape starlings and secret springs. Then her gaze came back to the child's hair. That was not typical at all.

'So, Margaret did run away with that Scot,' said Evie with a snort, in her Yorkshire brogue, which Emma recognised as similar to her mother's. 'I might have guessed.'

'I beg your pardon?' asked Mrs Roberts, smoothing down her skirt, eyes wide behind their glasses' horned rims.

'Same hair – see,' said Evie, lips twitching. 'Red.' It wasn't clear if this amused or annoyed her. Perhaps it was both.

Mrs Roberts shifted uncomfortably in her court shoes, shooting Emma an uncertain look, brown eyes hesitant. 'I'm sorry – do you mean to tell me this is the first time you're meeting your granddaughter?'

Evie's right shoulder lifted in a casual shrug. 'Stranger things have happened than a grandmother meeting her runaway child's offspring for the first time, I'm sure.'

Mrs Roberts looked agog. It had never occurred to her that child and grandmother might never have met – Emma hadn't said – then again, as the child hadn't said anything at all since the accident, that was hardly surprising really.

It was Evie, though, who reassured Mrs Roberts that everything would be all right, the same way she'd been reassuring most visitors who came to Hope Cottage since she herself was around Emma's age.

'We're going to get to know each other just fine, don't you worry,' she told them both, seeing Mrs Roberts out the door. 'It's home, and she'll feel that soon enough – it's in her blood.'

When they were alone, Evie let Emma introduce herself to the cottage slowly, meeting the whitewashed walls, the polished flagstone floors, the low, weathered beams above their heads and the secret nooks and crannies cut into the textured stone. These were filled with books, comfy seats, drying herbs and sleeping cats. Emma counted three before she was shown upstairs.

'This is your room,' said Evie, leading her to a spacious room under the eaves, where a forest green iron bed was dressed with a pale muslin cover, a lilac and bird's egg blue patchwork quilt at the foot. There was a small wooden wardrobe and, next to the bed, a three-legged stool where a jam jar held a posy of dried bell heather, which perfumed the room and brought to mind thoughts of long walks on the moors they'd driven past on their way into the cobbled village with its rolling hills and butterscotch cottages.

Emma tried to imagine her mother living here and couldn't. Her mother didn't allow pets. Their flat in a busy, noisy street in London had double-height ceilings and polished, black marble countertops. The furniture was sharp and metallic and they had black and white art dominating entire walls. The flowers were sharp and pointed, with exotic names like *strelitzia*. Words like 'spacious' and 'minimalist' and 'art deco' were used to describe their flat. She didn't know what the opposite word for minimalist was, but she knew that it applied here, to Hope Cottage. She sat on the bed, hugging her small backpack to herself like a misshapen teddy bear, and puzzled at the difference.

In the kitchen, Evie lit the fire and consulted The Book, flipping through the pages until she found the one she was looking for.

Transitional Tomato Tagine.

'This might do,' she told Pennywort, the year-old bulldog, who'd taken a seat at the table, his white and brown spotted head propped up on the table edge, keeping a solemn chestnut-coloured eye on the proceedings. She patted his head, then drummed a finger against her chin as she read the notes written by some long-ago Halloway hand.

Make at dusk, stirring counterclockwise, keeping your intentions firm, and your emotions calm. Slow, but lasting results.

Evie didn't mind waiting. Unlike the villagers who came with desperation in their eyes, who wanted, needed, instant change, she knew that time could be a mercurial friend when you asked too much of it too soon.

She slipped off the last of her good jewellery – her mother's silver ring – with a sigh. Pennywort put his head to one side and gave her a bulldog huff as she did, his dark eyes boring into hers.

'Don't look at me like that. What do I need trinkets for anyway?' she said, though she put it aside with some reluctance. That's how she knew it would work. She'd plant it tonight beneath the frost-covered tomato bed, where it would join Mrs Drummond's diamond earrings and Sandra Pike's antique vase, a token for better days ahead.

Emma entered the kitchen, and Evie saw her taking in the navy blue range dominating the room, the wrinkly dog sitting at the large scrubbed wooden table and Evie standing before it, a giant cream mixing bowl in her arms. In the background, Elvis crooned softly from an old wireless on the pale blue Welsh dresser.

'This is Pennywort, he keeps an eye on things, likes to ensure that we keep the cottage running shipshape,' she told Emma. Then she looked at the dog, 'My granddaughter, Emma.'

Pennywort, ordinarily a bit of a grump, gave Emma a very uncharacteristic bulldog grin, which the child returned, going over to touch his soft fur.

Evie nodded, deciding that they may as well start where all Halloways begin – gently though. That was best. 'So… what I'm going to need from you is a sprig of rosemary, a thumb of lemon verbena and three of the bottom leaves of the dark opal basil. You'll find them all in the greenhouse outside. The basket's there by the door.'

Emma hesitated. Evie saw the child's confused expression and asked, 'Do you know what they look like?'

Emma shook her head. Evie glanced at The Book as if it would lend her strength. It made sense. When Margaret left, she had vowed that she didn't want anything to do with the 'family folly', as she termed it; it was little wonder she'd never instructed her child. By Emma's age most Halloways would be able to identify dozens of wild herbs with their eyes closed.

Evie opened a drawer and took out an unlined notebook with a plain black cover and a pencil, and put these in front of the child. 'All Halloways start with one of these.'

At her look of confusion, Evie scanned the dresser next to the range till she found a plump volume, which she plucked off the shelf and handed to Emma as well. 'This was your mother's.'

Emma frowned as she opened the notebook and took a seat next to the dog. He gave her the sort of attention he usually reserved for food, his head butting her arm so that he could see as well.

The notebook was filled with tight black writing and careful sketches that observed the passing of the seasons and the uses of herbs and wild flowers. Some were pressed inside the pages, offering up a lingering scent of the Yorkshire moors.

There were recipes and remedies and ruminations. Emma's fingers traced around splatters and dribbles from long-ago bubbling pots, riffled through pages that had buckled from steam and smelt of spices and stews and summers gone by.

She paged through it eagerly, until a dark thought rose up and clenched her throat, flooding her with sudden fear. She stood up quickly, her breath coming in sharp gasps, thrust the notebook at Evie and shook her head. A wild, chilling realisation dawned upon her. This could not be her mother's.

Emma's eyes scanned the kitchen, taking in Pennywort, who was regarding her with bemusement, and the rest of the cottage, this cosy, somewhat quirky place that in no way looked like her parents' home in London. It wasn't possible; her mother couldn't have come from here. This was all some horrible mistake. The social worker, Mrs Roberts, must have got it wrong.

Evie must be someone else's grandmother. Her mother never cooked. She ordered pre-made dinners for the week, which arrived in neat cardboard containers that stacked perfectly in the fridge. They had labels on the front that told you in chunky black letters how much in calories, sodium, protein and carbohydrates they contained. All you had to do was divide the meal onto plates and warm them up in the microwave. They were expensive and healthy, and home-cooked, though not in their kitchen. This saved her mother valuable time so that she could be in front of her computer looking at bars and graphs and putting what she saw into spreadsheets. People paid her a lot of money to do that, so that she didn't have to cook, or so she said. Her mother never stopped to look at anything outside, like rainbows, or the unusual flower growing out of the pavement, or the drawing of a monster wearing underpants on its head in the shop window. She certainly didn't document the things she saw in pretty notebooks. How could she have, when she hardly saw anything at all? Whenever Emma stopped to point out such things, her arm was pulled and she was chastised to, 'Hurry up', though it wasn't always clear why they were in such a hurry as they were never, ever late.

'You don't think it's hers, do you?'

Emma opened her mouth, but no sound came out.

Evie hesitated. 'Your mother changed over the years. It's partly my fault, partly her own, partly this village and what it means to be a Halloway in a place where not much has changed in over two-hundred years… you'll learn about that soon enough, but for now all you need to know is that this was hers, and that there was a time when she wrote in this, when she liked nothing better than her life here at Hope Cottage.'

Evie opened the notebook to the back cover and approached Emma. 'I'm just going to show you this, okay?'

Emma took a hesitant step backwards as Evie handed her back the notebook, pointing to where an old, sepia-toned photograph was pasted inside.

Emma's mouth parted in surprise. It was a girl, close to her own age, with thick black hair, head thrown back in laughter, her arms wrapped round a somewhat younger and plumper Evie. They were standing before the same old, navy range in the kitchen. Beneath the photograph, written in childish script, was: 'Margaret and Evie Halloway, Hope Cottage, 1974.'

Emma crept forward, her fingers tracing over her mother's face and the Halloway name in wonder.

'Did you know it's a family tradition to keep the Halloway name for girls, even after they marry and have children?'

Emma looked up at Evie in surprise. She knew that lots of people didn't understand why she didn't have her father's last name – her father included, who'd felt a little betrayed that his child didn't have his last name. Officially her birth certificate said Emma Rose McGrath Halloway. It was something that always came up when her parents were arguing, when they thought she couldn't hear them. 'Girls are always Halloways, even I can't go against that,' her mother had said once when she'd had a bit too much to drink, trying to explain why she'd gone behind her husband's back and filled in Emma's birth certificate when he'd left the hospital for a cup of tea. He'd said she could have at least called her Emma Halloway *McGrath*.

'It's because of this,' said Evie, pointing to the enormous book open on the table. 'It's the Halloway Recipe Book. It's over two hundred years old, and filled with all the recipes Halloway women have made over the years – all our hopes, our secrets too. It's why it never leaves this cottage. Some say if it did, well… who knows what may happen?'

Emma's lips parted in surprise and she crept forward to see, smoothing her long red hair behind her ears. The book was enormous; the cover was made of pale blue cloth with tiny white flowers that had been faded by time to the texture of fine linen, soft as butter. It was brimming with pages that had been crammed together and stitched inside. Each page told a story, offering a window into the past: the types of foods that were fashionable in the 1800s; the sorts of spices that were favoured when King George IV was on the throne; surviving the rations and the two world wars. There were recipes from all the years in between, in times of plenty and times of lack. Some of the pages were crisp and white, others had newsprint in the margins, where old headlines and adverts rested alongside the recipes, telling them to 'Make Do and Mend' and 'Keep Calm and Have A Cup of Yorkshire Tea'.

'We used newspaper during the war years – when paper was a little scarce – we painted it white, then wrote on that. Then later, newspaper became scarce as well,' Evie said.

There must have been thousands of handwritten recipes. Some were elaborately hand-lettered in perfect calligraphy; others were scrawled, jotted in haste. Some had beautiful watercolour illustrations to accompany them; others were in simple copperplate, with no adornment beyond the date of their creation.

The recipe names made her pause. Some were austere and rather puzzling, like one called The Sinking Ship, which spoke of turning tides and changing fortunes; others were tongue-in-cheek and made her smile as she silently mouthed the words. She looked at Evie in surprise. They weren't like any recipes she'd heard of before. The ones she liked best were a little bit funny and had names like the titles of old songs, Come Together Stew, Mend Fences Flambé, Hit the Road Roulade and Just in Time Tagliatelle.

'They say what they mean, not what they are,' explained Evie, who had a fondness for naming some of the recipes she created after old rock 'n' roll tunes, influenced, no doubt, by the local vintage-music station, The Old Whistle, which was always on. 'A good recipe isn't just about making something that tastes good, you see?'

Emma shook her head. She'd always thought that taste was the most important thing.

'The trick to a great recipe is first having a clear intention of what you'd like to achieve. Food does so much more than feed the body, you know? It can feed the spirit too, help it to grow, if you have the right ingredients and a firm intention, that is,' Evie said, picking up the basket and beckoning Emma to follow out the back door.

When she opened it, though, she stopped short, shook her head and sighed, raising her eyes heavenward, as if to seek guidance up there. For there, by the low garden gate, were two women, waiting with rather expectant grins.

One was plump, with pale, nearly white, flyway hair and glasses as thick as the end of a jam jar. The other was tall and stout with thick, short dark hair and the somewhat mistaken belief that riding boots complemented any outfit.

'Ah,' said Evie.

'Ah, indeed,' said the tall, stout one, blue eyes dancing.

'Were you on your way to us?' asked the plump one, with a wide grin. 'Wouldn't that have been funny?' she went on. Even with the distance between them, Emma could see that her nail polish was a pearly sort of purple, and most of it was chipped away.

'Oh, I doubt that, Dot,' said the other, opening the gate, giving Evie an almost apologetic look as she said, 'We were in the neighbourhood…'

Evie's lips twitched. 'That's not hard, is it?'

Dot grinned. 'No, because we live here!' she said, directing her reply to Emma.

'Well, just up the road, anyway,' she added, indicating the cobbled high street in the distance.

Evie rolled her eyes. 'Emma, meet my sisters. Dot,' she said indicating the one with the bottle-thick glasses on the end of her nose, and 'Agatha Halloway,' she said of the other. 'Or Laurel and Hardy.'

'Ha ha,' said Agatha. 'What does that make you – Curly?'

Dot cocked her head to the side and considered her great-niece, noting the freckles, the Halloway eyes, the small frame, then frowned.

'Red?' she asked, looking at Evie as if for guidance.

'Red', repeated Agatha, who looked rather taken aback at the thought as well.

'That Scot…' explained Evie.

Two nearly identical pairs of round blue eyes widened. 'That cheeky madam,' said Agatha. 'She denied it like nobody's business, told me she was moving to London for work.' Her eyes grew sad and a tear leaked down her cheek.

Dot brushed the tear off her sister's face, though her own eyes had filled too, just as Evie's had.

Evie nodded. She couldn't help wishing things had been different – that Margaret hadn't left that day, hadn't felt the need to get away, hadn't felt the need to change everything she was.

'To be fair, it's a nice change,' said Dot, who had that air of someone who despite the worst of circumstances tries to put on a brave, kind face, glancing from Emma's mane to Evie and Agatha's wild crops of hair.

Halloways were not often described as the sort of people who had 'good hair days', unless the definition was one that meant it was a day that one of them hadn't broken a hairbrush, or made the local hairdresser consider closing up shop just because they had decided to make an appointment.

Silence followed this rather sore point. Which Dot, with her relatively sleek-by-comparison hair, often pressed.

'So… have you shown her The Book?' asked Agatha.

'She's just got here,' protested Evie. 'But yes, I did. We're taking it easy, mind – that goes for you two as well. I was hoping to introduce you both a little later, actually… Once Emma has had a chance to catch her breath,' she said pointedly.

Agatha gave Evie a long-suffering look; Agatha was not the type of person who believed in taking anything slow, or easy for that matter. 'Because there's an easy way to break the news to a six-year-old that she's just been handed over to a family who many think are witches?'

Emma gasped.

SIX

'To be fair, the child doesn't look scared any more,' said Dot, cowering a little under Evie's glower as the latter set down cups of tea in front of her and Agatha, with a heavy thud, then proceeded to pour a liberal amount of brandy into her own, despite the relatively early hour.

Evie pinched the bridge of her nose, closed her eyes and prayed for strength. 'That's only because I told her the *truth.*'

'Emma,' she went on, addressing the child, who had been watching the exchange like a ping-pong match since Evie's face turned tomato red and she began shouting at her sisters from the doorway, arms gesturing wildly, pointed fingers shaking; a few nosy neighbours started craning their necks over garden fences to witness the commotion, so Dot had shooed the four of them all into the cottage.

'You remember how I explained about The Book?' said Evie.

Emma gave a hesitant nod.

'Well, that's really what Aggie means. It's something all Halloway girls are born with – your mother too. We offer hope, which is a magic all of its own, and it affects the food we make.'

'The boys get other things,' chipped in Dot.

Aggie snorted. 'Like the power of evaporation – they disappear at will.'

'That's not true,' said Dot. 'Anyway, Daddy wasn't a Halloway, technically.'

Evie looked away. 'It isn't easy on the men, this, we have enough failed relationships in our family to attest to that, but that's a story for another day.'

'It isn't easy on the women either,' pointed out Aggie. 'I mean look at your mother,' she told Emma, whose ears perked up at her mention.

'Oh, she was excellent in the kitchen, a real natural,' enthused Dot, her eyes wide behind their thick lenses. 'She cooked with her heart, and you often felt what she did in what she made. Which, of course, came with its problems, especially when she was a teenager, struggling with her emotions. And later too, really, perhaps it was harder for her because it called so loudly.'

They nodded solemnly. 'It's why she resisted it so much,' said Dot, wisely.

To her credit, Emma didn't look quite as frightened as a child in her situation would have had every right to be.

'What do you think about this?' asked Agatha.

Emma shrugged.

'She doesn't speak,' said Evie, shaking her head in exasperation. It wasn't like she hadn't told them about it. They just kept forgetting.

Dot and Agatha shared a look. 'Not a word?'

'Nothing since the accident.'

'Ah, poor thing,' said Dot, standing up and consulting The Book. 'I seem to recall an excellent recipe that Mother used on our evacuee from the Blitz, what was his name – Johnny?'

'Jason,' said Evie.

'Ah yes, poor lad. He didn't speak either, in the beginning.'

'I've decided on the tomato tagine,' said Evie. Gentle was best.

'That slow burner?' said Aggie, tutting. She stood up and went to stand next to her sister, skipping through the pages. 'Why not something with a bit of zap, a bit of fizzle – how about this?' she said, settling on one that promised quick-fire results. Lightning Bolt Lemon Pie was exactly the sort of recipe Agatha would choose, the sort of thing only someone with a gambler's heart would try. 'It worked on old Bob Hogson, remember?'

'Oh yes,' said Evie in exasperation, pinching the bridge of her nose again. 'The family wanted a bit of peace and quiet from his constant moans—'

'Well, they got it, didn't they?'

'Yes, only they realised that his constant griping was the only thing that had been keeping him alive! He withered away soon after that with nothing left to care about.'

Evie shook her head, took The Book from her sister and flipped it back to the tagine, giving the page a firm pat. 'We just want a bit of calm. No whirlwind changes. Slow and steady wins the race,' she said, decisively.

Aggie looked at her in disbelief. 'Clearly, you know nothing about racing.'

Emma learned that Dot and Aggie were a part of Hope Cottage, just as much as Pennywort and The Book. Dot lived in a spacious bungalow with her husband Jo, who ran the used car dealership in town.

If you visited her house, you'd almost always catch her in her bathrobe and slippers, even at midday, though she always had her make-up on; she was a bit vain about her big, round eyes and full Cupid's bow mouth and always wanted them to be seen at their best. As soon as you were inside she'd ply you with tea, then dash off to get changed, all the while telling you secrets through the closed bedroom door. Dot liked nothing better than telling stories, and she could suck you in and make time go past faster than you could blink. Before you knew it, you were agreeing to another cup of tea and listening to the latest gossip. Some said that Jessica Flynn, the newscaster on local radio station The Whistle Blower, kept Dot on speed-dial for her nightly round-up of the village news, because no one knew more about the residents of Whistling than her.

She told her stories with drama and intrigue and an uncanny knack for voices. Emma learned, like many of the residents of Whistling, that you visited Dot when you had time to spare – and at your own peril if you didn't. Minutes and hours and afternoons could pass without you realising you'd fallen under Dot's spell. She served endless pots of tea and old-fashioned cakes that left your mouth watering for more; there were Eccles cakes, rich with nutmeg and currants, mountains of singin' hinnies, hot and rich with honey, and before you knew it, even though you'd just come for a cuppa you'd left after the last game of cards, well after dinner and well past dark.

But she was more than just a storyteller. Dot was the one you called when you needed calm and cheer, when it felt like all hope was lost. Aggie was the one who brought luck. Though, somehow, she'd never managed to stumble on any of it for herself. After husband number three, one would imagine she'd given up, but she was a romantic at heart.

'Aggie is the oldest,' said Dot. 'And should have been the one to run Hope Cottage—'

'Only I ran away with a drummer when I was eighteen,' said Aggie. She'd married Stan straight away. His band had had a few hits back in the sixties. Michael was next – he became a professional poker player. And Bill, in her thirties when she thought that maybe it would be a good idea to date another artist like herself. The short version was that it had not been.

Aggie lived in a flat just off the high street, where she painted enormous canvases filled with rushes of black swirling paint that she said sometimes reflected her moods. Shadow art, she called it. The first-time Emma visited her flat and stood in Aggie's studio, she realised she recognised them, or at least ones like them; there had been several hanging in her old London flat, her home with her parents.

'You know these?' she asked, as Emma stared at them in wonder. Tears came to her eyes as Emma nodded.

Aggie stared at her. 'Your mother was one of my first customers – we used to be very close, she and I. Same temperament,' she said, with a grin. 'I just wish she'd told us about you,' she went on, squeezing Emma's shoulder.

'That makes two of us,' said Evie.

'Three,' said Dot, who was wiping away a tear. They'd been doing a lot of crying and talking about Emma's mother, which was something that Emma found helpful; at least she wasn't alone in her grief.

'And I got married soon after, to Jo,' said Dot, who didn't have any children of her own. This had been a devastating blow; of all of them, Dot was the most motherly.

'So, running the cottage fell to me,' said Evie, 'but it's all of ours really – yours too.'

SEVEN

Present day

It was after midnight when Emma heard the door to the cottage open and low footsteps crossing the flagstone floor, en route to the fridge.

Emma switched on the light.

Sandro was standing with a stack of trays balanced one on top of the other, which he almost dropped, making at the same time a funny, rather high-pitched cry.

'Jesus,' he said, his eyes wide, when he saw her.

'Sorry,' said Emma, snorting. 'You scream like a girl by the way.'

He laughed. 'You try making a manly scream, Pajarita, when you think someone is about to attack you with that,' he said pointing at her crutch, which was casting a rather ominous scythe-like shadow across the wall.

Emma started to giggle.

'I hardly think the Grim Reaper would be after you just for those,' she said, and then frowned. 'What is it anyway?'

'The contents of the fridge from the Tapas Hut.' He set the trays down carefully on the table. 'My fridge blew,' he said, moving his hair from out of his eyes and giving her a half-grin. His handsome face now looked tired and unamused.

'It blew *up*?' Emma gasped, eyes widening in horror as she pictured an explosion. 'Is everyone all right?' She focused her still-hazy eyes on him with difficulty. He didn't seem injured.

He frowned, confused. 'Fine – it was just a fuse.'

'Oh,' she said, hiding a smile.

'Well, anyway, I just have a bar fridge in the annexe so I thought I'd put these in here.' He pointed to the large double-door fridge-freezer that sat across from the Welsh dresser.

Emma shrugged. 'Sure.'

'You're up late,' he noted. 'Hope I didn't wake you.'

'Couldn't sleep.'

'Would you like a coffee?'

'Why not?' she asked, trying and failing to open the pill bottle of her painkillers.

He unpacked the contents of the boxes, filled the coffee pot, then came over with a glass of water and got a pill out for her.

'Thanks,' she said. He shrugged, went off again and returned with a yellow striped mug, which he placed before her before taking a seat opposite, his dark eyes peering at her.

She blinked, and then looked away. His gaze was fairly intense, seeing perhaps more than she was comfortable with. In the background, there was an odd humming sound, which had her confused; she looked around, wondering if Penny was snoring, then realised it was the sound of the coffee machine.

'Is that sore?' he asked, pointing at her hand in its cast.

She shrugged. 'Sometimes. I can't wait to get the pins out.' She sighed.

He nodded. 'I can imagine,' he said, touching the cast, his fingertips brushing her wrist. She jolted from his touch, moving her arm away.

'Sorry,' he said. 'Did I hurt you?'

'No. It's okay,' she said, blushing. 'Touch is just weird, you know – since my accident,' and she explained about how things could get confused in her brain. Though, to be fair, when he'd touched her it had felt just like it should: gentle, nice really. Perhaps it was the surprise of such a normal response that had shocked her.

'That must be hard,' he said, shaking his head.

She took a sip of her coffee and sighed.

'You know, I can deal with that – though I wish I could read. It would be such a help just to be able to escape for a bit.'

'Why can't you?' he asked.

'The words sort of scramble across the page and I can't really make sense of the letters.'

'Geez, I'm sorry.'

She gave him a small smile. 'Thanks. What I really miss most, if I'm honest, is being able to enjoy food,' she said with a small, sad laugh. 'Not being able to taste or smell anything, that's the worst, really, it makes life seem… flat.'

His eyes were solemn as he regarded her. 'Especially for someone like you.'

'What do you mean?'

He shrugged, his hands taking in the expanse of the kitchen and The Book open on the scarred wooden table. 'Coming from a family of cooks, your career – the food column – I mean, it must feel a bit like you've lost a piece of your identity,' he said, eyes contemplative as they regarded her.

She blinked. That was exactly how she felt.

Then he smiled. 'Food's my life too, Pajarita – I think I'd be the same,' he said with a wink.

She grinned, forgot to tell him to stop calling her a little bird. Up close, she could see that his dark eyes had small flecks of gold in them, though she saw this, as usual, doubled, like rows of negatives from a film.

'You should let them help,' he said softly.

'Who?' she asked, looking away. She'd been staring without realising it.

'Evie, your aunts. Let them make a recipe for you.'

She shook her head. 'No.'

'Why not?'

She frowned, her ire rising. 'Because – because it's all rubbish anyway.'

'So then, what could it hurt?'

'That's beside the point.'

He took a sip of his coffee. 'I doubt that, Pajarita.'

'Why do you say that?'

He shrugged. 'Because if you really thought that it wouldn't matter, would it?'

After Jack had sent the heart-shaped dog biscuits, Emma wondered if he would come past, but he didn't. She tried not to be disappointed by that. Tried not to inject more meaning into the small gift than she should, reminding herself that they had both moved on. But it was hard. Hard not to think of him. A few times she saw him out of the window, jogging in the street with his dog, Gus, and almost found herself going out to call to him.

It was during Emma's third week at Hope Cottage that she got the email she was dreading from her editor at the *Mail & Ledger*. She passed her mobile to Evie, who was sitting at the table, plaiting dough for a recipe for strengthening a family bond ahead of the Christmas season.

On the vintage radio station, The Old Whistle, a medley of Christmas tunes from the likes of Bing Crosby and Ella Fitzgerald had been playing all afternoon. Emma had been humming along, realising as she did that sounds had begun to make sense again, music didn't feel like an assault and she didn't need to lip-read any more, which was a relief.

Though everything else was still a mess. Just that morning as she'd tried combing her hair, the bristles of her hairbrush had without warning shed their benign guise, becoming sharp needles that pricked painfully at her scalp, and she'd yelped with fright and pain as she flung the brush from her. Her hair was now shoved into a very messy, knotty bun, which she'd done with one hand. Attractive, it was not.

Her mobile was open to her latest email.

'Can you read it to me?' she asked Evie. 'I'm still seeing double.'

Evie nodded, dusting the flour off her fingers onto her apron and popping on her glasses. Emma took a seat next to Pennywort, eyed the plate of ginger snaps and bit into one, only to sigh; it was like eating warm sand, completely tasteless.

Dear Emma,

Thank you for letting us know about your situation. We were devastated to hear of your accident, and sincerely wish you a speedy recovery. Unfortunately, as the situation described is not quite temporary, we may need to make alternative arrangements with your weekly column, 'The Historical Cook'. Our staff writer, Jane Bunting, has been using some of your past material, reworked into themes such as the recent holiday food one, but I fear that it is not a long-term solution. As it is one of our most popular columns, we cannot simply put it on hold, as you can imagine. Please advise whether we should look at contacting a freelancer to fill your place – is there anyone you would recommend? Obviously, we would like to keep the same standard our readers have come to enjoy.

Best wishes,
Sue Fedler
Food Editor, the Mail & Ledger

'One of their most popular columns? Because of you – all your hard work!' huffed Evie, putting the phone down with a thud.

Emma felt ill. A replacement? It hadn't even been a month and they were already looking for someone else? After four years?

'I can't believe they'd write this,' said Evie.

'I can.'

What did she expect? It wasn't like she was permanently employed by the newspaper; she was a freelancer. She had a popular column that many food historians would love to write – she couldn't expect them to keep running her old copy for ever, repurposed into 'new' content. Still, after four years of loyal, faithful service that had helped to boost advertising and lift a rather flabby food section, she might have expected slightly more loyalty than this – at least a guarantee that as soon as she was well again they would welcome her back.

'I suppose legally they don't owe me anything, I'm self-employed – not permanent staff.'

Evie shrugged. 'Still, loyalty should count for something?'

She could recommend someone to fill her column, but it was a tricky situation as she didn't know how long her recovery was likely to be. It could be a few months, a year, perhaps even more – would it be fair on either of them if she came back after a prolonged period wanting her column back? She couldn't really blame the newspaper for wanting to make a plan; they were running a business after all. The doctors couldn't guarantee when she might get better, or if she even would.

There were other concerns too. She needed the money; even though the column wasn't her main source of income, it was key, particularly, in building her brand as a food writer and building a network of freelance clients. She had some savings that would cover the rent for a few months, but, still, letting go of the column would just make it that much harder to return to her old life, which she desperately wished to do.

Evie found her sobbing an hour later in the living room, an abandoned notebook and pen in her hand. Evie picked up the notebook and saw the uneven scrawl across the page. It looked like a child had written it, one who had recently learned the alphabet and was having some trouble, the letters shaky, some almost back to front.

She swallowed, took Emma in her arms. 'It'll get better.'

'When?' she sobbed. 'That took me two hours. The worst is it's all here,' she said, tapping her head with a finger of the hand in the cast, tears making steady streams down her face. 'I know what I want to say, I just can't get it out.'

Evie stroked her back, wiped her thumbs under Emma's eyes. 'If that's the case it's a problem we can deal with, love. You don't have to write it yourself, do you? You just need someone to transcribe what you say.'

Emma took in a shuddering breath, felt a surge of hope fill her chest.

'You're right.' She looked at Evie, eyes widening in realisation. 'You'd do that – for me?' she asked.

Evie scoffed, 'Of course I would, silly.'

It took almost two days to write her first column, something that usually only took her a few hours at best. Partly it was trying to remember past facts and references with a brain that was easily tired, and getting Evie to use her mobile to look these up for her as they didn't have Wi-Fi – something Emma was prepared to remedy in secret if she had to as Evie was a committed Luddite.

It was also hard to focus on what she was trying to say when so much seemed to call for Evie's attention. As soon as she would begin transcribing Emma's dictation, there would be a knock on the door.

The people who visited came with their troubles and looked for a sympathetic ear, and it was never easy for Evie to get away. Besides, the recipes required her full focus, as many were complex and needed ingredients that had to be foraged on long rambling walks and then took hours of preparation.

By the time she was able to give her full attention, Emma was often fast asleep or had lost her train of thought. Evie's knowledge of food, her own observations and ruminations, could also be a distraction and she couldn't help peppering Emma's dictations with them; they would come through after she read back what she'd written.

'I don't remember saying that!' said Emma, referring to her latest column, a look at food in Shakespeare's time, to which Evie had added in a snippet of her own about balancing the humours with the seasons.

'Oh? Well, I added it in.'

'Evie, I appreciate that – but this is about fact, not myth.'

'It's not myth!'

'Yes, it is!'

This happened at least three times. Afterwards there were tense silences, followed by a lot of cajoling and forced apologies, till finally they'd start again. It was like running around in circles, getting nowhere fast. It was frustrating all round, but at last the first column was done.

'I think it would be easier if you had someone else. Someone less… busy,' said Evie tactfully.

Emma looked at her, bit her lip. 'I agree, I appreciate everything you've done though, but it's—'

'It's not really working,' agreed Evie. 'Anyway, the person that I have in mind would be perfect, free in the early mornings so you'd have some quality, focused time, which I think would really make a difference.'

Emma nodded. That *would* make a difference; she felt at her best in the mornings, which was when Evie was often busiest, so they'd been forced to do it closer to the middle of the day when Emma's tired brain always needed a rest.

'Brilliant. Have you contacted an agency of some kind? I'm not sure I could afford that – but I could make it work, somehow, it would be worth it.'

'That's the best part – they'll do it for free!'

'Really?' she said, eyes widening in surprise. 'That's amazing, who is it – Dot or Aggie? I didn't think they had the time.'

Evie beamed at her. 'Not Dot or Aggie, no, but just as good.'

Emma frowned. She was beginning to suspect something. Next second, Evie confirmed it.

'Sandro!' she said in delight.

Emma felt her stomach drop. 'Oh God.'

Evie ignored all her protestations. 'It'll be great – don't worry.'

'But – but what about his English? I mean…' She bit her lip. 'I wouldn't be able to correct it on the screen…'

'Oh, don't be such a snob, his English is great, and if need be, I'll go over it.'

'Is there no one else?'

'Nope,' said Evie, who looked a little bit too pleased.

EIGHT

'You'll be all right on your own for a bit?' asked Evie for the second time that morning, as she made her way out the door. 'I can go later, or…' she said, her blue eyes hesitant.

Earlier, she'd watched as Evie took down the familiar set of dark green and white cake tins from atop the blue Welsh dresser, the tins that were filled every year with their traditional Good Cheer Christmas Cake, which took weeks of preparation and was one of their most involved recipes and – to the sisters' minds – their most important. Emma had had to stop herself from snorting, and it had been on the tip of her tongue to say, 'Oh God, you honestly still believe a silly slice of Christmas cake for everyone in the village keeps this place together?' But she had stopped herself, just in time, biting her tongue. She didn't want the argument; nor did she want to hurt Evie.

'Go, Evie,' she said now, mock-sternly. 'I'll be all right, it's just a couple of hours. I'll survive – trust me.'

Evie shook her head. 'What's this "Evie" business?' she asked Pennywort, who was sitting in his customary seat at the kitchen table. The dog gave a small huff. It was a very old argument.

Emma ignored her – they both knew she'd called her grandmother Evie since she was six years old.

'Go on now, go give Harrison Brimble his recipe for athlete's foot, or whatever it is.'

Evie laughed. 'It's plantar fasciitis, but all right, if you're sure.'

'Oh *plantar fasciitis*, well that changes things then, I can understand the need for a house visit now.'

'Ha ha,' snorted Evie, 'I'm sure he'll make it.'

She still looked a little worried, so Emma rolled her eyes. 'I'll be fine, stop being a mother hen. I'll probably take one of my many naps, lucky me.'

Seconds after she'd left, there was a knock at the door and Emma shuffled forward to open it. 'What did you forget,' she called through the closed door. 'Corn plasters, perhaps?' She opened it wide, only to see Jack Allen standing outside, a grin on his face.

'Corn plasters?'

She swallowed, gathering her cardigan closer to her body as the cold wind entered through the open door, making that whistling sound that rattled the drainpipes, causing her to shiver slightly. 'It's you,' she said, blinking, the laughter dying on her lips.

'Me,' he said with a small smile.

'Thought I'd come past, see how you're doing,' he said, running a hand through his dark blond hair, hazel eyes hesitant. His eyes trailing over her face, lingering on her injuries, and then frowning. She knew she looked a sight; while the marks on her face had started to fade, she still had several bruises, which had turned a yellowy-green now as they healed.

Aside from that, she was wearing a very old, patchy pair of joggers, covered as usual in dog hair, and there was a coffee stain on her sleeve. She felt herself flush, wishing that just once she could see him when she looked at least halfway decent. 'Do you want to come in?'

'Um…' He hesitated. 'Okay.'

Outside, there was the sound of a car slamming on its brakes and they both jumped, then peered outside to see. Across the garden wall, through the open window of the car, they saw Stella

Lea, the girl who'd hated Emma since she arrived here at six years old, declaring herself her enemy based on a two-hundred-year-old disagreement between their families. Things had only got worse since Stella and Jack dated a few years before, but that was over now, wasn't it?

Stella sat behind the wheel staring at them both, her face bloodless, her eyes blazing, looking for all the world as if she'd just been slapped in the face.

Emma blinked, then looked from Stella to Jack in shock.

Then, with a sudden screech from her tyres, Stella tore off down the road.

Jack closed his eyes, pinched the bridge of his nose.

Emma swallowed. 'Are you and Stella still together?' she asked.

Jack took a breath. 'It's… well, it's complicated. The short answer is not any more, but you know how she is – how she's always been about you.'

Emma nodded. Stella had always seen her as a rival. Unfortunately the feeling was mutual.

'I better go or else she'll turn this into World War Three…' He hesitated before turning to leave. 'Sorry. I'll see you.'

Emma retreated inside the cottage, where she closed the door and rested her head against the cool wood, breathing heavily, seeing Stella's expression behind her closed lids. She couldn't help but be sucked back into the past.

Those first few weeks when Emma first came to live at Hope Cottage there were many lessons to learn about the recipes her family made, her new home, and the people in it.

She learned that cinnamon didn't just provide warmth and flavour; it could help ease fear and anxiety. That celery wasn't just something you served at really boring parties; it could help lower blood pressure. And that borage didn't just make a colourful addition to salads; it was said to give courage too.

She learned that food made in the kitchen of Hope Cottage left at dusk, in dishes and on plates wrapped up in dishtowels over a covering of clingfilm, inside baskets that were secreted away to the sound of quick footsteps and desperate hearts. Those same baskets and dishes would return a few days later, in time for their next assignment. The blue casserole dish with the white daisies on its side, the cream plate with the rose pattern and the chip on the rim, the copper pot with the wooden handles, all clean and clear of food, but never empty, all the same.

When the co-owner of the Whistle-In Store, Harrison Brimble, recovered from a nasty fall despite all his doctors' dire speculations, it could only have been as a result of Evie's Get Up and Go Gumbo, according to Mrs Brimble, who left six ticket stubs for the vintage cinema in town inside the blue casserole dish. When posh Madge Sanders finally got a proposal out of Timothy Wastrel after ten years of dating, she was convinced that it had to be because she'd fed him every last bite of Dot's Make Up Your Mind Meringue, and she left French chocolate and perfume on the rose plate.

When old Mrs Morton's rheumatoid fingers eased up for the first time in months after she'd tried Evie's Better Than a Holiday Noodle Soup, she left five knitted Christmas jumpers inside the old copper pot. Evie, Emma, Dot, Aggie and Uncle Joe wore them every year at Christmas after that.

But there was a darker side too, which she found out soon enough when she saw Janice Honeymoon hand over a set of earrings that had once belonged to her grandmother after she asked for a recipe to help save her marriage. When Janice had left, she asked Evie, 'But why did you take the earrings when they meant so much to her – surely, we could have just helped her? It's a bit mean.'

Evie looked at her sadly. 'If only it worked that way. But there's a cost to what we do, for making our recipes. A sacrifice that needs to be paid.' If Emma was surprised at this, it was nothing compared to her shock when she watched Evie plant the earrings at dusk, beneath the cucumber frame.

'If you dig just a little in the garden of Hope Cottage you'll find the others too,' Evie went on. 'Tokens from a lover, cherished keepsakes, treasured heirlooms – not all of them would be worth something out in the world, but here they are all the same. They're precious because of what they meant to the owner. Aggie says it helps the garden to bloom, but all I know is that it helps the recipes. Without this price, this sacrifice, they don't often work.'

Few in Whistling would ever have believed that that was where all their offerings ended up, that they weren't all lining some treasure chest somewhere.

'It's the price we pay in order to do what we do. We can't use them – if we do, well, it just doesn't go so well for us. It changes the effect, poisons it – and us, somehow,' Evie explained. 'There have been a few Halloways, in the past, who tried it and found that out the hard way. I don't blame them exactly – it can be hard our way of life, and it can seem like an easy solution to use them, but it's anything but.'

They never accepted cash. Even if it was sent after a recipe worked, it was returned with a polite though firm refusal. In time Emma would begin to wish that they would take money; ticket stubs and perfume didn't mend the leak in the roof or keep the woodburner going. There were other costs too; besides their twice-mended linens and their faded dresses, there were the whispers that followed them everywhere they went, and the stares, and the rumours too.

It was on her first day at the Whistling Infant Academy that she discovered, like many Halloways before her, that she'd also inherited the old feud between the three oldest families in Whistling. No recipe in The Book had been able to change the fact that an Allen never spoke to a Halloway if they could help it, just like a Lea would cross the street before they would ever stand next to someone who came from Hope Cottage. Or that a Halloway would make a recipe for anyone, anyone at all, unless that someone was an Allen or a Lea.

The Leas thought the Halloways were witches; the Allens thought the Halloways were expensive frauds. There wasn't a week that went by when the vicar, John Lea, like his father and his father before him, didn't deliver a sermon to encourage his delegation not to seek a solution from the faded blue door of Hope Cottage.

Just as there wasn't a day that went by that Janet Allen didn't judge the people who went to the Halloways for help as blind fools. No one seemed to remember that once, long ago, they had all been friends.

It was Stella Lea, a girl with pale blonde hair in two long plaits and very serious, dark eyes, who conveyed a rather rudimentary version of this to Mrs Prudney, Emma's new teacher, who hadn't lived in the village long and therefore had no idea herself just what she was asking when she requested that she take a seat next to Emma on Emma's first day. And Stella refused and matter-of-factly said, 'Leas are never friends with Halloways, that's what Mummy said.' She crossed her arms. 'So, *no*.'

Emma had gone home hurt, confused and embarrassed at being singled out, but most of all unable to explain what had happened, though Evie soon guessed. By that evening Dot, who'd never met a rumour she didn't like to share, confirmed it.

Her round face was splotchy and red from her anger. 'It was that Stella Lea – refused to sit next to her in class.'

'You'll make other friends, don't you worry,' said Evie – calmly, but her ears had turned pink in ire despite her consoling tone.

'You wouldn't want an Allen or a Lea as a friend in any case – they're all idiots,' said Agatha, who wasn't the type to ever mince words.

Even Uncle Joe was there, Dot's husband, a shy quiet man who generally liked to stay out of the way. But he had a fondness for the little girl with sad eyes and had come to offer some silent sympathy and an awkward pat on her head, before he retreated fast to the living room with the latest *Whistling News* and its crossword puzzle.

'Well, I'm sorry but I couldn't stand by and just take that. I walked past Netta Lea outside the Brimbles' store,' said Dot with a sniff. 'Stella's mother,' she explained for Emma's benefit. 'I called her name, and when she turned I pointed at her, then drew three circles in the air, very slow-like, while I muttered, "Wisha washa wisha", giving her a very hard stare while I did,' she went on, pushing up her jam-jar glasses. Dot's lips twitched. 'I made her think I cursed her.'

Evie gasped. 'You didn't!'

Aggie laughed. 'She doesn't really think that? Could she be that daft?'

'She really does, the silly arse.' Then Dot gave a little snigger. 'It's gobbledegook, obviously,' she said, giving Emma a wink. 'But she doesn't know that. She looked like she was ready to pee her pants. She ran inside, howling like nobody's business.'

Emma's mouth gaped as she imagined the scene, Dot with her flyaway hair and jam-jar glasses making circles with a pointed finger, Netta Lea's horrified face (she pictured an older version of Stella). A tinkling laugh escaped her mouth, her shoulders started to shake and tears leaked out of her eyes. Soon they were all giggling. It was the first time she'd made a sound since she'd arrived.

'You might have made things worse though,' said Evie, sobering, giving Emma a nervous look at the thought.

Dot sighed, bit her lip. 'I know, I'm sorry. I couldn't help myself. That woman!' she said, gritting her teeth.

Emma patted Dot's soft, pale hand with its chipped polish, violet this time. Dot had become a firm favourite. Anyone who would 'curse' someone like Netta Lea, whose daughter had decided to be mean for no other reason than something that had happened hundreds of years before, for her was worth shouldering a few dirty looks for, she decided. Besides, it wasn't going to be easy anyway – not being able to speak had already made certain of that.

Dot's actions, however, did have one unintended effect, which was that they got the attention of Maggie Gilbert, who was the class chatterbox. She was slightly plump, with light brown, shoulder-length hair and sparkly pink glasses that were peppered with silver unicorns on the sides.

'Is it true that Dot Halloway cursed Stella's mam?' she asked Emma the next morning at the school gates, pushing up the glasses on her small button-like nose. Her green eyes were curious.

Emma nodded, with a shy grin. She didn't have the words to tell her it was only a laugh, but perhaps Maggie sensed the joke, because after that she decided that the quiet red-haired girl who smelt a little like cinnamon, and brought the best snacks of anyone she knew to school, seemed rather sweet, and so she took pity on her and welcomed her into her little group, which was made up of Gretchen Hannah, a serious girl with very straight black hair and a fondness for *Star Wars*, and Jenny Hughes, a tow-headed string-bean with a shy smile, who always had her head in a book.

Fairly soon no one remembered a time when Emma hadn't been part of the group, and life took a decided upturn after that, even though she still hadn't found her voice.

Emma's real trouble, though, started a few months later on the day she fell in love with Jack Allen. It was also the day she got her voice back and the day that Jeremy Lea's dog, Ripper, followed him to school and introduced himself to the children, and Emma in particular, showing that the Leas had passed down the family feud to every member of their family, even their dog, by going for her first and taking a sizeable chunk out of her leg.

In her swarm of fear and pain, she saw a slightly older boy with dark blond hair, who she hadn't noticed before, run in front of the dog and distract it by letting it bite him too.

She found out his name while they were being rushed to hospital, sitting side by side in the ambulance, where she forgot all about the pain in her leg and noted that his eyes were hazel with flecks of green.

'I'm Jack Allen, by the way.'

'Nice to meet you. Does it hurt?' she asked.

'Not really,' said Jack. 'He didn't get me all that bad.'

'So you can talk,' he went on, smiling slightly. 'You haven't before. Not for months – at least, that's what everyone's been saying.'

She nodded, eyes wide. 'I couldn't.'

'Well then,' he said, looking from the bite on his hand to her with a grin. 'It was worth it then, just so I could meet you.'

Her mouth split into a wide, starry-eyed smile. By the time she was being stitched up, and she remembered the old family feud, it was already too late; she'd already started picturing their wedding.

She'd wear pink, of course, even if it did clash with her hair. It would go nicely with Jenny's troll ring. This was a common playground game that usually ended with a few light-sabre noises from Jenny, daisy petals from Maggie and some important words of pronouncement and blessings from Gretchen, such as 'Favourable tax treatment' and 'Off-shore banking'. Gretchen, who hadn't quite made up her mind whether she was going to be a barrister or a tax solicitor when she grew up, listened in on a lot of her father's business calls.

At A&E Emma waved goodbye to Jack as his mother came to fetch him, then blinked when Mrs Allen gave her son a smack on the head for returning the gesture, shooting her and Evie a look of pure loathing as she went past.

'She hates me,' Emma said in hurt and surprise, all thoughts of their troll and *Star Wars*-themed wedding crumbling to ashes. They were the first words she'd spoken to her grandmother since she arrived at Hope Cottage.

Evie sighed, shaking her head. An Allen could do that to you, crush you like you were something nasty under the heel of their boot.

Evie's eyes were kind as she stroked Emma's hair. 'She doesn't hate you, she just hates where you come from, the Halloway family,' she explained with a sigh.

'But why?'

'It's a long story, and it happened many years ago. But I suppose the Allens started hating us when they came to us for help and it didn't work.'

'What didn't work?'

'A recipe. Sometimes, things go wrong. We try our best but we can't make guarantees. It's why we always say the words "I make no promises" before we agree to do one, because we can't know – who are we to promise such things? All we can do is offer hope.'

Emma looked at her, thought of all the things she'd seen and heard. 'Is that all it is – hope?'

'Sometimes. Sometimes that's all you really need. Hope can do a lot of things. It grows with just a touch of light, in even the most desperate, forsaken heart. We should never underestimate the power a little hope can bring.'

*

As Emma's first year at Hope Cottage drew to an end, Evie tried her best to be what Emma needed. When Emma came home in tears thanks to Stella Lea, Evie would wipe her eyes and take her for ice cream. Chocolate and pistachio, her favourite – just like her mother.

'It's not going to solve anything, but it does help,' said Evie with a wink one bright, crisp afternoon in spring, when the heather was turning the moors into a purple carpet. Evie listened as Emma explained the latest humiliating attack.

It wasn't that the day had been that much worse than any of the others, or that Stella had found a novel way of being mean; she wasn't all that creative as far as bullies went. Though some of her tricks were rather nasty. One involved pulling up Emma's dress while she was standing in line so that her underwear was exposed to the class, then running off before Emma could catch her, and getting back in line so that Emma was the one to get into trouble. She was always mocking her accent whenever Emma spoke up in class.

The latest, though, had been particularly horrid, and humiliating. 'Did you smell that?' Stella asked Jack Allen just as they were leaving the school grounds, pulling a face in her direction. 'I think Emma farted.'

Emma's mouth fell open, and she gasped. 'I didn't.'

When Emma turned red in her humiliation Stella pointed it out as proof. 'Look at her face – she did, yuck,' she laughed.

Seeing her mortified face, Jack gave a short laugh and told Stella to shut it. 'Just leave her alone, Stella.'

'Well,' said Evie, taking a lick of her lemon sorbet as they walked home from the cobbled high street, Emma's short legs busy keeping time with hers. 'You've tried ignoring her, which doesn't work – she's just become more of a bully – so perhaps it's time to tell her to leave you alone? If that doesn't work, I'll have to go and speak to the Leas myself.'

Emma shook her head. 'No, it's fine, I can handle her.'

Emma *had* told Stella to leave her alone, but it hadn't made one bit of difference. That was the problem. She had thought of another way though, one she hoped would shut her up for good.

'If you're sure,' said Evie.

Emma suspected that Evie had already gone to the school to speak to the teacher, Mrs Prudney, though, because in class at least, Stella now simply ignored her.

It was Maggie who explained why she thought Stella had become that much worse during the past year. 'I mean, when I first got here she wasn't nice or anything, but she's become really horrid since you arrived, like really horrid.'

'Is it because of the stupid thing between our families?' asked Emma.

Maggie shook her head and pushed up her glasses, their silver unicorns flashing. 'I think it's because you're friends with Jack,' she said wisely. 'She hates that.'

'Why?' asked Emma in surprise. Jack was in the year above her, so it wasn't like they spent that much time together, just a few conversations snatched here and there in the playground. Emma, of course, wished it were more.

'Well, she likes Jack, always has, and until you came along he never really spoke to any other girls.'

'Well, there was the time he asked if he could borrow my pen…' added Jenny, tucking a long strand of mousy-coloured hair behind her ears.

Maggie grinned, 'Yes, well, besides that, of course.'

They all laughed.

The next day though, when Stella snuck up behind her and her friends, a large pile of leaves in her hands, ready to dump them on Emma's head, Emma turned and stood up, saying, 'I'd rethink that if I were you Stella', then she raised a finger and took a leaf out of her Aunt Dot's book as she narrowed her eyes and muttered, 'Wisha washa wisha.'

Stella blinked and her face paled. 'What are you doing?'

'Oh, you know, just cursing you,' she said, cocking her head to the side as if in thought. 'I'm trying to decide whether to turn you into a pig or not.'

Stella's dark eyes bulged. Emma almost laughed. The girl was as silly as her mother. 'Isn't she one already?' asked Maggie.

Emma shrugged. 'She acts like one, that's for sure.'

Stella let out a little squeal, dropped the leaves, and she and her gang of girls ran away, to the sound of Emma and her friends' laughter.

NINE

It was the first week of November and Emma was sitting on the bench in the greenhouse, with her broken leg propped up on a cushion and a blanket over her.

Outside the rain lashed against the glass, the sky a pale grey hanging over the horizon like old cotton wool.

Her eyes raked across the seedling trays; even now, she knew what Evie had planted more out of memory than anything else, as her sight was still wont to play tricks on her. This time of year there would be marjoram and coriander, French tarragon and sage. When she was younger she would rub the leaves between her fingers and breathe in their scent, imagining just what she'd make with each. Her fingers twitched to do that now, but she stopped herself. What would be the point? She still couldn't smell.

Evie had helped her set up a makeshift office in here, among the pots and gardening implements, away from the busy thrum of the cottage. Her laptop was on the potting bench. On an old paint-splattered stool there was a fat blue kettle and a tin of Yorkshire Tea, next to which was a plate piled with freshly baked spiced biscuits. If she closed her eyes she could picture the taste – warm, with the snap of ginger, nutmeg and allspice. She didn't need to try one to know that all she'd get was the texture of warm sand on her tongue.

There was a knock on the clear glass door and Sandro came inside, dripping and shivering, giving her his wide, warm smile, a dimple appearing in his cheek.

'Hola, Pajarita.' Then, stamping his feet theatrically, 'It's freezing,' he said, rubbing his hands and switching on the heater that had been placed nearby. He shook his curly head like a dog, so that she laughed, replacing the awkward smile she'd given him at first.

'Sorry you got caught in the rain. Um. You don't have to do this if you're busy or anything – I can make another arrangement.'

'Don't worry about it,' he said, taking a seat next to her laptop.

'Have a biscuit.'

He did. Then he sat and stared at her, making her feel suddenly silly and nervous.

'I feel a bit like Barbara Cartland.'

He gave her a puzzled look as he fired up the machine. 'Who?' he asked, then clapped his hands together and said, 'Tea?'

She nodded, and he got up to boil the kettle.

'She was a romance novelist, pretty prolific, she used to dictate her novels,' Emma explained.

He popped tea bags into two yellow mugs, and cocked his head to the side with a frown as he considered. 'I think, maybe, I do know her – lots of pink, right? And wasn't there a poodle?' He mimed a little ball shape.

Emma laughed. 'Yes! Pity I can't really do pink. Although when I was younger, I did try.'

He looked puzzled. 'Why can't you wear pink?'

'Clashes with the hair. Red.' She pointed to it, for emphasis.

He shrugged. 'Does everything have to match?'

She shrugged. 'Maybe not.'

He took a seat, folding his rangy body onto the small chair, his dark hair an unruly mop falling over his forehead, then opened the laptop and grinned, showing his even white teeth. 'Okay, shoot,' he said.

She nodded.

He stared at her.

She swallowed. 'Could you perhaps not stare at me – that might make it a little easier.'

His lips twitched, but he looked away.

She breathed slightly easier. 'So, the topic of the column is lunch.'

'Lunch?' he said, snapping back to look at her again, an eyebrow raised.

'The history of lunch.'

'O-kay, sounds fascinating, Pajarita,' he said.

She gave him an eye-roll.

He looked surprised but began to type as she spoke. 'The history of lunch as we know it is a fairly modern invention; one might say it's yet to arrive in Yorkshire, as in the county where I grew up, saying "lunch" will brand you as a foreigner faster than you can eat your dinner. Where the word "lunch" came from is often in dispute. Some say that it hails from the word "nuch", a word that prior to the seventeenth century was used to mean a piece of bread, and later, "nuncheon" which was having a quick snack between meals, later it was the Earl of Sandwich who revolutionised—'

Sandro laughed, interrupting: 'I wondered about this, eh? Didn't realise it wasn't just me, because when I first got here, a few people asked, "Sandro, do you want to come for tea?" and I'm like, great, eh? Saying yes to everyone for the same day, thinking I'll just pop in for a drink… but next thing you know, I'm having to eat three dinners.'

Emma laughed. 'You didn't!'

'I did – you try telling your Aunt Dot you're full. And you know what's really confusing?' he went on, dark eyes amused.

'What?'

'Every time I'm invited for tea, I'm never given any.'

Emma laughed. 'Well, when we mean tea, as in the drink, we say, "Fancy a cuppa?" And we don't ask what type you'd like – here, tea only comes in one form, the best – Yorkshire Tea.'

'Ah.' He grinned, and the dimple in his cheek showed. 'Mystery solved.'

'When we say "tea" we actually mean the last meal of the day, and dinner is served sometime past noon.'

He sighed, 'Ay. No wonder I'm always confused.'

Emma laughed. 'I was too, trust me. When I first came here.'

'Weren't you born here?' he asked.

'No, I was born in London, then came to live with Evie when I was about six, after my parents died.'

A shadow fell across his eyes. 'I'm sorry,'

'Thanks. It worked out. Evie was great.'

'I can imagine – she's barmy.'

Emma laughed. 'Barmy – picking up the lingo?'

'Bob's yer uncle.'

Emma laughed. 'You know, the first time I heard that expression, I was about six, from old Harrison Brimble. He said it to me about something, and I didn't speak at the time so I didn't ask, but for ages afterwards I thought that I had a mystery uncle named Bob.'

He laughed. 'Really?'

'Afraid so. I can only imagine, you being Spanish, how strange some of it must seem.'

'A little, but I like it.'

'Why did you move here?'

He shrugged. 'Just wanted a change.'

'So, you came to Whistling?'

He shrugged. 'Yeah. I like it, especially the moors. It's peaceful out there, wild, time feels different in a way, slower, it's good.' His dark eyes were solemn, and she found herself staring. She did know. The moors were one of her favourite places on earth.

'Sorry, I interrupted you,' he said, turning back to the column, and she snapped back to reality.

'You said something about a Mr Sandwich?'

She laughed. 'The Earl of Sandwich,' she said with a grin. 'The accidental inventor of the world's most famous lunchtime meal. Who allegedly, while working late one night or at a party with friends, depending on the version you believe, asked his butler to bring him a piece of beef with two slices of bread around it as he was busy and wanted something he could eat quickly and easily…'

His eyes were huge. 'That's how the sandwich was invented – barmy, so barmy.'

After their third cup of tea they were done.

'Thank you for doing this,' she said, surprised that she'd enjoyed it as much as she had.

'No problem,' he said, 'I had a lot of fun, Pajarita.'

'Have you heard the news about the Galways?' asked Dot, later that afternoon, when Evie had cajoled Emma into getting out of the house for a bit.

The Galways lived just outside the village in a run-down council flat. Their son Jimmy had been a few years younger than Emma at school, and last Thursday was the first time she'd ever seen Mary Galway come knocking on Hope Cottage's door.

They were sitting in Dot's cosy living room, a tray of Eccles cakes before them. Despite this, Emma was feeling uncomfortable; her head was pounding, she was in desperate need of another nap and her foot in her cast was itching. She'd been using one of Dot's knitting needles to scratch it, only of course the knitting needle felt a bit like a heat rod due to her muddled senses. She sighed, wiggling her foot, trying to concentrate on something else.

Dot's favourite time of year was Christmas and she'd already put up her decorations, despite it being only November. The tree was festooned with baubles in her favourite colours, pink, lilac and silver, and the room was festive and inviting, with a cheery fire and some soft music playing in the background. Growing up, Emma had spent many evenings here, playing cards with her aunts and secretly feeding Pennywort bits of Dot's excellent teacakes.

'No?' said Emma. 'What happened?' She shot a look at Evie, thinking, despite her better instincts, of the other day when Mary Galway had come by.

'She moved out.'

'She didn't!'

'Oh yes. I saw her down at the Brimbles' store, you wouldn't even believe it was the same woman. Apparently she went down to Fritz, where the Caleb boys live, you know, and fetched Jimmy back herself. You know he ran away because he and Steve are always at odds? He got involved with a bad crowd who live in that dodgy area, by the old factory that closed down. Anyway, I heard that she gave those Caleb boys a talking-to, told Jimmy to get in the car, and then she told the boys that if they came near her boy again she'd give them what-for.'

'But that's not all.'

'It isn't?' asked Emma, surprised.

'No – she's left Steve. Said she'd had enough of him being a bully. She's gone and got herself a job and a flat too.'

'Mary Galway?' said Emma in shock. 'The same woman who is liable to burst into tears if you look at her wrong?'

'Our same lass,' agreed Dot.

'The same one who walks into doors because she is so afraid to look up because she might see something she doesn't like? That Mary Galway?'

'Yes!' cried Dot. Then she looked at Evie, eyes shining. 'What did you make?'

'Moxie Maker Chicken in Cream.'

'Really?' asked Aggie, who had been engrossed in a novel, her legs in their customary riding boots thrown over the back of the chair. She marked her place with one long paint-splattered finger and then folded the page before closing it.

Evie frowned. She was the type of person who believed that those who didn't use bookmarks should sleep outside with the rest of the swine.

The book's cover had a photograph of a woman with wind blowing through her hair, wearing an old-fashioned gown that was a bit loose at the front so she was having to hold it up, while behind her a muscular blond, who looked like he bathed in olive oil, was looking at her suggestively.

The book came from Dot's secret library, which she kept locked in the pantry on a shelf sandwiched between rows of detergent and mothballs. They were lent out to a very select group of people (Aggie and Evie and Ann Brimble mostly), which had at one point included Emma, to her shame; she'd devoured them all when she was about fifteen, and still had a covert fondness for slightly steamy historical tales. She blamed Dot's library for some of her unrealistic notions about men.

But right then she was shaking her head at her aunts and Evie, 'You can't be serious, Mary Galway didn't do any of that because of a *chicken casserole.*'

'How else can you explain it?' asked Aggie.

'Perhaps she just had enough of Steve – I mean he'd always been a bully, perhaps enough was enough.'

Aggie looked at her. 'If only that were true. I've often found that courage tends to wane the less you use it.'

'Maybe hers had been storing up.'

'I told her it would make her strong,' said Evie.

'And she believed you?'

'You'd be surprised at what a little belief can do.'

'Maybe,' admitted Emma.

'Well, either way, Mary Galway has finally found the courage she's been looking for for half her life. She stood up to her husband, and fought for her son. Told Steve that she was filing for divorce,' said Dot.

Aggie looked at Emma, her eyes wide. 'I don't know, love, sounds a bit like magic to me.'

Emma rolled her eyes.

Later that evening, her phoned pinged with an email from her editor, a response to the column she'd sent. She handed the phone to Evie to read aloud, biting her lip. 'What does it say?'

Evie's eyes scanned the contents, and then she gave a little snort.

'They love it. Apparently, the copy-editor, Abby Fairbrother, sent a note along with it as well.'

Inwardly, Emma cringed, wishing she'd got Evie to have a look at it before she'd asked Sandro to send it on. Abby was a bit of a pedant.

'Abby says Yorkshire must agree with you – it's one of her favourite columns so far, and the grammar, for once, was exceptional, hardly any corrections.'

Evie's lips twitched.

'Oh, shut up,' said Emma, stifling a giggle herself.

*

After Evie went to bed Emma sat at the kitchen table, next to Pennywort, who watched her with his solemn brown eyes. In front of her was the box of Christmas decorations that Evie had taken out of the attic. Idly, she rifled through it. Many of the decorations she, Evie, Dot and Aggie had hand-made over the years, a tradition of Hope Cottage. There were baubles dipped in gold. Delicate willow-wreath animals including a bunny, and a bear and a little mouse. She touched them and smiled, remembering the day she and Aggie had sat making that. Her eye fell on The Book, open to the recipe Evie and her sisters had just started to make and which would take nearly six weeks. The day before, Evie and her aunts had put the first cake layer in to bake, and it had now been soaked in port; it would rest for a week before they added the next layer of hope. It was the Good Cheer Christmas Cake recipe Emma had scoffed at in her mind when Evie had taken down the green cake tins from their home atop the dresser, though she hadn't had the heart to say anything aloud. Perhaps a part of her couldn't for other reasons too; perhaps on some level it was because the recipe was a cornerstone of the history of the cottage, and whatever she felt about The Book, the intention behind the recipe had always been kind. It was the only recipe that they made every year for the entire village, regardless of feuds or disagreements or differences, and she couldn't help remembering the first time she'd helped to make it too, on her first Christmas at Hope Cottage. With snow beginning to fall outside the window, and the radio playing soft Christmas jazz, it didn't seem all that long ago now.

TEN

December 1996

It was the week before Emma's first Christmas at Hope Cottage. Bing Crosby was singing 'Winter Wonderland' on the old wireless. Snow fell on the cobble path outside, covering the rolling green hills in a blanket of white and topping the roofs of the cottages. There were Christmas wreaths on the pastel-coloured doors that lined the high street and twinkling lights on all the garden walls and streetlights.

Inside the cottage, Evie was dusting flour like fairy dust onto the large wooden table, and Emma was separating eggs into a bowl.

In the corner, by the hearth, was the enormous tree Harrison Brimble had brought them the week before, and Ada Stone had made the willow wreath that twinkled with fairy lights and cranberries on the outside of their front door; it had been hung just beneath the cat-shaped knocker.

That's how it worked during Christmas at Hope Cottage, Emma was finding; people showed their appreciation for what the Halloways did throughout the year, with small gifts and tokens – though sometimes, as in the case of their enormous tree, not so small.

The range hadn't stopped all week, keeping the windows steamed up. Today the air was full of the scent of cinnamon from the spiced cake Dot and Aggie were mixing on the table, adding in the spices and currants as they consulted The Book.

'That's a lot of mixture,' said Emma, staring at the enormous cream mixing bowl the size of a trough.

'Well, it needs to be – it's for the whole village.'

'Everyone?' asked Emma in surprise.

'Yes. It's the one time of year we make something for everyone in the village,' said Evie. 'It's our way of helping to bring some good into people's homes during this time.'

'And everyone gets a piece – even…?'

'Everyone,' said Evie, not mentioning the Allens or the Leas.

'They won't eat it anyway,' said Dot, who knew exactly who Emma meant.

'Why not?'

'Oh, an Allen will never take a crumb of food from us ever again,' said Dot. 'Not after—'

'What?' asked Emma. 'Evie said that it was a recipe that went wrong, many years ago.'

'Oh, it did. It went about as wrong as a thing could go, really.'

'What do you mean?'

'Well, it was a long time ago, during your great-grandmother's time – Christmas time too, I believe, when Geoff Allen came to Grace Halloway for help during a desperate time in their lives.'

'It was their business, wasn't it?' asked Dot.

Evie nodded. 'Yes, the Allen Printworks, the Allens used to own one of the largest printing companies in the country. It had been in the family for many years, only their son John had a bit of a gambling problem, and had got himself into some trouble. They were in danger of losing everything to his debts when they sought out Hope Cottage, looking for a recipe that would help change their situation.'

'What happened?' asked Emma.

'Well, it's hard to say really. Sometimes, even though we try our best, things go wrong, and well, that one did. The Allens lost their business, they reopened it some years later, but it was a good, hard slog to do that and they never forgave us for what they went through – the price Grace Halloway charged was most of their savings.'

'No,' breathed Emma.

'I'm afraid so.'

'But why money – it's not what you usually take,' said Emma, horrified.

Evie shook her head and corrected her. 'We take what is valued most. It's not about what is important out in the world, but what matters most to the person looking for change, you see? For Geoff Allen nothing was as precious as money.'

'But I mean – it was all they had! Couldn't Grace Halloway have just given it back to them, if it hadn't worked anyway?'

Evie shook her head. 'She couldn't, even if she wanted to – you know that's not the way it works.'

Dot made a strange sound.

They all turned to look at her.

She shrugged. 'Well, the rumour went that there was another reason she wouldn't have been able to…'

'Why's that?' asked Emma.

'Because somebody had already dug it up.'

Emma gasped.

'We don't know if that's really true,' said Evie, dusting the flour off her hands and putting the cake in to bake in the old range. Afterwards it would rest in the tins for a week before they began the next stage of the recipe.

'Margaret said she looked and couldn't find any—' started Aggie.

Emma looked up at the mention of her mother's name, saw Evie shoot her sister a warning look, and before she could ask any more they'd sent her on an errand to the Brimbles' store.

The weeks leading up to Christmas were the busiest time at Hope Cottage. Every morning there were new faces at the door, and new recipes to be made.

'Why is it so much busier lately?' asked Emma, as their fourth caller for the day left the kitchen. Mrs Watson, with tears in her eyes, wishing to repair her bond with her estranged sister of some thirty years.

'I think it's because when things slow down during this time of the year, you get a chance to look at your life and what's important,' said Dot. 'And what's not.'

'Like?'

'A silly grudge.'

Emma nodded. That made sense.

'Personally, I blame all those Christmas films,' said Aggie, who had her feet up on the kitchen table, her face tired, flour in her short dark hair.

'There's so much pressure this time of the year on families – and, well, if yours isn't getting along too well, or you haven't got one, it can be hard.'

Emma looked away. It was a year since she'd lost her parents, and it had been hard. Evie, and her aunts, had come to mean so much to her in the space of a year, but it didn't change the fact that this would be the first Christmas she had had without her mother and father, and lately she was missing them even more than ever.

Evie saw her face, and played with her hair. 'It's okay to miss them.'

Emma nodded; she could taste the tears in her throat. 'Oh lass,' said Aggie getting of the chair and coming over to give her a hug. 'I'm sorry – I didn't mean to make you sad,' she said as Dot shot her sister an angry look.

Emma wiped her eyes. 'No, it's okay,' she said, and sniffed. 'I think it makes me feel better knowing that I'm not the only one,' she went on, thinking of all the people who came here looking for something to help them too.

'No,' said Evie, simply, stroking her hair. 'You're definitely not alone.'

As the years passed, Emma collected stories about her parents the way some people collect photographs, storing them carefully in her mind so that later she could take them out, and mull them over while the rest of the cottage was asleep, wondering if she was more like her mother or her father.

She'd learned from Evie that her mum had been fiery, with a quick temper. 'She wasn't a chatterer, you know, like some girls,' she said, pausing as she kneaded dough one clear day in spring, while she and her sisters made lavender biscuits for Tom Harvey, Uncle Joe's partner at the used car dealership, who was struggling to sleep lately. 'She used words sparingly, even as a child, as if words cost money. But she was quick to stand up for what was right, and didn't back down for anyone, regardless of age or size, or...'

'Common sense,' agreed Aggie, her feet up on the table, slurping a coffee, her head buried in a book from Dot's secret library.

'Why?' asked Emma.

'Well,' said Dot. 'When your mam was about your age now, nine, she broke into a neighbour's back garden – Clifford Hobb – to rescue Gizmo. He was a rather sad, lonely Alsatian who was tied up to the fence outside, even during the worst of the winter.

The owner kept him as a guard dog, you see, didn't really think of him as an animal with feelings and needs.'

'Oh no!' exclaimed Emma. She was a huge animal lover.

'Well that's what she thought, too. When she heard about poor Gizmo, all she said was "Tisn't right" and when she heard his cries on the way home from school, soon after, she decided that enough was enough, and she hopped the fence, and broke him out.'

'What, really?' exclaimed Emma, mouth open in surprise.

'Yep,' said Evie. 'Took him home with her. Our eyes nearly popped out of our skulls when she brought him inside, poor thing. See, his owner ran the old metalworks factory, Hobb's Steelco, before it closed down. Kept a fair few of the villagers in work at the time, so none of them were willing to risk his wrath and report the treatment of the dog.'

'But that's unfair – that shouldn't have meant he just got away with it!' exclaimed Emma.

'That's what your mother thought too,' said Aggie.

'We'd reported him though,' said Dot.

'Not that anything was done,' Aggie said, and sniffed.

'He'd been tipped off by someone, and took the dog inside the day someone came by for an inspection, and we were told it must have been a false alarm,' agreed Evie.

'My foot,' huffed Aggie.

'So, what happened after she brought him home – was he cross?' asked Emma.

'Furious,' said Evie.

'See, she left a note, telling him exactly what she'd done.'

Emma's eyes bulged at her mother's daring.

'She also told him that she was going to be keeping Gizmo from then on if he didn't want to treat his dog better.'

Emma shook her head in amazement. 'What did he do?'

'Well, he came here, mad as hell. We were ready to box him ourselves, obviously not about to let him intimidate her, but somehow she made him listen and in the end he agreed to let her keep the dog.'

Aggie grinned, 'Well, he was furious, of course, but he couldn't very well threaten a nine-year-old girl, so he left it.'

Emma liked thinking of the brave young girl who hopped fences and saved animals. It was hard though to reconcile her with the image of the woman who was always busy in her home office, typing away on her computer, and whose life was strictly regimented, with appointed mealtimes and play dates. She supposed that growing up changed people.

It was harder to collect stories about her father because they didn't know that much about him, but she'd pressed for as much as she could.

'Well, what I can tell you straight off the bat is that he was handsome, and Scottish,' said Dot one bright, cold morning in late October as she sat next to Pennywort, a mug of spiced pumpkin coffee in her hands – a Halloway tradition that had begun shortly after they visited America in the autumn for the first time, and came home with a pile of new recipes, inspired by their travels. Emma especially liked the Plucky Pumpkin Pie and Get up and Go Gumbo.

Dot's eyes were vague, lost in thought. 'He was a stranger to Whistling, so I suppose to your mam he would have seemed exotic.'

'He had really beautiful eyes too – sort of a—' she began.

'Sea-green colour,' said Emma, remembering, and having to swallow the lump of sadness that the image caused.

'He had a good sense of humour though. When they first got together she was always laughing,' remembered Evie.

Later she found a surprising source, who told her many more stories about her father. Her Uncle Joe, who had employed her father at the used car dealership when her parents had just met.

'He'd come to visit his friend Gordon for the summer. Liam and he had been to school together before Gordon moved to Whistling as a lad. Well, from what I can remember, he took one look at your mother and decided to extend his stay, got himself a job, here,' said Uncle Joe, one afternoon when Dot had sent her past to drop off some papers that he needed. They got to chatting, after he offered her a cuppa. 'The job came with a room – just above the shop, so to your dad it was perfect, I suppose, just what he needed.'

After that, Emma popped in more regularly to visit her uncle and to hear more about her dad. He'd show her the new cars that had come in for sale, and she'd sit in his small back office, which had a view of the high street, and they'd chat.

'He was a good man, hard worker too. He was studying part-time, something to do with management, marketing, that sort of thing, I think. Good head on his shoulders, but he wasn't all work, you know? He was funny too, could be a bit of a practical joker at times.

'On my birthday, the year he worked for us, he took the liberty of breaking into my computer and changing everything to extra-large font, and he and one of the sales guys put up a rail all around the office, just in case I fell. I was only fifty-nine!'

Though, of course, that sounded ancient to nine-year-old Emma, but it helped her to remember some of the practical jokes her father used to play at home when she was growing up.

Like the time he switched the containers of the ready-made meals her mother ordered – for jelly beans, chocolate cake and marshmallows – and how her mother had opened some of them and laughed till tears leaked out of her eyes. The two of them had seemed to hold hands and giggle for a long time after that.

Or the time he'd come home with three pairs of funny slippers for each of them, just out of the blue one winter's day. Hers were large green monster claws, his were red dragons with ridges on the back and a tail, and her mother's had been a smiley shark, because that's what he sometimes called her when she was sorting out people's finances, 'Sharky'.

Lots of his jokes weren't wildly hysterical, but they never needed to be; they were dad jokes, and she missed them, and when she chatted to Uncle Joe, it felt like he wasn't gone or forgotten.

'Did I tell you about the time he wrapped up everything in my office in newspaper?' he told her one day after school.

'Everything?' Emma said with a laugh, picturing the scene.

'Every last little thing. The computer. The phone. My mug, the chair, the walls, the wheels on the chair…'

By the time Emma was ten, she could spot wild garlic at a hundred paces, and knew nineteen different varieties of poisonous mushroom just from their scent alone, yet she still hadn't found a way to convince Mrs Allen that she and Jack could be friends.

By the time she was eleven she'd started making some of the simpler recipes from The Book. But she was impatient to do more; she wanted to be the one to say the words, stir in the bits of hope, so Evie would set her to work on mincing herbs. 'You'll get there, but it's important that we get the basics right first,' she said, peeling a potato, the skin a perfect spiral falling onto the worn table.

It wasn't long though before she decided to try making a recipe from The Book by herself, when she was alone at the cottage while everyone was over at Dot's playing cards. Her aim was simple:

to mend the feud with the Allens, a noble, if rather self-serving, pursuit. But though she worked hard, using a complicated recipe that spoke of mending fences and healing rifts, and she sacrificed her favourite box of pencils under the mulberry bush, there was still nothing she could do to get an Allen to accept food from a Halloway.

'Are you mad, Jack?' said Stella Lea, her dark eyes nearly popping out of her skull in utter horror, knocking the slice of carrot cake out of Emma's hands.

'Hey!' Emma cried in protest.

'Do you want to be poisoned, or worse *cursed*?' said Stella, ignoring Emma. 'Don't you know anything?'

Jack looked startled. 'Um – well,' he said, staring at the slice of cake on the ground, a small flicker of fear in his eyes.

Emma felt a small stab of guilt, which she squashed. It was for everyone's good, she told herself. 'It's just cake,' she said, face reddening slightly from the lie, as Stella marched away.

'She doesn't know what she's talking about – here, have another slice,' said Emma, holding out her lunchbox to Jack.

'Why do you want me to have it?' he asked, a slight trace of suspicion in his voice.

Emma blinked. 'I just thought you'd like some – you don't think I'd do anything bad to it, do you?'

He stared at her for a few seconds, then looked away. 'Course not – um, I'm not hungry, but thanks though, see you,' he said, beating a hasty retreat.

Emma felt like crying. All she wanted to do was help.

'Well, what did you expect?' said Maggie, who'd witnessed the whole thing. 'I mean he is an Allen – you know they're a bit funny about…'

'What?'

'Well, about your family – the food they make, you know.'

'I know, but I was hoping…'

Maggie gave her a look. 'What?'

'Nothing,' said Emma. 'There's no point if he won't even try something I've made.'

It was a pity, she thought, when Evie found out, not because she was punished – she wasn't; Evie knew her disappointment was punishment enough – it was a pity because it just might have worked.

Emma had got good at sensing what someone needed just by looking at them. A drop of the shoulders, a downcast head, would benefit from a recipe designed to ward off melancholy. Someone with holes in their clothes and dust lining their pockets would be wise to try one that brought about some luck.

Emma went to sleep dreaming about the recipes in The Book, and woke up excited to see which ones they would make that day. In her notebook, which was now full of sketches and observations and imaginary recipes of her own, she doodled future ideas, which very often included one to change an Allen's mind. Never dreaming that one day, there'd come a time when she wouldn't want anything to do with The Book, when she would begin to blame it for everything that went wrong.

ELEVEN

Present day

Evie and Emma's aunts had started on the second layer of the Good Cheer Christmas Cake, which was now soaking up the combination of honey and hope. Long ago, it had been Emma's task, as a little girl, to pour it into the tin, her face solemn as she said the words. Now, though, she escaped to the greenhouse before they could ask her. It was cosy here with the heaters on. Emma had a thick, cream woollen scarf around her neck and one fluffy pink mitten on her uninjured hand. Outside, there was frost on the grass, and the sky was clear and indigo.

'Evie said you've bought a farmhouse?' asked Emma as she and Sandro got to work on her column.

Sandro smiled. 'Yeah, it's great, or it will be when it's fixed up. It has these dormer windows…' he said, his dark eyes lighting up.

Emma's mouth fell open. 'It's not the old stone farmhouse with the blue shutters, is it? At the edge of the village?'

He looked at her in surprise. 'You know it?'

Emma's eyes widened. 'Yes. I've always loved that old place, it's so pretty there, with the views of the moors, and the castle, you can smell the heather in the summer, and just feel like you're in another world—' She stopped, blushing.

His eyes though were wide, staring at her. 'No, you're right – that's exactly it.'

They shared a grin.

'So, you bought it?'

'Yes – it was one of those cases, you know, when your heart is leading your head, it's pretty much unlivable just yet – but hopefully, soon.'

'I think that's great – I admire it, to be honest, having that sort of faith.'

'Well, you're in the minority.'

'Why do you say that?'

'No reason,' he said, shaking his head, a cloud crossing over his dark eyes.

She couldn't help wondering who'd objected. Something told her that perhaps it was a woman. She didn't know if Sandro had a girlfriend; her aunts had said there had been a girl, but the way they'd spoken, it seemed like it hadn't ended well.

'So, you've bought a farmhouse, deep in the heart of the Dales – what brought you here, really?'

'Oh, the usual, you know. Tax benefits, sunshine…'

She laughed. Then guessed. 'Love?'

He nodded, gave her a sad smile. 'Yes. But it didn't work out.'

'What happened?'

He didn't say anything for a while, just stared at her with his rather intense brown eyes, and she reddened slightly. 'Sorry, it's none of my business, obviously…'

He shook his head. 'It's okay, Pajarita,' he said, running a hand through his curly hair. 'We were just… incompatible, eh. She wanted the city life, wasn't really keen to leave London, and I'm more of a country boy at heart. And I suppose there was the small problem of her sleeping with my landlord, as well,' he added, with a wry laugh.

'What?' Emma gasped.

'Yes – bit of a shock that, after I'd moved here to be with her.'

'Jesus, I'll say,' she said, pulling a face. 'I can't imagine anyone wanting to cheat on you—' she started, then went slightly red. 'Oh God…'

Had she just inadvertently told him she found him attractive?

'Thanks.' He grinned, the dimple appearing in his cheek.

She laughed as well, rolled her eyes. 'I just meant when you're not driving me nuts, you're, you know, okay I suppose.'

He threw his head back, roaring with laughter. 'Thanks, that just touches my heart.'

She giggled. 'I live to please. Why stay then, in England I mean?'

'Well, I came down here, just to clear my head – I was planning on leaving, but then I saw the valley and I've always wanted to open up my own restaurant… I was sitting in the teashop when I ran into Dot.'

'Dot Halloway? My Dot?' she exclaimed, sitting up.

'There's another?'

She laughed. 'Well, no… definitely not. Go on.'

'Well, next thing I was telling her all my plans and she was telling me to come to the cottage to see her sister, that they would help me. She pretty much marched me over here, Pajarita, your family are forceful – forceful,' he repeated with a wink, though he seemed to approve, quite a bit.

Emma's mouth fell open. 'They made a recipe for you?'

He looked at her, his eyes wide. 'Course they did! Had to give up my favourite guitar pick and everything,' he said with a wink. 'Worth it though.'

'Just a pick?'

'Santana's pick,' he said with emphasis. 'Eh.'

She just stared. She had no idea who Santana was. He looked at her, shook his head. 'Ay, Pajarita…' he muttered, clearly horrified at her ignorance. 'Anyway, soon after that I approached the council about the land, got the van – hired Nico – and it all fell into place. I had some money saved up, you see. Then Evie offered me the annexe, and the rest is history.'

There was a knock on the door that afternoon. Emma opened it and was surprised to see Jack Allen standing there, a thick blue and white striped woollen scarf wrapped around his neck and mouth, the tops of his cheeks pink from cold and a bakery box in his hands.

'Hi,' he said, his hazel eyes crinkling at the corners.

'Jack,' she said, her mouth opening in surprise.

'Can I come in?' he asked with a grin, stamping his feet from the cold.

She blinked. 'Of course.'

She was taken aback, though. Jack was usually a bit reluctant to come inside the cottage; his mother had forbidden it when they were young, and so over the years they'd spent many hours chatting just outside. It was hard to believe but even after all this time he'd never actually been inside for longer than a minute or two.

Thankfully, Evie and her aunts weren't home. Perhaps Jack had waited until they'd left. Old habits are hard to break, she thought.

Jack stared around at the stone walls, looked from the range to the alcove, saw The Book on the table and gave a short, amazed laugh. 'Hope Cottage,' he said, echoing her thoughts from earlier. 'And there's The Book.'

She gave him a half-smile. 'Was it what you expected?' she asked, pulling out a chair for him to sit and adding, 'Tea?'

'Please,' he said, and she went and filled the old copper kettle and set it on the range, and got two blue mugs from the dresser.

'Gosh – old school,' he said eyeing the kettle.

Emma shrugged. 'Evie doesn't trust a kettle that boils in thirty seconds. There's something about the ritual of lighting the fire, and waiting for the water to boil... though she bought me a little modern kettle for the greenhouse – that's where I work now – which was sweet of her.'

He looked around. 'I'm not sure what I expected... potions and strange things in jars, maybe.' He laughed. 'A cauldron...'

She laughed. 'Really?'

His face coloured slightly. 'When I was little, yes. The way my mother spoke about this place... it's silly when I think of it now.'

His eyes scanned the dresser, fell on Pennywort asleep on Emma's bed, and he shook his head, smiled. Then he put the box on the table and opened it. Inside there were four perfect little muffins, topped with little reindeer in white fondant, with red glitterballs for noses.

'I saw these in the bakery and I thought of you... remember that time when we got there just when it was opening and we got these...?'

She bit her lip. 'Course I do.'

She had never forgotten, that was the trouble, none of it.

'So, um, what have you been doing with yourself?' she asked, handing him his mug. Tearing her gaze away from his.

'I joined the family business – the Allen Printworks.'

'Oh?'

He gave a small, self-deprecating sort of laugh. 'I sold out...'

Jack had always spoken of escaping the family business, doing something in art and design, perhaps going to New York.

Emma shook her head. 'It's easy to think you'll do things differently when you're young.'

'You did.'

She shrugged. 'Yeah, well...' She didn't point out that she had felt like she had no choice – because of *him*.

'The funny thing is, I enjoy it, more than I thought I would anyway. I run the sales department now and…'

Emma wasn't really listening. She couldn't take it any more; she had to know. Couldn't just sweep what had happened the other day away and pretend it had never happened.

'Jack?' she interrupted. 'What happened with Stella?'

He sighed. Ran a hand through his hair. 'It's a long story, but we ended it a little while ago, and well…'

'She isn't taking it very well,' Emma guessed.

'She, um… well, she thinks I ended it because you're back.'

Emma swallowed. He reached out, touched her hand. Emma looked up, into his hazel eyes. 'And did you?'

He stared at her, 'I don't know. Maybe.'

'Jack,' she said, feeling her heart start to race.

A noise from behind made them both start.

'I didn't know you had a visitor,' said Evie, her voice, a little cool.

Emma closed her eyes. 'Jack just came over to say hello.'

'That's nice of him,' said Evie. Her tone, however, implied otherwise.

Jack swallowed. 'I just stopped by to see how Emma was doing,' he said. 'I better get going though.'

'You don't have to leave,' protested Emma. 'Stay a while.'

He shot a look at Evie, who'd actually crossed her arms. 'Can't, sorry – got to get back to the office,' he said, leaning over and giving her a kiss on the cheek. 'Nice seeing you again, Mrs Halloway,' he said before he left.

Evie harrumphed. 'Mrs Halloway?'

Emma let out an impatient breath. 'Well, it's not like he could just call you Evie.'

'What do I care what an Allen calls me?'

Emma rolled her eyes. 'You could have been a bit nicer to him, you know – it couldn't have been easy coming in here.'

Evie scoffed. 'Yeah, but as usual it was just so very easy for him to run away when things got a little tough.'

'Yes, and who made it tough?'

'Love, it wasn't me that made it hard.'

'You did tonight.'

Evie sighed. 'I know… look love, I'll be his best pal, I promise, if Jack finds a way to be the man you need. If he stood up for you to his family, no one would be happier than me. I'm just afraid that you'll get your hopes up again, only for them to come crashing down.'

She was still angry later that evening, trying to block out Evie's words, when she decided to finally try having a proper shower. Since her accident, she'd got by with a flannel, soap and a sink full of water. It did the job, but it was tiresome, and Evie had to wash her hair for her every few days. What she craved, really, was to be more independent, to not have to rely so much on Evie for everything, particularly now when she was so annoyed with her. The trouble was that she shared Evie's fear about having her hopes crushed by Jack again, but she was trying not to think about it, trying to make sense of what she felt.

Wrapping her damaged arm and the cast on her leg in plastic bags, she ran the water and stepped gingerly under the spray, careful to keep her broken leg as far away as she could. It felt fine at first, the water warm, invigorating; but then, without warning, everything changed – suddenly it was like she was being tortured alive, by hundreds of stinging insects. The pain stealing her breath away, like nothing she'd ever felt before, she scrabbled to open the glass door, falling, gasping, wet and howling on the floor.

It was a long while before she could scoop herself off the linoleum, or even risk putting a towel across her skin, terrified as she was of what it might feel like. When she sat up though, once the shock had worn off, her stomach plummeted and hot, angry tears pricked her eyes: she realised she'd landed on her already damaged wrist.

Evie took her the next day to see the doctor who was monitoring her recovery. Emma sat with her heart in her mouth as Dr Norton examined the arm. He'd had to take off the cast, and she could see that her hand looked swollen, the skin a mottled shade of purple and red.

He peered at her from above his black-framed glasses. 'It didn't break again.'

She exhaled in relief, not realising that she'd been holding her breath.

'You'll have to go back into a full cast though. I'm sorry, I know you were looking forward to having it off soon.'

Emma closed her eyes. 'Will it set it back – the recovery?'

'A few weeks, yes, but nothing serious. Just no more showers, all right – stick to what you know. For now, we know that water isn't always your friend.'

Emma frowned. 'But for how long – I mean, I need to be able to shower at some point, to live a normal life.'

His eyes were sad. 'I'd suggest taking smaller steps. Holding your hand under the tap, for instance – if it stings, well then at least it's felt on a reduced area, you know what I mean?'

She nodded. It made sense. 'Small steps.'

'Small steps,' he agreed.

When she got home, she found Sandro waiting for her in the greenhouse. Her laptop was open. He greeted her with a wink. 'Hello there, soldier. I heard about what happened. I'm sorry.'

She gave a small smile. 'Thanks.'

She felt completely worn out from her trip to the doctors. Her brain felt loose and flabby, like a punctured balloon.

He shook his head, eyes concerned, no doubt noting her flat, straggly hair, her pale skin and the purple, bruise-like shadows beneath her eyes.

'You look exhausted,' he said, standing up. 'I know we said we'd do the column now, but let's leave it till tomorrow, okay? Get some rest. I can go in a bit later tomorrow so you can do a longer session. I can get Nico to open up for me.'

Emma took a seat at the garden bench.

'No – don't worry, I'm fine, we can do it now, I'll rally. How about one of your super-volt coffees?'

He grinned. 'Super-volt?'

'Yep – couldn't taste it the other night, but my brain was buzzing for hours.'

He laughed. 'You sure you want to carry on?'

She nodded. As much as she'd dearly love to just sink onto her bed, she didn't want to make him give up any more of his free time for her.

'Who's Nico?' she asked as he made their coffee.

'He's an employee – helps out with the Tapas Hut, good kid.'

She nodded. 'I must come and see it. Dot and Aggie said I'd like it.'

'Yeah? That would be great.'

His mobile started to ring. Emma saw the name flash up on the screen, *Holly*.

Sandro switched it to silent.

'Aren't you going to get that?'

His eyes were dark, unreadable. 'Nah. Here you go,' he said, handing her a mug, and they got to work.

An hour later, despite the strong coffee, he was shaking her gently awake.

'W-what?' she said, staring into dark, concerned eyes.

'We can pick up the rest tomorrow morning, but for now, bedtime,' he said, firmly.

She blinked, sitting up. 'But I can't ask that of you.'

He gave a soft laugh. 'You haven't – I'm offering.'

'But why?'

He shrugged. 'Why not? We're friends, right, Pajarita?'

She grinned. 'Not that I deserve it. I was pretty horrid to you when I first got here.'

'Not really. Anyway, I'm tough, I can take it – and I mean, you've been through the wars, I get it.'

She swallowed, trying to find the right words. 'Well, anyway, thanks.'

See you later.'

When he left, she heard him speaking on the phone. 'Sorry, Holly – it wasn't a good time, what's up?' And before she climbed into her bed, the silk screen blocking out most of the wintry sun's rays, Pennywort snoring softly, she wondered briefly who Holly was before she fell into a deep sleep.

The next morning, Sandro looked at her. 'I got something for you.'

'For me?' she said, surprised, as he bent over and placed something next to her on the small gardening bench.

'It's nothing much, but I was thinking about what you said the other day – how hard it is for you to read – and I thought, well, this might help. You mentioned that sounds are okay now…'

It was an old portable CD player. She looked at it in surprise. 'It's old – but it works. I thought you could listen to audiobooks, maybe? I went past the library.' He gave a little laugh as he admitted, 'I had to join. I didn't really know what you might like, so I got a few.'

He handed over two audiobooks, one a detective story, the other an epic saga called *Midnight in Prague*.

She turned them over, looking at the pictures, her voice wobbling slightly, and she felt tears prick her eyes. 'Thank you.'

He touched her hand. His eyes were gentle, kind. She felt herself staring, and then frowning in confusion when he suddenly stood up.

'So, where did we leave off?' he asked, taking a seat at the laptop.

That afternoon, while the snow fell down, and Evie and her aunts worked on a recipe to bring a family together over the holidays, she put the first CD in the player and sat back in the alcove, with Pennywort's head in her lap, listening to the detective story Sandro had brought her, a smile on her face. For the first time in ages, she felt almost normal.

TWELVE

Through the frosted window, Emma watched as Jack jogged past with Gus at his heels, the bear-like Newfoundland matching his pace. The household was still with that quiet hum that cloaked the cottage in its slumber. It was icy cold, but she didn't bother with her robe, or putting on a hat; there wasn't time.

Hesitating just for a second, she unlocked the door, crossing the garden quickly to open the low iron gate.

Jack stopped and circled back, pushing his hair out of his eyes.

'Hi,' she said, a little hesitantly.

His face was serious. 'Hi.'

His eyes were dark in the pre-dawn light. They were standing on either side of the low gate, a hand's breath apart.

His hand came out to touch her face, his long fingers gentle. She closed her eyes. She knew she should move away, but she couldn't.

'I love you,' he said. 'It's only ever been you, you know that?'

Then he cupped her face in his hands and kissed her. She sank into it, her hands coming up to touch his hair; somehow they, and her leg, were miraculously healed. She felt deliriously happy, and warmth spread throughout her chest. It was everything she had ever wanted.

Her eyes snapped open. She was back in her bed, Pennywort snoring loudly on her pillow and letting out small yips in his sleep, which must have woken her up.

One of her hands came up to touch her flushed cheeks. The other was still in its cast. It was just a dream, she told herself. But it had felt so real, so wonderful. Her body had been healed, and she had Jack in her arms… She sighed, lay back against the pillows and tried not to think about him – and failed. She closed her eyes and groaned, cursing the dream, how it had made things so simple, when it had always been anything but simple between them. Even from the start.

THIRTEEN

Whistling Moors, 2002

There were touches of frost on the heather, and the moors were quiet in the darkening afternoon, as thirteen-year-old Emma saw Jack Allen approaching. He passed the old farmhouse at the edge of the village. In the distance, she could just make out the amber lights of the town, and the top of a church spire.

'Hi,' he said, his hazel eyes warm as she neared.

'Hi, Jack,' she said, pushing her frozen fingers into her pockets. When she breathed puffs of white fog billowed out. She felt her stomach clench, like something was inside her, bouncing on a trampoline. She wondered why they called it butterflies, when surely a swarm of bees would be more appropriate?

They started walking along the path, which cut through the moors and across to the next village.

'Have you spoken to your mam?' asked Emma. She'd been up, tossing and turning, worrying about it. Hoping that just for once Janet Allen might be persuaded to change her mind.

He shook his head. 'I tried, but all that happened was I got a ten-hour lecture.'

Emma felt her stomach plummet. 'So, I won't be coming then.'

She kicked at a stray rock. Had she really thought that she'd be able to go to Jack's thirteenth-birthday party? Not really, said a small voice within. Still, every year the Allens threw a birthday party for Jack at their large triple-storey home, usually in one of the converted barns. It was one of the highlights of the young social scene in Whistling and Emma had always longed to be able to go, but due to their family's long feuding history, she'd never been invited. Perhaps, she thought now, she never would. She scowled at the ground.

Jack ran a hand through his hair. 'I'm sorry.'

'It's your party – you could have insisted that you wanted all your friends there,' she said.

'If I did that she would have just cancelled it, I'm sure.'

Emma looked away. If it had been her, she'd rather have cancelled it than not have Jack come.

He touched her arm. 'We can do this, if you like, celebrate just the two of us.'

She smiled, her black mood lifting somewhat. He was right, surely it was more special if it was just the two of them?

'I didn't bring your present though,' she said, biting her lip.

He shrugged. 'That doesn't matter.'

'Did you try your father this time?' she asked. 'I thought maybe if you asked him—'

Jack shook his head. 'He wouldn't agree, not if it meant a fight with my mother.'

She nodded. She'd known it was a long shot right from the start. Just being friends with Jack was hard enough; it was only in the last few months that he'd started taking more chances to see her, like they were doing now. She supposed boys were different. She would have risked – had already risked – several arguments and fights about Jack with Evie and her aunts just so she could see more of him.

They used to speak every day after school; Emma used to hang back especially just so they could. But Janet Allen had put a stop to that a few months ago, when she saw the two of them laughing outside the school gates. She stopped her car so abruptly it left a trail of dust, and jumped out, leaving the door open in her haste. A few people around them gasped, some laughed, as Mrs Allen slipped in her heels as she marched across the cobbles towards her and Jack.

She shoved a finger under Emma's nose. 'Stay away from my son!' she roared. Emma jumped back in shock.

'Mam!' protested Jack. 'We were just talking – calm down.'

'Calm down? Calm down! Get in the car this instant Jack Robert Allen, how dare you embarrass our family like this,' she said, wrestling him towards the car. Jack tried to pull his arm away. 'You're the one being embarrassing,' he hissed, his face red with shame.

But Mrs Allen's grip was vice-like and she shoved him into the car. Seconds later they'd sped off, and Emma had been left alone and mortified, with the sound in her ears of dozens of her schoolmates whispering and laughing at her.

After that, Jack had avoided her for a week, to her hurt and dismay. Till he passed her a note in the corridor, telling her to meet him by the abandoned farmhouse after school.

'I'm sorry about what happened,' he said when they met. 'And for not speaking to you. It's my mother – she's become impossible, she said that if she caught me talking to you again, I'd be grounded for a year. I've tried to explain that you're different. I mean, you don't even really believe in any of that nonsense about your cottage and the food your family make, do you?' he asked.

It was one of the first times they'd ever spoken about it – so directly, anyway.

Emma felt her throat constrict. She'd always played it down around Jack. She hadn't really known that he had thought it was all nonsense until now.

'Um, no, not really,' she said, ignoring the small part of herself that was screaming, 'Liar!' inside.

'Exactly – well, that's what I told her, but she won't hear it.'

Since then they'd met every few days for a long walk after school. Now that Mrs Allen was sure that he wasn't speaking to her, she'd stopped coming to fetch him, which was a relief for Jack, who'd found the situation embarrassing. 'I mean, no one else gets fetched.'

Emma could well understand his mortification. She was that glad though that he thought their friendship was important enough to him that he had arranged a way for them to still keep it – even if it had to happen in secret. It was better than the alternative.

As they walked home now though, six months later, Emma thought of the weekend approaching, when, she, as usual, would be the only one in her year not going to Jack's birthday party. She couldn't help but wish that it was different.

Jack was moaning about how he would have given anything not to have Stella Lea come. 'She's always whining – it drives me mad, but no, "The Leas and Allens have always been friends",' he said, imitating his mother's voice. 'So, she's coming, of course.'

Emma shook her head. It wasn't fair – why did Stella Lea get to go and not her?

Emma's attitude towards The Book began to change after she and Jack began to spend more time together. Evie noticed the change when Emma started to come home late, with no explanation of where she'd been, smelling of fresh earth and heather, her face guarded, her tone terse, monosyllabic when questioned.

Perhaps, thought Evie, it was the way Emma's eyes averted when she saw The Book, or the way that just for a moment they would flash with resentment when she was asked to help with a recipe, where before they would have sparkled at the thought of helping someone.

Evie blamed the spate of near-miss recipes that season. It could happen sometimes, like an unseasonal rainfall. When John Pendle came for a recipe to help his farm flourish, his crop got blight. When Katie Harvey wanted to win the harvest pageant, she came down with measles. Many more would occur before that spring, and soon, Evie saw the doubt begin to creep into Emma's eyes; noted in fear the way Emma began to tally each one up, a grim satisfaction upon her lips as if it explained something deeper.

That was the year Emma began to resist, and wouldn't step inside the kitchen for days.

Evie watched as she fought herself, her fingers twitching, her shoulders tensed, until at last she'd light the fire in the old range, and finally allow herself to do what she loved.

Evie saw how each time it took longer and longer for Emma to get back into the kitchen. Her notebook – once so full and minutely observed – lay blank and abandoned for weeks, sometimes months, on end.

'She's been spending time with young Jack,' whispered Dot, one dark, cold November afternoon. Pennywort was dozing with his head on the table as she peeled the carrots for a recipe for Mrs Morton's bad sight. Aggie shook her head. 'I saw them myself,' Dot insisted. 'It's like Margaret all over again,' she went on sadly.

'Maybe not,' said Evie. 'I'll have to speak to her.'

But it was like trying to stop a train by standing on the tracks.

'So… you and Jack Allen,' she began.

'Yes?' asked Emma, feeling her face flush as she took a seat across from Pennywort, who laid his head on her arm and promptly closed his eyes again.

'I hear you've become quite good friends.'

Emma looked up. 'Is that a problem?'

'No,' said Evie, as she began to chop an onion. 'It's just, well, we can't help noticing that lately, you haven't wanted to cook anything and I wondered if Jack—'

'It doesn't have anything to do with him.'

Emma looked away; she heard his words inside her head. *I told my mother you thought it was rubbish – you do – don't you?*

'Okay,' said Evie, in the tone of someone who was looking for more. Emma looked up. 'Maybe it's because, well, sometimes they don't really work anyway.'

Evie nodded. 'That's true enough, but then that's the truth with all things, love. No one succeeds at everything all the time, even this,' she said, pointing at The Book. 'Though sometimes things do work, just not the way we think they should.'

FOURTEEN

Whistling Village Hall, 2005

Sixteen-year-old Emma was standing in the back of the hall, in a black and beige dress that inverted like a tulip, her long red hair shining under the amber lights. She stood next to Gretchen, who was dressed in a pantsuit, and Maggie, who was wearing a lacy pink and black dress that stopped at the knee. Jenny was sitting in the corner, absorbed in a novel, as usual, while the rest of them were all watching Jason Thorpe spike the punch from the bottles he'd filched from his parents' liquor cabinet, which were hidden in a sports bag at his feet.

The town hall had been transformed for the annual winter dance. This year's theme was Enchanted Forest.

Sculpted willow trees created a canopy overhead that had been covered with fairy lights and fake snow.

Emma's eyes scanned the room and, with a little jolt in her chest, she saw Jack staring back at her from across the dance floor. He was standing next to Stella Lea, who was dressed in a pale blue dress that seemed at odds with her sour expression. He gave her a small smile, and she looked away with a flush.

A slow song came on, and a geeky boy with dark hair who lived in the next village, and was wearing a Superman T-shirt with his formal trousers, came over to ask her to dance.

Emma agreed, despite Gretchen and Maggie's sniggers; she didn't quite know how to say no politely. When the song finished, she felt someone touch her shoulder. It was Jack.

'Let's go outside,' he said.

She blinked, surprised, but nodded.

It was freezing outside; she'd left her coat in the hall. He shrugged out of his jacket and gave it to her.

'Who was that?' he asked.

She shrugged. 'No idea, he just asked me to dance.'

'So you said yes?'

She grinned at him, and then looked away. They were walking down the cobbled path towards the Brimbles' store, now closed for the evening. Just the shadowy moon lit their path.

'Why? Were you jealous?'

He stopped, his face serious. 'Yes,' he admitted.

She looked up at him from beneath her lashes. 'Good.'

Before she knew it, he was leaning over and kissing her. His lips were warm, his breath scented slightly with rum. Her head started to spin and her heart to thrum. She'd waited for so long for this moment.

It was her first ever kiss, and when they finally tore apart to breathe, she thought she might never be this happy ever again.

His breath was warm on her neck. 'So, that's what it's like to kiss Emma Halloway,' he said with a grin.

She felt her stomach flip as she looked into his eyes. 'Did you wonder about it?'

He grinned. 'Always.'

Suddenly a pair of strong hands wrenched her away from Jack. She gasped in horror as she saw Neil Allen, Jack's father, standing across from them, a stony expression on his face. A face, she realised, that looked so very similar to Jack's, only older, and far angrier than she'd ever seen Jack look.

'Dad—' Jack started, his eyes widening.

His father's face grew harder still. 'You're drunk – I can smell it from here. At least that explains this stupidity. In front of the whole town too.'

Emma's eyes widened. She could see Janet Allen marching towards them, her face livid. She left behind her Stella Lea, whose mouth, like that of many of her schoolmates, was hanging open at the sight of Jack Allen and Emma Halloway kissing in the moonlight.

'I'm not drunk,' protested Jack. 'Dad, this is ridiculous, Emma and I are friends.'

'Friends?' said Mrs Allen, nearing, her eyes snapping to Emma's, a look of pure loathing on her face, as if being friends with a Halloway was far worse than finding her son drinking. 'I thought I told you to stay away from my son,' she said, pushing Emma away from Jack.

'Mam—'

Suddenly there were thunderous footsteps, and a cold voice behind hissed, 'Touch my grandchild again, Janet Allen, and I'll make whatever stupid curse you think we put on your family, seem like a joke,' growled Evie, her voice low, and deadly.

There were several gasps all around.

Evie's blue eyes were wide, her dark mantle of shaggy grey hair fairly snapping with electricity and, for just one heart-stopping moment, there wasn't a person watching who didn't wonder if the rumours about them were true. Even Emma.

'Come,' she said to her granddaughter.

Emma hesitated for just a moment, her eyes meeting Jack's. How had what until then had been the most special night of her life turned into one of the worst?

'I don't care what you say!' shouted Emma, later that night. 'I love him.'

Dot's eyes were anxious as she tried to intervene. 'Evie—'

Evie shot her a silencing look. Dot and Aggie had come over quickly when they'd heard the news. Uncle Joe had made himself scarce in the living room, telling them to, 'Go easy on the child.'

'You love him?' she repeated. 'You're sixteen, for goodness' sake.'

'So?'

'So, you don't know what you're talking about.'

'Evie, is that helpful—' began Dot.

'What?' spluttered Evie, rounding on her sister, her eyes blazing.

'Come on, love, it's not like it's a surprise – we've all known she's felt this way for years,' said Aggie with a sigh, pinching the bridge of her nose.

Emma looked at her aunt gratefully and dashed away a tear.

Evie sighed, her anger starting to ebb. When Janet Allen had touched Emma, she had looked as if she could have cheerfully murdered her, but suddenly, all the fight seemed to go out of her. 'Oh lass, he's an Allen, I just don't want you to get hurt and I just don't see how else this is going to end.'

Emma looked up. 'B-but he feels the same way.' She looked back down at her feet. 'I'm sure he does.'

'Maybe, lass, I'm just not sure that's going to make such a difference.'

'You'd like that, wouldn't you!'

'No, actually I'd very much like to be wrong.'

Emma's lip wobbled as she turned on her heel, marched upstairs and slammed the door, hoping to drown out Evie's words with the sound of it shuddering closed.

When she saw Jack the next day, fear grabbed hold of her heart at the look on his face. It was like a wall had formed in the space between them.

'I can't see you any more.'

Emma felt like she'd been plunged into ice.

'W-what?' she breathed. 'Jack, no – we can fight this – fight them!'

He shook his head, wouldn't look her in the eye. 'No, we can't.'

She grabbed his arm. 'Why – why won't you even try?'

He looked up, the mask slipping from his face so that she could see the pain his words were costing him. 'I just can't, Emma. Maybe things would have been different if Evie hadn't said what she said – it just made it so much worse, they're so angry with me. It's like I've betrayed them or something.' He looked down and whispered, 'They told me things, things I never knew… that I didn't want to believe.'

A creeping sort of dread started clawing at her throat. 'About what?'

'What your family did to mine…'

Emma's mouth fell open. 'But Jack, that was a long time ago, and it's all rubbish anyway.'

'Yeah well, they lost everything they had on that "rubbish". Their whole business. My dad said it took forever for my grand-father to rebuild it, and even now it's not what it was – and it's all thanks to what they did. God Emma, I know it's not your fault but I just wish you hadn't come from that family.'

It was three weeks after the dance. Emma, in the twilight garden, cast a furtive glance over her shoulder. There was soil trapped beneath her fingernails. Beneath the squashes, a new token had been planted. The necklace that had once belonged to her mother. Tears coursed down her face, but she was determined; she should have done this years ago. She didn't have much time before Evie came home. Her fingers left dirt on the well-worn page, the book open to an old recipe called simply Faded Love, a recipe that promised to help a heart learn to forget. Though she had eaten every bite of the intricate dish, which had asked for artichoke hearts and fresh juniper berries, as the weeks passed she realised that it had made no difference at all; all she still felt was heartbroken.

She spent as much time as she could away from the cottage, walking the moors. It was a favourite walk, one where as a child she'd gather wild flowers and herbs; but now she was older, she spent more time, she supposed, gazing inward than out.

She liked to come here, so that she could be alone and think. Sometimes she'd imagine that she owned that old farmhouse, with its broken-down roof and faded blue shutters and doors. Sometimes, she imagined getting as far away from Whistling as she could, going back to London, and away from here where people judged you more on your last name than who you were inside.

It hadn't been easy going back to school after the winter dance, all the stares, and the rumours. The constant whispering. Stella Lea had taken to calling her a witch again; she mostly just tried to ignore her, as usual. Maggie, Gretchen and Jenny tried their best to shield her from some of her schoolmates' taunts, but they could offer no real solace for the fact that Jack wasn't really speaking to her any more. It was this that hurt Emma more than anything else.

Leaving the wild and empty moors, she walked back towards the village, thinking she'd spend some time with Aggie in her studio.

As she walked into the village, her hands trailed over an old poster with a smiling cartoon drawing of a grain of wheat, announcing the harvest festival, now long since past. She saw Harrison Brimble, with his long grey hair and misty eyes, give her a little wave from his store. She passed the new pizza bar that had just opened, the scent of pepperoni and mozzarella cheese wafting thickly on the air, and she saw inside her friend Jenny, sitting next to her brother Ryan, laughing as they ate. Maggie said the owner didn't check for IDs when serving alcohol, so it was rather popular with her peers. She wondered if she'd ever feel like a normal teenager again. When Jenny looked up, Emma averted her eyes; she didn't want to have to go and say hello, and pretend to be happy. She headed up the street, past the old clock tower to Aggie's flat, which was a converted old house of honey-coloured stone, the windows and doors painted in a pale mint green, the garden full of hollyhocks, roses and French lavender. She pressed the buzzer, and went upstairs when Aggie's voice boomed through the speaker for her to 'Come up, our lass.'

When she saw Emma's face, her mouth pulled down. 'Bad one, was it?'

That was Aggie, she just let you be. It was a comfort not having to pretend otherwise. Emma nodded, taking a chair by the window of Aggie's studio, which had a view of the village square below and the clock tower. She could see people milling about doing their autumn shopping, baskets under arms.

Aggie poured them both a sherry. 'Medicinal,' she said with a wink.

Emma took it with a small smile. 'I'm starting to understand why my mother ran away,' she said glumly, as Aggie went back to painting an enormous, shadowy feather using swirling black paint.

Aggie dabbed her brush into her palette, and said, 'Has Evie ever spoken to you about that?'

Emma shrugged. 'Sort of, she just told me that my mother turned her back on Hope Cottage, and that the day she left, she said she was going to burn The Book.' She sighed; even now, she could sympathise. 'It's funny, when I first came to live here, you and Dot said something about how hard it was to be a Halloway and a teenager.'

'Yeah – well, it was hard, especially for your mam, I mean you have to deal with Stella, who is nasty enough, but she had Janet Allen in her year, can you imagine?'

Emma's mouth fell open. 'Janet Allen was in the same year as my mother?'

Aggie nodded. 'Oh yes – though her last name was Cairn then. Not that it made a difference, she grew up in the Lea household.'

Emma's eyes bulged. 'She grew up with the Leas? How come?'

'Adopted, apparently. The vicar's best friend from Scotland passed away when Janet was about twelve. There was no other family really, I believe, so they took Janet and her brother Gordon in.'

Emma looked at Aggie in surprise. 'Scotland?'

'Aye, it's how your mother met your dad – it was the year she turned twenty, Gordon's old school friend, Liam McGrath, came to stay the one summer, and they met at some dance or something – and fell for one another.'

'What!' she exclaimed. 'My mother met my father through Janet Allen?'

She sat thinking hard. She'd heard, from her Uncle Joe that her father had come to Whistling all those years ago to visit his friend, a friend who'd moved away now, but her uncle had never mentioned that he was the brother of Janet Allen.

'Yes. Though from what I heard, Janet wasn't too happy about it – she tried to split them up, and caused a real ruckus.'

Emma frowned. 'But why? Why try splitting them up?'

'Well, I suppose the real issue was that Janet despised your mother because she believed that Neil Allen – the boy she was in love with, Jack's father – had a crush on her.'

Emma's mouth fell open. 'Did he?'

'I don't know. I don't think it was like you and Jack but I think it was part of the problem, and of course she was raised as a Lea so she also believed that your mother was a witch, you know? She didn't want her brother's best friend to end up with her so she tried to break them up, told him all about the family, all the worst sort of rumours – like that we were frauds and crooks. I believe, looking back, it was worse because your mother was pregnant at the time with Liam's child, so she felt even more betrayed by Janet, who had always made her life a living hell at school.

'When your mother told Neil about how Janet was trying to poison Liam against her, Neil took Janet's side. I think he said something about your father having a right to know the sort of family he was signing up for. After that, Margaret just snapped, she tried to burn The Book, then she and Liam ran away, and from what you've told us, she just sort of gave up on being a Halloway, I guess.'

Emma looked down. It was the first time she'd ever really thought that, maybe, she was a little like her mother after all.

FIFTEEN

Present day

'How does that feel?' asked Dr Norton, touching Emma's hand, now finally free of its cast, which lay abandoned like a snakeskin on the carpeted floor.

She'd almost passed out when he took the pins out, but it was more from the shock of the thing than real pain.

'A little tender, but okay.'

'You'll have to go easy on it – practise the exercises I showed you. I won't lie, they may hurt, but they're worth it if you want a full recovery.'

She nodded. She'd do anything just to feel like herself again. 'If only the rest would hurry up,' she said. She was tired of having Evie do everything for her, tired of feeling like a burden. Even now, Aggie had to take time out from her day to drive her to York to the doctor, because there was no way she could manage the two bus exchanges with her scrambled senses and broken leg. After six weeks, she just couldn't help feeling despondent at how slow the progress had really been.

He had large, thoughtful eyes, and a bushy beard that hid a kind smile. 'The rest will just take time, be patient with yourself.'

Patience. It had never been her strong suit.

He looked at her, seeming to read her thoughts. 'It's common with this type of injury to have feelings of sadness, even depression.

You don't need to suffer through it. I could refer you to someone if that's the case.'

'I'm okay,' she said.

He was staring at her, his face clearly showing that he didn't believe her. She sighed, and everything that she'd been trying to suppress came bubbling up: 'I just want to feel like me again, I just wish I could know for sure when or if I was going to get better. I mean – I can deal with this,' she said, indicating her injured hand. 'It's not great, it's sore and I wish to God I hadn't fallen on my writing hand, but there's an expected date for recovery, you know? It's not knowing when the rest will get better that just drives me a bit... mad. I just want to smell something, anything. Even my dog's bad breath. Taste something, even if it's rubbish – it would be heaven if it were rubbish, because it would be so much better than nothing. Yesterday my aunt told me that I was getting too thin. I hadn't even noticed I was. At the beginning of the year I tried for ages to shift a few pounds – and now I just look sick, and frail. I'm twenty-eight, but I feel like I'm an old woman. I nap three times a day. I haven't had a proper shower in six weeks, and...' she thought of how she sometimes snapped at those around her, when they were just trying to be kind, 'I've become mean at times.'

Dr Norton's eyes were sympathetic. 'Well, it's easy to be nice when you're not in pain. The people in your life love you and they will understand, especially if you explain. You may need to face that for a while this is the new normal. And, I think you need to be careful not to get in your own way.'

Emma frowned. 'What do you mean?'

'Measure your progress since the accident, see that as ground zero, and don't compare it to what you were before – it won't serve you, not now. The brain is a remarkable organ, capable of so much, but we've got to help it along by being kinder to ourselves.

If we're constantly beating ourselves up we'll see that effect on our bodies, so it's vital to look for small moments of happiness we can glean where we can – even if that just means being grateful for the people who can help us.'

Emma nodded. She knew he had a point, but when you couldn't taste or smell anything and your sense of touch was so confused, it was hard to look on the bright side sometimes, especially as she felt like a burden most days.

Perhaps he was reading her thoughts again, because he asked, 'You're a food columnist, yes?'

She gave him a puzzled look. 'Yes?' Wondering what that had to do with anything.

'What about cooking?'

She blinked. 'Pardon?'

'Well, that shouldn't be too strenuous – in fact the movements would be quite good for your hand. I know you can't taste anything yet, but there's always a bit of joy in making things for others—'

'I don't cook,' said Emma shortly.

His grey eyes widened. 'You don't? That's curious – I mean, you write about food for a living, don't you enjoy it?'

'Ah,' began Emma. 'Well, I used to…'

She hadn't, not for years. It was all so entwined with how she felt about the food the women in her family made, and all the trouble it had caused her over the years. She just couldn't approach it lightly, even if she wanted to; but still she'd never been able to properly abandon her love for it. It was such a deep part of her, which was why she channelled her love for it into her columns instead. In many ways her columns and articles had been a way of trying to make sense of it all.

Dr Norton didn't notice her distress.

'I think it would be good, the gentle movements will be good therapy for your hand, and I mean, I'm sure I don't have to tell you,' he laughed, 'but I've always found that there's something about cooking that really feeds the soul.'

Emma looked at him, at a loss for words. 'Did my family put you up to this?'

'Pardon?' He looked a bit taken aback.

'Nothing,' she said with an attempt at a casual smile. 'It's just, I don't see how cooking would make any real difference to my situation.'

'It couldn't hurt, could it?'

She looked away. Oh yes it could.

They were driving back to Whistling, the windows fogged from the heaters. Outside, snow was beginning to fall, and her breath billowed out in little puffs. Aggie looked over at her with a concerned frown as she stared out the window, a glum look on her face as she peered at the world through her hazy eyes. 'You don't look all that happy to have your cast off, I would have thought you'd be chuffed to bits,' she said, as she changed lanes, her blue eyes puzzled.

'I know,' sighed Emma, who was annoyed at herself for the black mood she couldn't shake. 'Ugh, I know. I should be – and I am – but well, it's just... this is the first time I've been out of the cottage in weeks and I thought, I don't know... I thought that by now, there would be some real progress, you know?'

Christmas had always been her favourite time of year, and yet she dreaded the idea that it would come round and she would feel no differently, unable to enjoy any of it.

Aggie frowned. 'But you got the cast off your hand – surely that *is* progress?'

Emma nodded. 'It is, and I'm grateful, it's just slow, that's all, especially all the other things – there's been no real progress with that, beyond not having to read people's lips any more. I thought that by the time the cast on my hand was off, I'd be able to write again, feel a little more like me really, but I've still got to do a lot of therapy. And even then, it's not like I can see things straight, or taste or smell anything.'

'Tell you what, love, come back to my place for a bit – have a glass of wine, it might do you some good, change of scenery, you know?'

Emma gave a small smile. That did sound good. 'Okay. Thanks Aggie.'

She was glad to step into Aggie's flat on the high street, with its weathered beams and stark white walls, its dark wooden furniture and colourful prints, throws and rugs in shades of orange, turquoise and coral.

Upstairs, her art studio was still filled with stacks of her black and white canvases, and shelves full of paint. Emma had always loved these paintings, since she was a child and had come to Aggie's studio to watch her work. While Dot was the gentlest of the lot, and Evie the wisest, Aggie was feisty, and loyal to a fault. There had been times, particularly when Emma became a teenager, when she had sought out Aggie because she just didn't judge when Emma came round and sat in the studio with a 'monk' on, as they said in these parts. Aggie would let her rail about the Leas or Janet Allen, often throwing in a healthy dose of venom at them herself. Aggie didn't say things like, 'Cheer up, love', which Emma appreciated; it was good to be around someone who just let you feel what you felt, without feeling the need to put on a 'happy face'. Emma looked at Aggie now, realising how much she'd missed her while she'd been in London.

Emma braved the steps, sweat pooling in her hair as she dragged herself up with several hops, her elbow grazing the wall even with Aggie's help, till finally she made it to the top and her aunt led her to a red leather chair by the window in her studio, from where Emma could see, despite her hazy vision, and the pounding that had started again behind her temples, the village square and, in the distance, the clock tower.

Aggie poured her a glass of Merlot and took a seat across from her. She had strung fairy lights on the beams, and in the corner of the studio, Emma could see the bleached driftwood tree that Aggie had made, which come the first of December would be filled with her tiny willow sculptures.

Seeing it, Emma couldn't help feeling her spirits lift. Some things never changed. She took a sip of the wine and looked out of the window. 'I can almost see the clock tower in focus if I do this,' she said, squeezing one eye shut. 'Almost.'

Aggie gave her a sympathetic look, took a sip of wine. Then she frowned. 'Hang on, you've reminded me. I've got something for you,' she said, getting up and rummaging in her art desk, moving aside sketchbooks and the usual found objects she used as inspiration for her art – strange feathers, pebbles and used ticket stubs. 'Aha!' she cried when she found what she was looking for, buried in one of the drawers. It was a piece of folded-up newsprint, from what Emma could see.

'I thought this might be interesting for your column – well, if you ever wanted to do something on our history. The *Whistling News* ran the story as part of a heritage piece about the town a few months ago, and I saved a copy.'

'Oh?' said Emma, taking the article from Aggie, squinting and then handing it back to her with a sigh. The print darted across the page like moving insects, no matter how hard she squinted at it. She sighed again. 'Still can't read.'

Aggie shook her head. 'I know that. You don't have to read it – look at the photograph.'

Emma frowned and looked, holding it back from her face so that she could try focusing her eyes. Written in large black copperplate, the article's title was 'Whistling Celebrates its Bicentenary'. Underneath this was the byline of Jessica Flynn, who presented the six o'clock news every evening on the local radio station as well. The article was accompanied by a large sepia photograph, clearly from the nineteenth century, that revealed a man standing in the middle of two women next to the clock tower in the centre of the village.

He was wearing a top hat, and had his arm around one of the women, the younger of the two. Both women had hair that parted rather severely down the middle.

'It was taken to celebrate the inauguration of the clock tower,' said Aggie. 'That's Grace Halloway,' she went on, pointing to the older woman.

Emma's mouth popped open. Grace had dark hair, and a serious expression on her face. The other woman was younger with lighter hair, her expression more festive, cheerful. 'And that's Alison Halloway.'

Emma looked. It was hard to really make out the photo with her impaired vision, but she tried her best. 'Who's that with his arm round her?' she asked.

'I thought that might interest you – that's John Allen.'

'John Allen?' said Emma in surprise.

'Geoff Allen's son.'

Emma frowned, trying to piece the story together, remembering the legacy of the failed recipe – the one that had ended the friendship between the Halloways and the Allens. 'Was he the one who owned the printworks?'

'That was his father, Geoff. John was the one with the gambling problem.'

Emma looked up. 'The one who came to Grace for a recipe?'

'Yes.'

'So, this must have been before it all went bad, then?'

Aggie nodded. 'It must have, though look at Grace's face. I've seen photos of her before – she's not usually that stern. Something tells me she wasn't too pleased about something – maybe it was the fact that he had his arms all round her daughter?'

'Maybe,' breathed Emma. 'I mean – things were different then, nowadays the first thing you do when you're in a photograph is throw your arms round the person next to you and smile, but back then that would be quite taboo, unless…'

She looked at Aggie in complete shock. 'They were a couple?'

'Maybe.'

SIXTEEN

Hope Cottage, 2005

'Evie hasn't been feeling all that well, have you dear?'

Evie, who had been lying under the kitchen sink, tightening a pipe with a wrench, paused her grunting and sat up. She pushed back the red bandana that was attempting to keep her wild, salt and pepper hair at bay, frowned, then suddenly nodded as she saw her sister's pointed look, and gave a faint little cough. 'Hem. Not for days. I didn't want to say anything…'

'She looks positively feeble,' said Dot, eyes wide with worry.

'Barely moved a muscle,' Aggie agreed.

Emma rolled her eyes. 'Yesterday, Evie hefted that big chest up the stairs all by herself, went on a nature walk with Mrs Brimble until late in the evening and still had energy enough to chop all that firewood when she came home,' she said, pointing to a sizeable log pile in the corner.

Dot didn't look fazed in the slightest. 'It's just the surge, isn't it?' she said.

'The *surge*?' spluttered Emma, raising a brow.

'Y-e-s,' said Dot, nodding her head wisely. 'I saw it on *Grey's Anatomy*. The dishy one – McSteamy?… well, it happened to him, it's all so dreadfully sad, the surge, it's the last bit of energy someone gets, you know…' she whispered, sotto voce, 'just before they pop their clogs.'

Emma's lips twitched. 'Pop their clogs! What am I going to do with you lot? Evie is perfectly fine.' She looked at her grandmother, her expression softening. 'You are, aren't you?'

Evie gave another fake cough. 'Hem. N-o.'

Emma rolled her eyes. 'It's just a few hours away,' she pointed out. Once again.

'What's that, dear?' said Evie, eyes wide and innocent.

Emma gave her a pointed look.

'My university. It's only a few hours away and I'll be coming home every weekend, if I can.'

'What's that got to do with the price of eggs?' said Dot, raising her own brow.

'This is not about that – is that what you thought?' said Aggie, the picture of innocence. 'Can you believe that?' she asked her sisters.

'Like we would ever be so – so…' Evie searched for a word.

'Obvious?' suggested Emma, crossing her arms and giving them the squinty eye. 'You wouldn't, just for example, hide my acceptance letter away from me in Pennywort's food bin – for over a week – for instance?

'Us? Never!' cried Aggie.

'We would never be so deceitful,' said Dot.

'Where's the trust?' said Evie, shaking her head, and getting back to work on the sink.

'Really? Just like you wouldn't tell me that you were feeling rather poorly yourself and in desperate need of someone to mix your paint for you?' she asked Aggie.

'Not just the paint. Those canvases don't carry themselves.'

'Ha ha, nice try.'

Aggie harrumphed. 'Why do you have to go anyway?' she said, giving up the pretence.

'I want to learn, make something of myself. See a bit more of the world. I mean I grew up in London, but I hardly remember it, and this is a great opportunity for me—'

Evie set the wrench down again, and scoffed. 'You grew up here.'

'With us,' said Dot.

'You know what I mean,' said Emma, feeling a sudden stab of guilt. 'I'll be coming home all the time, you'll see.'

'Look,' said Aggie, 'we support you, you know we do. But does it have to be in London? Couldn't you go to the local one instead? I mean, we couldn't help noticing that you decided on that university shortly after young Jack and Stella got together over the summer.'

'That has nothing to do with it!' protested Emma.

They all shared a look. Surely it had everything to do with it. There had been no talk at all of her attending university in London till then. She'd applied, of course, they'd all encouraged her to try all her options, but it wasn't until news broke that Stella Lea and Jack Allen were together that Emma had announced, the day after, that she would be going to King's College in London.

Emma sighed. 'I just want a bit of a change, it's not for ever,' she said.

They nodded. Evie glanced at The Book, a thoughtful look on her face. Emma saw it.

'No recipes! I've made up my mind, don't try and change it and please don't fight me on this.'

Of course Emma's decision to go to King's College had everything to do with Jack Allen – and her desire not to be subject to the sight of him dating Stella Lea. While she was there, she made a decision to put all thoughts of him firmly from her mind.

Still, there were times in a lecture room when she'd glance round, sure that she'd seen a boy with familiar hazel eyes, only to find they were not familiar at all; or she'd see a boy with dark blond hair in the corridors and her heart would begin to race, before she could remind herself that she was done thinking about him.

She focused instead on her studies, which she rather enjoyed. Here she sought and found other explanations for the things she'd witnessed as a child, things that made her think that perhaps there was a chance that she was normal, after all. And perhaps, deep down, that just maybe there was hope for her and Jack one day too – if an alternative explanation for her family existed. Where, for example, if a recipe from The Book was said to ease aches and pains and it contained at its heart a compound of ginger, which helped to ease inflammation, surely that was the real reason it worked? Not because of anything else?

In time, she convinced herself that what her grandmother and her aunts did was nothing more than a big bowl of myth and lore, all sprinkled with rumour and speculation and a town that really should know better by now.

She convinced herself of a lot of things. If she was feeling down it had nothing to do with the smell of cocoa or wood fires or roasted marshmallows, scents that always reminded her of Hope Cottage. It was simply, she was sure, because she needed an earlier night for a change. If she found herself getting tears in her eyes while she stared at a book with a pale blue cover in the cookery aisle, it wasn't because she missed that old swollen tome back home, it was because she hadn't had a good night's sleep in a while.

There were other things too, that she could explain. Like how grinding her teeth at night wasn't to stop herself from suggesting a remedy or thinking of the perfect recipe when someone complained of an earache or a fall-out with a friend; it was simply stress, a common ailment of life.

In fact, after a while, Emma became so good at convincing herself that something was blue when it was green, she barely noticed the effects any more.

Learning about the history of food and writing about all the weird and wonderful lore that came with it, she told herself, was almost as good as the real thing. Better perhaps, because this way she could be just like any other young woman in the city.

If some days her fingers itched for the feel of flour or the curve of a wooden spoon, she distracted them by typing up notes and paging through old-fashioned books that spoke of the art of cooking. Somehow, she couldn't quite bring herself to make anything, didn't trust herself not to get sucked back in some way.

During the last month of her final year of study, while she was still making up her mind about what to do once she was finished – make the move to London an official one or look for work somewhere close to home? – her Aunt Aggie had her first art exhibition in several years.

Emma came home to attend the exhibition, still undecided. There was a job going as a lifestyle editor for a weekly paper based in York who seemed interested in the articles she'd sent through. And in London, she'd gone for a promising interview at the *Mail & Ledger* about a potential food column, but she hadn't yet heard anything from either of them on the night she attended Aggie's exhibition.

Aggie's large, black and white 'shadow' paintings, which, she had explained to Emma once, 'reflect the shadow selves we all hold inside of us', had a small but loyal following, Emma included.

This first exhibition in years coincided with her seventieth birthday and was held in the remodelled Whistling Art Gallery, a converted old building that doubled up as an art and design school during the day. It had a loft space for the gallery on the tenth floor. As the occasion was also celebrating a more-than-forty-year career, there were quite a few loyal fans like Emma who'd made the trip to Whistling.

Emma stared at her aunt's latest collection, the curious, almost ethereal shadowy shapes, which were somehow both whimsical and slightly vintage looking, yet at the same time modern and alluring. A bit like the woman herself, she thought. To strangers the images of the shadowy faces of women, bending over a book, a table laden with food or a child with a dog in her lap, could be anyone, but Emma knew they were of them, the Halloways. Some, however, were so abstract they could have been flowers or butterflies, yet somehow the feeling they conveyed was the same: hope, heartache, love. You felt it all when you looked at one of Aggie's paintings.

'They're beautiful,' she told Aggie, eyeing one of a little girl whose hair was flying out from her head as she swung on a swing, a shoe fallen on the grass beneath her feet.

Aggie kissed her hello, then shrugged. She painted what was in her heart. 'I remember, when I was a bit older than you are now, my agent at the time suggested I try using colour, and attempting more of an art deco sort of style – it was the fashion then, you see, but I couldn't do it. What's the point? Should you sell a few more paintings or do what matters to you? Of course, Stan, my first husband, disagreed, he wanted me to chase the money.'

Emma frowned. Took a glass of pink champagne from a passing waiter, and asked, 'Was this the one who moved to Vegas to become a professional poker player?'

Aggie had had three husbands; sometimes it was hard to keep up with who was who.

Aggie shook her head, took a sip of her champagne and stifled a laugh. 'No, that was Michael, the second one.'

'Ah,' said Emma, with a grin.

It was then, while she was holding back a giggle, that she looked up and saw him across the crowded room. Jack Allen.

He was standing next to a group of students from the art and design school, his dark blond hair longer than she'd ever seen it. He was dressed in dark jeans and a black knitted jumper. When he saw her, his eyes widened in surprise, but he held her gaze. Emma tore hers away, trying and failing to tune back in to what Aggie had been saying.

'You all right, love?'

'Fine, fine,' said Emma, taking a sip of her champagne, her heart thundering in her chest.

She didn't concentrate on much else after she'd seen Jack; she stood helplessly alone while Aggie went off to mingle with a group who'd approached her, launching into an explanation about the techniques she'd used or what inspired each painting.

Emma looked up and saw Jack looking at her, wondering what on earth he was doing here, at an exhibition for a Halloway, of all places.

As if to answer her question, he walked over to her, and she had to fight an urge to run away. It had been some time since she'd stared into those familiar hazel eyes, but the feelings they brought were just the same; butterflies launched inside her stomach as her face flushed with a mixture of excitement and mild anger that, after all this time, he still had the same effect on her.

'Hi,' he said, almost shyly.

She made to take a sip of champagne, but found to her chagrin that her glass was empty.

'It's nice to see you again,' he said.

'Yeah, and you.'

'So, um, I heard you've just finished uni – is that right?'

She nodded. 'Yeah, this last week.'

'I've still got another week myself – I took a gap year first, did some travelling…'

She frowned, and then remembered something. 'So you did study graphic design, then?' she asked, realising that was probably why he was here tonight.

'Yeah, the college moved into this building a couple of months ago, it's been great.'

'I wouldn't have thought that you'd come to my aunt's exhibition. With, you know, everything…' she said, alluding to the tension between their families.

He ran a nervous hand through his hair. 'Oh, we're supposed to show support to all the exhibitions, help out, hand out flyers, that sort of thing,' he answered.

She nodded.

He was staring at her, so she looked away, swallowing slightly, wishing she had another glass of champagne to steady her nerves. Wishing he'd stop staring at her.

He moved closer, and she could smell his aftershave, fresh, spicy, sandalwood. 'So, um, does that mean you're back?'

She felt her stomach flip. Did he want her to be back? She cleared her throat, took a step back. 'I'm not sure. I haven't really decided yet.'

He touched her arm. 'Well, it would be great if you were.'

The breath caught in her chest; where he touched her seemed to burn. 'Would it?'

'Yes, it would. I-I've missed you.' He ran a hand through his hair, then coloured slightly, as if he hadn't meant to say that. 'Missed just hanging about with you, you know.'

She closed her eyes. It didn't change the fact that the last time they tried 'hanging about' as he called it, it had ended with him telling her that he couldn't see her any more, because of a stupid two-hundred-year-old family feud, one that made her wish she came from a different family.

'Yeah, well.' She gave a thin smile. 'I'm not sure me going to uni was what stopped that, Jack, but anyway, I um, I've got to go – Evie's waiting for me,' she lied, turning on her heel and, without a goodbye, leaving Jack standing staring after her, his mouth open slightly.

Emma made for the nearest lift, stepping over a piece of paper that had fallen on the ground in her haste, not bothering to see what it was as she shrugged it off her shoe. The lift doors were just beginning to close when Jack put his arm through the gap and bolted in beside her.

She sucked in air in surprise. Her heart started to race and, as the doors came to a close, Jack standing next to her, she hit the button for the ground floor.

'Are you following me?' she asked, crossing her arms and moving as far away from him as she could.

'Of course, I am,' he said, a furrow between those hazel eyes.

She turned to look at him in exasperation as the lift started to descend.

'Why?'

He looked at the ground and then back at her. 'Em – come on, you know I still c—'

But he didn't get to finish what he was saying. Just then the lift juddered to a very wild and rocky halt, making an alarming screeching sound, like nails on a blackboard.

'Jesus Christ,' said Emma, her heart jack-knifing in her chest. She lost her footing for a second and her elbow hit the side of the elevator, making her wince in sudden pain.

'Oh shit!' said Jack, turning pale and closing his eyes for a beat. 'I didn't even think – shit, this lift is out of order, oh fuck.'

Emma's heart was in her throat, and she had to fight every nerve in her body not to give in to her sudden panic and claustrophobia. She wasn't good with small spaces. Not good at all.

She blinked. 'It's out of order?'

He gave a short nod. 'What happened to the sign?'

She just gazed at him in horror. 'What sign?'

'There was an out of order sign on the door – didn't you see it?'

She shook her head. She was beginning to panic now, her head swarming. She vaguely recalled stepping over a piece of paper on the ground just before she got in, but she'd been in too much of a hurry to think of picking it up. 'I stood on something outside the lift, maybe it fell on the floor.'

He closed his eyes. 'Shit, sorry – I should have remembered myself. I wasn't thinking.'

Emma was only half listening to what he was saying as she tried to calm her breathing, feeling dizzy. There were white spots in her vision and her extremities started to tingle as if she might faint. There was an emergency bell, which she rang, repeatedly, while looking for an emergency number; but she couldn't see one as the sign was so badly scratched and worn.

Jack phoned someone at the party to tell them they were stuck, and Emma heard him say, 'Okay, well, I suppose we have no choice.'

He turned to her now. 'They heard the alarm – thank goodness – and someone will be on their way. That was Ben, he was stuck in this lift a couple of weeks ago, he's a friend from college. Anyway, he said it could take anywhere from a half-hour to a couple of hours,' said Jack taking a seat on the lift floor, obviously about to get comfortable for the time being.

Emma slid down beside him, her face pale, palms sweating. He took one of her hands and gave it a squeeze, 'It'll be okay, Ems.'

She swallowed, gave him a nod, squeezed his hand back. Whatever she might feel about Jack Allen, right now she was simply grateful that he was here and that she wasn't alone.

She put her head back against the lift wall as the panic started to mount. Her vision doubled, and she felt like she might throw up.

'Christ, you've gone really pale,' said Jack.

She opened her eyes. 'Small spaces,' she said. 'Freak me out.'

He nodded, then scooched closer, putting his arm round her. Part of her wanted to tell him to stop, but it was the part of her brain that was not stuck in a lift that could plunge them to their deaths, so she ignored that voice and was grateful for the small comfort Jack's arm afforded.

'Well,' he joked, 'if there was any one person I wouldn't mind being stuck in a lift with, it's you.'

She gave a short laugh, then closed her eyes again; she'd glimpsed the metal walls, and her heart started to race again.

He rubbed her back, and it was such a small, sweet gesture that she couldn't help giving him the first real smile she'd given him all night.

'Thanks,' she said.

'For what?'

'For looking after me.'

'Course.'

After a while, she started to calm down. His fingers on her arm went from soothing to gentle tickling and she became conscious of how close they were, the warmth of his body, how she fitted so easily against him, his scent, fresh and spicy, inviting.

She looked at him, saw his eyes, so full of concern for her, and swallowed. This time it had nothing to do with her fear of being stuck in an enclosed space.

He tucked a strand of hair behind her ear, and a sudden shiver went down her spine.

'Jack, I don't think this is a good idea,' she said, butterflies launching again in her stomach.

He gave her a half-smile. 'Like that's ever stopped us before,' he said, his fingers tracing the edges of her face, and then he leaned over and kissed her. Her head swam as she sank into the kiss, her hands in his hair as she pulled him closer.

When the maintenance crew came to get them out an hour later, Emma blushed. Her lips were bee-stung swollen from having been kissed so thoroughly, and she could only imagine the state of her hair, which had come out of its low knot.

Jack stood apart from her as he thanked everyone for their help, and she felt suddenly cold, missing the warmth from his body, which had been so close to her only moments before. In the crowd of onlookers she saw Aggie looking at her, a bit too knowingly.

She smoothed her hair as best she could, and then looked at Jack, who smiled at her, his eyes full of promise, as she said goodbye.

After that they couldn't get enough of each other. Jack knocked on the cottage door the next morning, just after Evie had left, bringing a box of lemon cinnamon buns for breakfast. 'Couldn't stop thinking of you last night,' he said, and Emma felt lighter than air.

Still he hesitated over coming indoors. 'Let's go for a walk,' he suggested instead, clearly not keen on the idea of being found in the cottage by Evie later. Emma could understand it, though she hoped that this time things would be different.

That first morning, they walked the moors for hours, pausing to kiss and sit in the purple heather, with only birdsong for company.

'I know you can't control where you come from, any more than I can, and it's unfair of them to put all that old crap on us,' he said, taking her hand, and looking into her eyes. He meant the old family feud that had got between them before. She bit her lip. It was what she'd wanted him to say the night before, what she'd wanted him to say for years now.

She felt like she was sixteen again, though this time they were bolder than they'd ever been, with Jack sneaking her into his large annexe at the back of the Allens' converted barn in the evenings; though a part of her hesitated at the idea of hiding what they had once again, she didn't want to expose what was so new to the wrath of his mother either.

They stayed up late, making love and talking about what they wanted from their future.

'You have to take that job in York,' he said, kissing her shoulder, as they sat before the fire in his small, cosy living room. She'd told him all about the position and how undecided she'd been.

'I hated not being able to see you all this time.'

She smiled, buried her face in his neck. 'I didn't think you noticed.'

'Oh, I noticed,' he said, pulling her towards him.

'Didn't you have Stella to distract you?' she asked. She'd meant the question to be casual, but the truth was it had devastated her when she'd found out that he'd got together with her – the girl who'd been so cruel to her when she first arrived in Whistling, who made her life hell, who was, somehow, always waiting in the wings for Jack.

He looked away, sighed. 'Stella was… well, she was never you. That's been over for a long time.'

Her heart skipped a beat at his words.

'What about you? Left anyone broken-hearted at uni? I'm sure there's half a dozen lads crying into their pillows now.'

She laughed. 'Not really.'

There was Pete, a boy she'd met at party, but they hadn't really progressed beyond the friend stage. He was sweet and kind, and had been the sort of person she could call if ever she wanted to see a film or catch a show. Her uni friends thought he was a bit boring, and truth be told she sort of liked that about him; but he wasn't Jack.

'Did you cry into your pillow?' she asked.

He grinned. 'All the time.'

The week passed in a happy blur. If Evie suspected anything, she didn't say so; perhaps she was too pleased to see Emma looking so happy.

She and Jack spent all their free time together, mostly at his place. She was careful to leave early in the morning, before anyone could see her, so she could sneak back into Hope Cottage.

Evie found her doing that the second week she was back. She was waiting for her in the kitchen, an anxious look on her face, dark shadows beneath her eyes.

'I hope you know what you're doing,' she said, as Emma tried and failed to come up with a plausible excuse for where she'd been.

Emma expected her to rail and rage, but she didn't. It was worse. Evie just looked sad.

'I do, it's different this time. We're older now and it's what we both want.'

'I don't think that was ever in doubt,' said Evie, picking up her mug of cold tea. Pennywort's head was dozing on the table. 'But just be careful, love, the trouble with most Allens is that they never change.'

Emma gritted her teeth. 'He has! We were sixteen the last time we got together, just kids really – his parents made him feel guilty, that's all. It's not like that now, he wouldn't stand for that.'

Evie nodded, pinching the bridge of her nose. 'I'm not fighting you, love, I just hope for your sake it goes differently this time, but—'

'But you doubt it?' spat Emma, crossing her arms.

Evie gave a slow nod, stood up and made her way out of the kitchen. 'I just wanted to tell you to be careful.'

Emma stood, shaking, flooded with anger. Couldn't Evie just be happy for her? They were making it work. Things *had* changed. Their relationship had deepened, grown into something stronger, more intense. Still, as Emma watched dawn crest the horizon through the window, she couldn't help the small niggle of doubt that crept inside her heart. They still hadn't gone anywhere as a couple together these past few weeks, hadn't been seen in public. Jack came past whenever Evie wasn't home, never venturing inside, and she waited until dark to go to him at his parents' home, so that she could sneak in.

It was just because they were keeping it between them for now, she told herself as she left later that morning, walking down to the village, thinking that she'd go and see Maggie or perhaps get a cuppa at the teashop.

Maggie wasn't at home, so she made her way inside the Harris sisters' teashop, pausing when she saw Jack sitting there with his parents. She blinked in surprise.

She felt nervous, but she offered him a smile, taking a step forward. His eyes widened and he shook his head, vigorously.

Emma frowned. She hadn't been sure if she *was* actually going to go over and say hello, but Jack's response, the way his hazel eyes seemed filled with fear, stopped her heart.

She took a step back. Just then Janet Allen looked at Jack, who had turned to his menu, the tops of his ears red, and then she looked up and saw Emma, and her face grew pinched in its displeasure. She heard Janet hiss, 'This place used to be great. No wonder it's gone down. They'll let anyone in here,' loud enough for Emma to hear, and a few people turned to look at her. Emma stood rooted to the spot, her face burning, waiting for Jack to say something, anything, in her defence.

He didn't.

She turned and left, heart thumping in her chest. By the time she was back at the cottage, tears of humiliation had traced their way down her face and she was cursing herself for being the worst sort of idiot – the one who never learned.

He came to the cottage an hour later, for once not caring if Evie was there when he knocked.

Emma stepped out and closed the door behind her; even though the cottage was mercifully empty, she was not willing to invite him inside.

'Oh God, you've been crying. Shit,' he said, noting her red-rimmed eyes. 'I'm sorry – you just surprised me, that's all. I was going to tell them.'

Emma snorted. 'Yeah, I'm sure,' she said, coldly.

He closed his eyes, 'Em, it's not like that, my parents have had some bad news. Looks like we're going to have to close down the stationery division of the business – we just found out – it puts the company at a very rocky point. Mum especially feels terrible as that was her department, you know, and now there will be people losing their jobs… I will tell them about us, I just want to wait until she's not so stressed, you've got to understand, it's not the time just yet, but that doesn't mean I don't care or—'

Emma stared at him, shook her head. 'Jack – I'm sorry that your parents are going through that, truly.'

But this was really everything she feared happening all over again. 'But I mean, there will always be something won't there? And why should telling her about something that should make any mother happy – the fact that her son is in love – cause her stress? Or add that much more to her load? Why am I always last with you, when you're always number one with me? I'm sorry but I'm done, done being this secret thing of yours. I think it's best if I take that job in London after all.'

His face blanched. 'You want to leave, just because I've asked for a bit more time?' His face hardened.

Emma was incredulous. It was too much.

'Is it just a bit of extra time though? Is it really?' she spat. 'I mean, how long do you fucking need? I've waited for *years* for you to speak up, to tell them how you really feel, and guess what, time's up, Jack.'

His eyes flashed. 'Is that so? It hasn't been a right fucking mess, and we didn't try a few times? Christ, Emma, if you really feel like that, then yes, perhaps you *should* go.'

SEVENTEEN

So, she did. She left for London on the next morning train, her heart feeling like a ball of lead at her feet, heavy and painful. She barely saw beyond the flash of green through the windows of the speeding train as it took her away from him, and away from Hope Cottage, and the life she'd hoped to build.

Her first week in London, she stayed on her friend Stevie's sofa, a girl she'd been to uni with, and went to see about the flatshare Stevie knew of at her brother's building the next morning, thankful that it hadn't been rented just yet – though in retrospect, that should have been a warning sign. The place was almost derelict, smelling of mould, and – she'd discover later – also the noisiest place she'd ever known, as the building was on a through road that allowed police cars and ambulances to put on their sirens so they didn't have to slow down for the traffic lights across the street. Which they did every hour, on the hour.

Still, by the following week she'd taken the job at the *Mail & Ledger* and had her own tiny room in a rather dodgy but slightly better flat with four other flatmates. She had paid some of her rent with a small loan from her Aunt Aggie, which she had vowed to pay back. After some time she got in contact with her old friend Pete, who was more than happy to resume their acquaintance and didn't seem to mind, or notice all that much, that she seemed to be only half there with him, the other half of her left behind, in a broken-hearted heap, in Whistling. He remained oblivious even when they decided to take it further.

Even that decision was a rather civilised affair as far as she was concerned, decided over coffee one morning while they ate eggs Benedict and pancakes – a Wednesday-morning breakfast ritual they kept at a cafe called Scrumptous before he went to his job as a tax solicitor in the building across the street. 'I think, you know, we get along rather well you and I,' Pete said, his blue eyes earnest. His dark hair was neatly combed to the side. He was wearing beige slacks with loafers and a skinny black tie. Handsome in an understated, always-indoors-and-pale sort of way. At his side was a copy of the *Guardian*, folded in half, which Emma knew he bought mostly for the crossword. 'And well, I was wondering what you thought about making it less platonic between us. I think we're quite suited despite our differences?'

She wondered if somewhere in his office cubicle across the street, there was a spreadsheet with the pros and cons of their relationship in neat columns, and whether he'd carefully weighed it all up before he asked, and she hid a grin.

There was something soothing about him for Emma. A quiet assertiveness she liked; even his formal tone was a bit endearing, and by the time they'd moved on to the pancakes, she'd agreed. It wasn't the most romantic of propositions, but she thought that maybe, in a way, this was better, more sensible really, without all the drama. Four years passed in much the same way. Pete grew more affectionate, slightly less formal. Though he still wore a bit too much beige.

He was the sort of man who wasn't drawn to an excess of anything. In the kitchen in his flat, he had precisely four of everything – bowls, plates, spoons, knives, placemats and chairs. She'd asked him once what he'd do if he ever had more than three people over for tea, and he'd simply shaken his head and said, seriously, 'I'd suggest we go to the pub instead as this flat only has enough room for four.' He didn't quite get the joke.

His wardrobe was colour coded. From light to dark. He owned five pairs of work slacks. Six work shirts. The extra one, presumably, in case he spilled something. His flat was sparsely furnished – a bed with a very firm mattress, and two pillows, no flounces or throws or quilts; one brown leather sofa (no fluffy cushions; unnecessary, he said); a small dining table, free from adornment; and a framed poster on the wall of a pretty Amsterdam street full of people riding their bicycles, which Emma thought displayed a slightly more romantic side of him. She later found out that the poster had been a gift, but she didn't hold that against him.

They were comfortable in each other's company. Both weren't that interested in watching television – and instead would often curl up together with a book for her and a crossword, or a financial magazine, for him. When she'd told Maggie, over the phone, about her life, she'd sounded incredulous. 'Jesus Em, even my nan has a more exciting love life, Christ, and she's seventy. You live in London – what about the parties, the nightlife, staying up all hours and then getting a drunken cab at dawn with your knickers in your pocket? You're young, not some old married couple.'

Emma just laughed. She didn't fancy the whole nightlife scene that much really, and quite liked keeping her knickers away from her pockets, if she could help it. Mostly she quite liked that Pete was always where he said he was. She didn't have to worry about him, which, after a lifetime of drama, felt rather nice. On Tuesdays, they went for a curry at Kapoor's, which was a block away; on Thursdays he made dinner – it was always steak and salad – on Fridays they went to watch a film or visit the theatre – he was rather daring in his choices, and a pretty good sport about hers, not minding if they went to a girly sort of show or something camp or wonderfully intellectual. He was easy company, Pete.

In many ways, he was good for her; he was like an alarm clock for one thing, and a human calendar reminder, so she became an early bird by default when he slept over, and he often told her useful things like, 'Time to go get your new pill, you've got a week left' or 'It's your Aunt Dot's birthday tomorrow, don't forget,' and oddly, she really liked that about him, even if he did sometimes nag a bit.

He was very ruled by routine, and could get amorous after dinner, though she wasn't always receptive to it, which made her feel guilty. She'd excuse herself, saying she was busy, needed to finish up an article or column, she was stressed, not in the mood.

Sometimes though she'd see that look in his eyes, which she tried to ignore; there was longing in it, like he was waiting for something. She realised now he'd been waiting for her to feel the way about him that he did about her. She'd been grateful for having him in her life; she'd appreciated him, his kindness, his steady presence, the way everything was so black and white with him, with no shades of grey. It had made things simple in a world that, to Emma, never used to feel that way before. She realised now though that wasn't the same thing as love; and he deserved that.

Sitting in the kitchen at Hope Cottage, Emma wondered now how different things might have been had she stayed in Whistling four years ago, had she never gone to London. What if she'd waited like Jack had asked, given him time until things had calmed down at his parents' business before they broke the news? It wasn't like she hadn't understood him asking for the extra time; despite what she felt about Janet Allen she hadn't wanted to be a source of stress in the woman's life – it was simply the fact that she was a source of stress to begin with that bugged her, because she'd never really done anything to deserve it.

It was this that she objected to most. Him asking for yet more time had felt like yet another excuse for them not to be together – but perhaps she'd been wrong to try and push it then? Should she have trusted him? Had she given up just when she was about to get what she'd wanted all along? Or was it just another attempt on her part to make a justification for him? Would it have made a difference if she'd stayed? Will it make a difference now? His parents' business had clearly bounced back. He seemed less hesitant to be seen with her in public now, and he'd even come into the cottage, and risked Evie's wrath in the process.

She put her head in her hands and groaned. Pennywort came to sit next to her, putting a paw on her shin. She looked down and touched his soft fur, looked into his solemn chestnut eyes. 'I'm in trouble, Penny,' she said aloud. The old bulldog gave a little huff. Almost as if he was saying, 'What's new?'

EIGHTEEN

Maggie was sitting with a mug of Halloway-tradition pumpkin-spiced coffee in her hands; a tradition from Emma's past that she would have given anything to be able to taste. Maggie had an amazed look on her face. Her blue bobble hat was drying out on a radiator.

Inside the cottage was cosy, the windows steaming slightly, but outside there was a blustery, icy rain falling, which had melted the snow and turned the early afternoon dark.

Mikey was playing on the floor with Pennywort, giggling as the old bulldog pretended to chase him, his little legs hurtling him around the table as he giggled. The old dog gave the toddler a head start while he caught his breath.

Emma grinned watching the two of them.

'Careful Mike,' said Maggie with a sigh, as he knocked into a chair, then screwed up his face, about to cry, only to change his mind when he saw Pennywort crawling on his belly to come and get him, and start laughing again instead.

Maggie who'd been poised to scoop him up, breathed a sigh of relief. Watching her, Emma cocked her head to the side. Her best friend was 'Mummy' now; it was sweet and a little strange, nice too.

Emma had just filled her in on what Aggie had told her about the recipe that had gone wrong, and the photograph of Alison with Geoff Allen.

'That's incredible. I mean – sorry – but it's weird in a way, like history repeating itself with you and Jack.'

Emma nodded. 'I know.'

'Talking about ancient history, I see that you and Stella are on fabulous terms as usual. I ran into her at the butcher's and she was spreading her usual charm.'

Emma frowned. 'What do you mean?'

'Let's just say the things she has been saying about you aren't very nice. I think she blames you for breaking her and Jack up, but that was over a while ago, or at least so I heard.'

Emma found herself blushing.

Maggie's mouth fell open. 'It's not true is it – oh Emma!'

'What?'

'Well, it's just always this way, isn't it? You, and Jack, and…'

'And Stella,' Emma said, blowing air out of her cheeks. She didn't need reminding.

Stella had always been there in the background, waiting, perhaps, for Jack to choose her. She was the girl his mother approved of, the girl who, sometimes, Emma wished she'd been – how much easier would her life have been had she been her? Though she couldn't help thinking how dull it would have been without Evie, her aunts and this cottage.

She didn't want to think about Stella Lea, or the way her face had looked when she'd seen them together the other day.

So she changed the subject, asked Maggie about how her work was going, and got a lengthy earful about the tricky route she had to plot from Rotterdam to Vienna taking out a key road because of a collapsed bridge, which had been pretty stressful and involved incredible skill and organisation to keep everything running smoothly.

'So, tell me, did the MD finally get it on with the sexy mechanic?'

'Bert?'

Emma grinned. Was there a less sexy name than Bert?

'Yeah. Last time you said they danced at the office party and there was some real fizz…'

'Tell me about it. It's worse. Actually there's a bet going on that it'll happen by around Christmas. Poor thing, she finds any excuse to go down to the yard, making goggle eyes at him, while he rolls up his sleeves, looking all James Dean – well, for a man in his sixties with a bit of a paunch.'

Emma laughed. 'That's cute though.'

'Yeah,' said Maggie. 'So you want in on the pot?'

Emma snorted. 'Okay, here's twenty,' she said, opening her purse. She liked hearing about the internal office politics and dramas in her friend's job; as a freelancer she'd missed out on a lot of these over the years.

Later, after Maggie had left, she sat and looked at The Book, thinking about the recipe that had gone wrong and why it always seemed that history repeated itself, no matter how hard they tried.

NINETEEN

In the corner of the kitchen stood the new Christmas tree, which Sandro had helped Harrison Brimble to deliver earlier that day. Emma had stood beneath its branches breathing deeply, but she still couldn't smell anything.

As night deepened, she had made a start with the decorations, but hadn't yet finished, and so she was still busy past midnight when Sandro got home, bringing with him a blast of the icy cold air and a glimpse of the snow that had begun to fall, cresting the tops of the garden gate.

His beanie-hatted head popped round the kitchen door. 'You're listening to one of the books I got you, eh, Pajarita?' he asked, pulling it off and rubbing his gloveless hands together.

She gave him a grin, pausing the CD player, a little wooden nutcracker in her hands. 'It's great, thanks.'

'Coffee?'

'Yes, please.'

She was tired. It had been hard trying to concentrate enough to thread the decorations on the tree with her hazy vision and she had a pounding headache, but she was determined to finish it; besides, she loved putting up the decorations.

He came over to give her a blue mug with a sleepy Snoopy on it, and to help. 'From tomorrow, or I suppose now really,' he said, checking his watch, 'it's twenty-five days till Christmas.'

She returned his grin. 'I know, crazy hey? That's why I'm doing this now – you see the tree is always up by the first in Hope Cottage,' she said in a slightly misty voice.

'But most people follow that tradition too.'

'Oh good, it's nice to find one area of normalcy here,' she joked.

He laughed. 'You're pretty normal.' Then he laughed harder at her raised brow, and said, 'Why didn't you ask Evie or your aunts to help with this?' He'd clearly noted that she was struggling to get the decorations exactly where she wanted, and had dropped one. He told her to simply point to where she wanted the last bits so that he could hang them for her.

'I should have, probably,' she sighed. 'But this was always my job, I've always liked doing it.'

He gave her a soft smile as he looked at the tree. 'These are lovely. So much nicer than the shop-bought things,' he said of the handmade decorations, many of which she'd made as a child with her Aunt Aggie.

'Thanks, it was always fun. Christmas has always been my favourite time of year.'

His eyes were warm. 'Ah me too, the food, a cosy fireplace, hot chocolate, presents, bliss.'

She grinned. Exactly.

Afterwards, he took a seat on her bed, next to Pennywort and the CD player, which earlier had been playing one of the audiobooks he'd given her.

'Which one were you listening to?'

'*Midnight in Prague.*'

'Ah, okay.'

'I've just started this one. The other was a bit too…'

He pulled a face. 'Gory?'

She nodded.

'Well, don't let me stop you,' he said, leaning back and getting comfortable. Pennywort grunted, then went to lay his head in Sandro's lap.

'Any point in telling you to bugger off?' she asked him, sitting down next to the dog.

He shook his head, his dark eyes amused. 'Nope.'

She snorted, and hit play.

He settled a blanket over them both, which mercifully didn't cause Emma's skin to confuse it with something else, so it felt just as it should, cosy and warm. Then a few minutes later, he asked, 'So… it's about two bank robbers?'

'Not exactly. He's on a secret mission for MI6, she's an undercover agent for the KGB, they're both on a mission in Prague.'

'But she has a flower shop – there was all that faff about the roses.'

'Just a code. I'll rewind it, shall I, so you can start at the beginning.'

'Okay,' he said, getting even comfier.

She rolled her eyes.

She felt tired when she went to the greenhouse the next morning. Snow had fallen during the night, making a white carpet that she shuffled through with her crutch, her foot covered in a rather lurid pink legwarmer that had once belonged to her Aunt Dot, to stop her bare toes from getting frostbite.

'Hola, Jane Fonda,' he greeted her, with a twinkle, and she couldn't help laughing as she closed the door behind her, her breath billowing out in puffy white clouds. The heater was on already and she shuffled closer to it, her teeth chattering. She had a pink and green bobble hat on, and her uninjured arm was in its fluffy mitten.

The heater was blazing out warmth, but she was still chilly a few minutes later so she put a soft green blanket over her, stretching out with her broken leg on the garden bench. Sandro made her a coffee, which he placed on an upturned paint can.

'Thank you,' she said, picking up the cup gratefully. She was in need of one of his rather intense coffees today, more than ever.

Sandro, despite having had very little sleep, looked fresh and energised. His curly hair was slightly damp from the shower, and he was wearing a royal blue hoodie that made his dark eyes sparkle in the early-morning light.

They started work on her latest column, about the history of Christmas food in Europe. He paused as she dictated.

'So, wait, Christmas wasn't celebrated in England until the Victorian era?' He looked amazed.

Emma grinned. 'Well, it was, but it was more of a feast, and not this big family celebration like it is today. Businesses didn't really give their workers the day off, we didn't have a Christmas tree or decorations…'

'Really?'

Then a short while later: 'Wait, so just because there was a photograph of Queen Victoria decorating a tree, after she married Albert, suddenly everyone wanted to have one?'

Emma shrugged. 'We do love our royals, you see – and if it was good enough for the queen…'

He grinned, gave a little shrug.

A little later he paused again.

'You're serious? It was actually against the law to make gingerbread?'

'Well, ginger was seen as something holy – it's a spice that we got during the Crusades, from areas that had been mentioned in ancient times in the Bible, plus it was really expensive, so in some parts of Europe in the sixteenth century only guildsmen were allowed to make it. But the rules were relaxed over the holidays, and as a special treat people were allowed to make them at home. During this time the making of gingerbread cookies evolved. They were then made into Christmas decorations as well.'

'Incredible, you know I used to make them as a boy, with my *abuela* – she had this tiny kitchen that looked over the mountains. It was because of her that I grew up wanting to cook.'

Emma grinned. She could picture him standing in his granny's kitchen. He was probably really cute with all that curly hair and dark eyes.

'Me too,' she said. 'Well, because of Evie.'

His dark eyes lit up. 'We should make some sometime, don't you think? Some Christmas biscuits, eh? Compare?'

She blinked. 'Um, not with my hand, you know?'

She hadn't baked anything, not for years, and she wasn't about to start now.

'We could work around that. I can help,' he said, warming to his idea.

'I'd rather not, okay?'

He frowned, staring at her in confusion. 'It's just biscuits, what's the worst that could happen?' he asked, as if he guessed, as if he knew what she feared.

'Just drop it please?'

His eyes widened. He was taken aback. Their easy camaraderie from earlier dissolving at her tone. His face tightening. 'Fine.'

They carried on for a while, but things were strained between them. When his phone started to ring, he looked at her a little coolly.

'Are we done? I've got to get going.'

She nodded, feeling a bit ashamed of how she'd snapped at him – but why did he always have to push things? 'Yes, I think so, we can finish later.'

'Good,' he said, closing the laptop and departing. There was no friendly, 'Adios, Pajarita,' either, just the too-quiet stillness of the greenhouse, and Emma's regret. Why had she made such a big deal out of something so small? She put her head on her knees, thinking, then again, when was cooking or baking ever simple at Hope Cottage?

'Will you grease the tins for me, please?' asked Evie as Emma took a seat at the kitchen table next to Pennywort. He was watching the sisters as they mixed together the third layer of the Good Cheer Christmas Cake, Evie muttering the words of hope and good tidings, Dot mixing in the currants and allspice, symbols of the hope and cheer, with the rum. It would be baked, then soaked in port over the following week, before it was added to the other layers in the giant green tin.

Emma hesitated, but gave in at Evie's impatient scoff. 'It's just greasing some tins, you aren't giving up your firstborn.'

On the radio, Louis Armstrong was singing 'Baby it's cold outside', and the blustery cold beyond the kitchen windows seemed to agree, as people bustled past wrapped up in heavy layers, bobble hats and heads down.

'How are your hand exercises going?' asked Dot, getting flour on her cheek as she pushed her jam-jar glasses up her nose, pulling a sympathetic face.

'Okay.' The truth was they hurt like hell. But there was no use complaining about it – it just made it worse when you actually had to do them.

The phone began to ring and Evie answered it. It was mustard yellow, one of those old-fashioned ones that attached to the wall. It had been there for decades.

'It's for you,' said Evie, with a frown.

Emma got up, crossing the flagstone floor and wiping her buttery fingers on a nearby dishcloth.

'Hello?'

'Emma?' said a voice that sounded vaguely familiar.

'Speaking.'

'Hi, this is Jessica Flynn – I'm the station manager for the local radio station. I do the news broadcast at six o' clock as well.'

Emma's eyes widened. 'Jessica – hi, yes.'

'I'm a big fan of your column. I heard that you were in town for a while, and I was wondering if you'd ever thought about doing a show of some kind? Perhaps we could meet for a coffee if you're keen, have a chat?'

'I'll tell you what – I'm not very mobile at the moment…' Emma explained a little about her accident. 'But if you don't mind coming here?'

'To Hope Cottage?' Jessica's voice sounded breathy, excited almost.

'Yes, if that's all right?'

'That would be great! I mean –' she laughed – 'I've always wondered…'

Emma laughed. She knew that a lot of the local residents – those who hadn't ever come for a recipe – wondered about what it was like inside. They would probably be a little surprised at how normal, if a little old-fashioned, it was. 'I'll give you a tour.'

When she hung up they were all looking at her in expectation.

'That was Jessica Flynn, asking if we could have a chat about my column and the radio—' She looked at Dot, then Evie, somewhat suspiciously. 'Did either of you put her up to this?'

They all seemed genuinely surprised. 'Not at all!'

The next morning, Jessica came past. Emma welcomed her inside, taking her navy wool coat, which had a fine dusting of snow on the shoulders.

She was tall, with dark hair and a long, patrician nose. Her dark eyes lit up when they saw the kitchen. Her mouth opened slightly, when she saw The Book.

'May I?' she asked, shrugging out of her coat, which Emma took from her and placed on a hook behind the door.

'Sure,' said Emma. 'Just – well…'

'Off the record?' Jessica guessed.

Emma nodded, gave her a small, embarrassed smile. 'If you don't mind – there's enough that's been said about this family, don't want to stir up any more.'

Jessica nodded. 'I can appreciate that.'

'Tea?' said Emma.

'Please.'

Emma turned to make it as Jessica had a look through The Book.

'Remarkable – I mean, as an object of history alone…'

Emma nodded as she popped a bag of Yorkshire Tea into a blue and white striped mug. 'It's funny – I had this discussion with my friend, Maggie, the other day as well. I think it's partly why I became a food writer myself – I've always been fascinated with the history of food. Evie always used to say that ours was an edible history.'

Jessica smiled. 'I like that. Well, it's why I wanted to talk to you – about your column. I wondered if you'd be interested in coming on, sharing some of your research – something about Christmas food – as we go into the season?'

Emma handed her the mug and Jessica continued, 'Ta. Well, as I was saying, the Halloways always play such an important role in Christmas in Whistling, you know, with their traditional Good Cheer Christmas Cake – is it true that it takes four weeks to prepare?'

'Six,' said Emma, biting her tongue so she didn't elaborate more, or tell her that she thought the elaborate tradition was nothing more than hokum.

Jessica's eyes widened. 'Six, well! It's such an institution; people really believe in it – I heard Sally Bradley say that she missed it the one year and nothing went right for her. Failed her exams, her flat was flooded, she had a fall-out with the people at work…'

Emma shook her head. 'I doubt it was because she didn't have it, but—'

Jessica grinned. 'You never know, right? Well, I've never chanced missing it since –' she laughed – 'just in case.'

Emma laughed too.

'Anyway, it would be really interesting to have you on board, talking a little about your own history and that of Christmas food. We were thinking maybe a two-week special just before Christmas, and thereafter perhaps a weekly slot the following year, if it all works out? We've got a slot open on Tuesday afternoons, and I thought a well-known resident could be good – the pay wouldn't exactly be grandiose; as you know, we're a tiny station run out of a barn.' She laughed again.

'You're thinking of a regular slot?'

'Yes, I mean, we could do it on a trial basis, perhaps? How long are you in town?'

Emma shrugged. 'I'm not sure, a while still, I suppose. But I'd be happy to do the Christmas special – it's always been my favourite time of the year. As you said, we could decide later about something more regular down the line if it works out. She went on to explain more about her health, and how she'd probably need Sandro's help to prepare the material.

'Alessandro – from the Tapas Hut?' Jessica's eyes lit up.

'Yes – he's been helping me with my column, he's a friend.'

'Oh?' Jessica said. Her eyes were shining with the light of an idea. 'Do you think he'd be willing to do one of the shows with you? It might be nice to get a European perspective – as well as a bit of flavour with him owning the most popular restaurant in town?'

Emma shrugged. 'I can ask him.'

'Great.' She beamed. 'Well, here's my card, let me know. We can meet at the studio – you know that old barn at the back of Jeff Hogson's house, right? – and discuss the details and prep for the show.'

Emma took it, and then said. 'Thanks, that sounds great. You know I read one of your articles in the *Whistling News* – about the bicentenary. It was really fascinating.'

'Oh yes – did you see the photograph with Grace Halloway and her daughter?'

Emma nodded. 'Yes, actually, I wanted to ask you about that – I mean, the man in the photograph, John Allen?'

'Yes?'

'Well, it was funny because –' Emma laughed awkwardly – 'Well, I mean…'

'There's been a long-standing feud between your families.'

'Yes,' said Emma, glad it was Jessica who'd said that, and not her. 'Well, I've always been interested in finding out what really happened – there's so much speculation, and rumour, as you can imagine. It's silly but looking at that photograph I saw a slightly different story…'

Jessica nodded. 'John Allen had his arms round Alison Halloway?' she said.

'Yes, exactly, and well, I thought that was a bit strange.'

'So, did I – I remember asking about it too, when I saw. I thought you knew?'

'Knew what?' asked Emma.

'That they were engaged.'

Emma gasped. 'Engaged – are you sure?'

Jessica nodded. 'Quite sure. I wanted to fact-check it after I heard, and I found an old announcement in the paper. I'll send it to you if you like – I have it scanned somewhere.'

'Yes, please,' Emma said, then frowned as she thought of something. 'You said you heard about it though? Who told you?'

'Oh, Dot, of course. She's the one who gave me the photograph.'

TWENTY

It was midway through the first week in December when Emma heard a loud bang, and then a curse, from the kitchen. She shuffled inside from the alcove, Pennywort at her heels.

'Everything all right?'

There were Christmas cards strung up with string on the old blue Welsh dresser, and already some of the villagers had begun to send their small gifts of appreciation for Evie and the aunts' help over the year. Some of these, like a set of garden gnomes with rather soppy expressions, or the lurid pink lava lamp sent by the retired hippie John Adams, Emma thought they could really have done without.

Evie turned to her with wide eyes. Her salt grey hair seemed to pulse around her shoulders. 'Not really – I just noticed that I'm out of cream for the Stand By Me Soufflé. It's for Alfred Bright, the butcher, he's been having trouble with his business; he's riddled with anxiety, poor lad, now that the new supermarket has opened up, which has been killing his profits. I'm going to have to pop down to the Brimbles' store.'

Poor Evie had been run ragged these past few weeks with the number of villagers who'd come past looking for recipes to solve their problems.

Before she could overthink it, Emma said, 'I'll keep an eye on it if you like?'

'Would you?' asked Evie, looking relieved. She bit her lip. 'It needs to be stirred every few minutes.'

Emma shrugged. 'That's fine.'

Evie hesitated, then, 'And you need to keep your intentions firm – calm, as you say the words,' she said, pointing to the instructions on the open page.

Emma sighed, rolling her eyes. 'Do I really have to do that?'

'*Yes*, he really needs this. If you don't want to, I'll have to call Dot, but there's not a lot of time and I'd hate for him to be disappointed, he's going through such a rough time.' She looked so worried that Emma's heart finally melted.

'Okay, fine. I'll do it. What do I have to do again?'

Evie beamed at her. 'Just stir it every few minutes, clear your mind of any negative thoughts and think of peaceful things.'

'Peaceful things?'

'Anything that conjures up serenity – water, the moors, whatever.'

Emma nodded. 'Okay.'

Evie still looked worried, so she gave her a reassuring smile. 'I've done this before. Don't worry.'

When Evie was gone, she looked at the pot, shook her head, hearing Dr Norton's voice in her mind: 'I don't have to tell you how cooking feeds the soul…'

'Well, here goes,' she said aloud, lifting the ladle and giving it a gentle stir. She breathed in and out, clearing her thoughts of all but her most peaceful thoughts. She pictured the sound of a waterfall, the ocean, the moors, Sandro's eyes. Her eyes shot open. She blinked.

'Peaceful thoughts,' she told herself firmly and concentrated on Pennywort's soft fur, deciding that dark, beautiful, Spanish eyes had no business swirling around inside her skull, particularly as they didn't conjure up a whole lot of peace, she thought with a giggle. Then, 'Stop it! Ocean waves… waterfalls…'

'You know, it's funny being back here. I've started to remember things, things that I thought I'd forgotten,' said Emma the following afternoon. She couldn't help reminiscing now that Christmas was drawing steadily closer. It was the start of the second week in December.

Evie was making plum jam, which would be used as an accompaniment for the roast turkey for the Christmas Day feast down at the Tapas Hut, which she and her aunts were helping to cater. There were little glass jars lined up on the scarred wooden table, around Pennywort, who watched with one eye open, his nose sniffing the air hopefully. She gave the old dog a pat and said, 'Like what?'

Emma glanced at The Book; looked to a corner of it, at the char mark that she'd noticed earlier. 'I remembered that you said my mother tried to burn The Book, you told me when I was little. Aggie told me later that it was after Janet Allen started a rumour about her.'

Evie spooned a little of the jam onto a spoon, blowing onto it till it cooled, then popped it into her mouth. She frowned, then swallowed. 'Oh, it was more than a rumour, more like a campaign, really. She had half the town believing Margaret was evil incarnate, it was hard for her – she started to really resent where she came from, so in a fit of rage, she tried to burn it. Luckily I was there in time to save it, mostly.'

'Mostly?' asked Emma, with a frown.

'Oh, well, I think she managed to tear out one of the recipes…'

Before Emma could ask more, though, the phone started to ring. Evie crossed the flagstone floor to answer. It was Dot. 'Keep your hair on, I'm coming,' she said with a sigh.

It was Thursday afternoon, which always meant poker.

When she hung up, she sighed at the mountain of jam she still had to decant.

'Don't worry – I'll do it, you go.'

'You sure?' Evie asked. Emma shrugged. 'It's only jam. Say hi for me.'

She spent the rest of the afternoon decanting the jam. Sandro popped in to get changed, his eyes widening when he saw her busy in the kitchen.

He took a seat and started to help. Despite their disagreement the other morning, they were still mostly fine around one another, if a little stilted.

'Don't you have to get back?'

He shrugged. 'It can wait.' He tried a little bit of the jam, closed his eyes in bliss.

'Is it good?' she asked, staring at the pot a little mournfully.

He nodded. 'Try some.'

She did, sighing deeply. Still nothing.

He smiled. 'It'll come soon, I'm sure.'

She nodded, hoping he was right.

'It's amazing what they did for that old man, eh Pajarita. Mr Grigson – did you hear he proposed to the old librarian? They came round to book the Hut for their wedding in the spring.'

Emma made a little noise, a kind of snort.

He frowned. 'What?'

'You don't really think one of their mad recipes would make that happen, do you?' she asked.

He shrugged. 'Some things you just can't explain by coincidence, you know?'

'Actually, I think you can.'

He rolled his eyes. 'Ay, Pajarita,' he muttered, but he let it go.

They spent the next hour putting the jam in the containers, working together companionably.

'How about some *Midnight in Prague?*' he asked.

She grinned. 'Really?'

'He was just about to diffuse the bomb, before you started snoring the other night.'

'What? I don't snore,' she said, blushing.

'O-kay,' he said, walking over to the alcove, out of harm's way, and putting the audiobook on.

An hour later he glanced up and saw the time. He jumped up. 'Ay, Pajarita, I better go – I lost track of time, Nico said he needs to catch a train today.'

'Oh,' said Emma, feeling a little disappointed that he was leaving.

'See you.'

After he'd left, the kitchen was too quiet, and still, and she felt a little lost.

She started putting the jam in the pantry and then took a break, by flipping through The Book, looking at old recipes, pausing when she found again the section of torn bits of paper where recipes had seemingly been ripped out.

Evie had said though that there was a recipe missing – which was rather specific; she knew that Evie would know all the recipes in The Book – but still, something about the way she had said it had made her think that one particular recipe was important. If her mother had tried burning The Book and failed, why tear out just the one recipe? Unless, perhaps, it was one she deemed more important than all the others.

Dot was in her reading chair, a glass of wine and a plate of mince pies next to her, when Emma came past to see her that Saturday afternoon, her red hair clashing magnificently with the pink bobble hat she was wearing, her bare toes, on the leg with the cast, icy cold despite the lime green knitted sock she had on.

The countdown to Christmas had really begun now in the village, and all through the streets people had put up their lights and wreaths. Some were more garish than the others, like the house next door, which had reindeer, a giant Santa who said, 'Ho ho ho' when she walked past the front garden, and a cascade of angels pasted inside all the open windows.

The short walk up the cobbled street had tired her out, and she sank gratefully onto the sofa, resting her crutch alongside it.

Uncle Joe was asleep next to her, his crossword at his side.

She gave his bald head a kiss. 'Aggie showed me this,' she said, giving her aunt the article that Jessica Flynn had written, which she'd pulled out of her jumper pocket. Dot pushed up her thick lenses and nodded. 'Oh yes,' she said, reading it. Her nail polish, though chipped as usual, was a bright and festive rose gold.

'Well,' she said putting it down after she'd read it. 'I was wondering when you were going to ask me about the founding members of the Halloway clan and what went wrong. Evie, bless her, told me not to say anything – but I said you had every right.'

'Dot,' said Uncle Joe, slightly warningly, from the sofa, his eyes still closed.

'Well, she *does*. Anyway she's older now, so…'

Jo sat up, gave them a meaningful look and then took himself off to his bedroom.

'He doesn't want me to dredge up old ghosts – wants to protect you, old dear, always had a soft spot for you.'

Emma grinned. 'That's sweet, but why would it be dredging up old ghosts?'

Dot frowned. 'Did Evie ever tell you about your great-grandmother Alison Halloway?'

'Not really.'

Dot nodded. 'Well, you know of the recipe that went wrong between the Allens, the Leas and the Halloways, obviously.'

Emma blinked. 'The Leas too – I didn't know they were involved.'

'Oh? But of course they were, they've always been at the heart of it, right from the start. Well, it's why it keeps repeating itself – the others don't want to hear it, but…'

'What?' asked Emma. 'What keeps repeating itself?' Her heart started to beat faster, though a small part of her knew, had always suspected.

'The same cycle – it began all those years ago and has played itself out once again with you, and Jack… and Stella.'

What do you mean?'

'Well, you know the story of Grace Halloway, yes? How she came to the village of Whistling, some two hundred years ago, with nothing but her child and a set of old recipes to her name, but was given the tenancy of Hope Cottage anyway.'

'By who?'

'The Allens, of course.'

Emma gasped in surprise. 'What?'

'Oh yes, many years ago they were the most prominent family in these parts, and old Geoff Allen owned much of the town. Grace scrimped and saved and bought the cottage outright a few years later, but it must be said, he gave her a very good deal. Like I said, they were great friends. Grace's husband had passed away, and she was bringing up her child alone, the same age as his boy – John.'

Dot continued. 'The vicar, Angus Lea, had taken over the parsonage, and all three became very firm friends. They helped start the school, where all their children went.'

Emma shook her head. No one had ever told her that.

'Suzette Lea, the vicar's child, fell in love with young John Allen – he was rather a dashing figure I believe, bit of a ladies' man, though if he loved anyone it was Alison. Times were different then though, you see, and it had long been promised that John Allen and Suzette were to be wed. John, of course, defied his father, and asked Alison for her hand. Geoff said he'd write him off without a penny if he did, nothing personal against the Halloways, but to old Geoff a promise was a promise, see.

'It caused untold stress on all of them. John started gambling, drinking. Soon he'd racked up so many debts that he was in danger of being sent to prison or killed by the people who he owed money to. Geoff settled these, but the cost was great, it put his entire business at risk, which was when they came to Grace for help.'

'For a recipe,' said Emma.

Dot nodded. 'Grace made it, she said the old words, "I make no promises." She warned them that it could go wrong, and it did – spectacularly, horrifically wrong. They lost everything.'

'But I mean, surely Grace couldn't be blamed? It's not like she could have controlled it.'

Dot nodded. 'I think Alison felt differently, like they could have done more, so she risked it all for love. Some say that she dug up the savings that the Allens had handed over for the recipe, and she gave it to John. They were going to run away with it, you see.'

'No!' cried Emma.

'I'm afraid so. Well, when she did that, I believe it tainted it – there has to be a cost, in some way or another, and it fell on all of us.'

'What happened to them?'

'John was found, and robbed by one of the debt collectors who'd been looking for him. He hadn't got the memo that John's father had paid his debts, perhaps, or maybe he didn't care, perhaps he saw that there was more money to be taken. Either way, John died of his injuries, and thereafter Suzette was sure Alison Halloway had done everything in her power, even killing the man she loved rather than let him be with her.'

'Why didn't anyone ever tell me this?' cried Emma.

'Because no one could prove it. Margaret tried, of course.'

'My mother?'

'Oh yes. She was determined to find that recipe.'

'To put things right?'

'In the beginning, yes. Later I think to ensure that Janet Allen and Neil, I suppose, stayed cursed for the rest of their lives. I'm not sure she realised it would continue to affect us, no matter how hard she tried to run away from it all, that it would just keep finding us all.'

TWENTY-ONE

The dark tells stories about the night, making monsters out of shadows and ghosts out of whispers. It tries to convince you of its power, it tells you things it would like to believe – that it can snuff out the stars, and hold the world in its fist – but no matter how hard it tries; it cannot hide from the light.

It takes so little to banish the dark, thought Emma the next morning as she watched the first light come in from the window, the colour of pale lemon, transforming all that it touched. Making the silver baubles on the Christmas tree by the hearth glow and shimmer. It fell upon her bed, onto her arm, and as she stared, she marvelled at the colours of her skin, the smooth lines and freckles, the pale hair, all in sudden, sharp relief.

When Sandro brought her a cup of coffee in a clear glass mug sprinkled with little snowflakes – her favourite Christmas mug – and placed it on the little three-legged stool by the side of her bed, he paused, and then looked at her in concern, dark eyes wide.

'You're crying.'

She turned to him and smiled. 'I am.'

'You're happy about this. I don't understand, Pajarita,' he said softly, taking a seat at the edge of her bed. 'It's just a Christmas mug.'

Her pulse started to rise from how near he was, the intensity of his dark gaze, and she swallowed as he peered at her.

'It's because I can see… well, properly now.' She gave a shaky, amazed sort of laugh. 'Everything used to be in double and now – it's not.'

'It's a miracle,' he said.

She nodded. There would have been a time when she would have laughed at him for saying that word, but now, she thought, surely that's what this was? After weeks of unfocused vision, to wake up and just be able to see so clearly and easily – what other word described it as perfectly?

She looked at the mug of coffee he'd put on the stool. It was steaming slightly, the picture of domestic bliss, so simple, and so wondrous, all on its own.

'I don't think I realised just how beautiful things can be.'

'Like what?' he asked.

'Everything. There's so much colour, so much detail. Take you, for instance,' she said, then blushed.

He grinned, and she saw the dimples in his cheeks, the white and even grin. 'So, you think I'm beautiful?' he teased.

She blinked, buried her face in her hands for a second. 'No.'

'No?'

'Oh God,' she said, grinning despite her blush. 'I meant only that I thought I could see you before…' She looked away, didn't explain, couldn't explain really, how, or why he'd seemed to stand out so sharply in relief. Perhaps because he'd been so different – and, at first, so unwelcome here in her childhood home, where so few things had changed.

'But I couldn't, not really,' she said, looking at the laughter lines around his dark eyes, the faint trace of stubble along his jaw, how his nose was slightly crooked. The way his eyes seemed to look into her.

'Like that,' she said, pointing at the tattoo on his wrist. 'I never saw that before.'

He pushed up the sleeve of his black jumper, revealing fine dark hair and smooth, tanned skin, and the symbol of a man, holding what looked like a rainbow in his outstretched arms. 'It's the Indalo Man,' he said. 'For luck.'

'And does it bring it?'

He looked at her. 'Sometimes. Sometimes, you just have to make your own,' he said with a wink.

She thought about that after he'd left. When Evie came in from feeding the hens, she found Emma sitting at the kitchen table staring at The Book, her fingers tracing over the old recipes, marvelling at all the different handwritings, seeing, perhaps for the first time in years, the magic Maggie and Jessica Flynn had seen when they looked at it.

'What's this?' asked Evie in surprise.

Emma looked up, then her face changed and her eyes went sad. 'You're older.'

Evie blinked. 'So I am, it happens, my lass.'

'I didn't see before,' Emma said sadly.

'But you see it now?'

'Yes.'

'Well, that's good.'

She saw other things too that day. Like the grey in Pennywort's fur, how his eyes had turned slightly glassy, and how he struggled to get up to the table, and needed a little help sometimes. But how he was still the same solemn dog who watched over them like he always had.

She saw too, that the kitchen needed painting and the old navy range in the centre of the room looked like it was ready to finally fall apart, but also how cheerful the room looked with the tree by the hearth, the rows of Christmas cards on a string on the dresser. The boxes full of plum jam, the tins full of the

Good Cheer Christmas Cake, ready for its next layer, stacked in a corner of the large table.

She saw the trays of tapas in the fridge, and Sandro's guitar in the lounge.

'I think I'm going to go for a walk,' said Emma, getting her coat and her crutch.

Evie blinked. Aside from short walks up the street to Dot's house, Emma hadn't voluntarily left the cottage since she'd been home – over twelve weeks now.

'Are you sure? Can you manage?'

Emma shrugged. 'I won't go too far, just the village.'

'Okay,' said Evie.

'I can see your grin from here, Evie Halloway.'

'But you *can* see it.'

Emma gave her a wide grin of her own. 'Yes.'

It was like seeing the village for the first time. The rows of pale stone cottages, ribboning the fields; beyond these, the wild moorland, which stretched on for miles into the distance, covered in snow. She could hear, even from here, the cry of the last golden plovers. The moors were wild and empty, with only a stone crossing to mark the boundary along the village. It had always been her favourite part of living here; walking them had been a reprieve at times, from the stares and rumours. Out there, the only things looking at her were skylarks and short-eared owls, who didn't know or care what her last name was.

As she walked into the snowy village, which looked like something that could fit inside a snow globe with its pretty cottages and cobbled paths, she saw that not much had changed in the years since she was here last.

There were still peeling posters on the lamp-posts, which were strewn with Christmas wreaths made of holly and cranberry leaves and twigs. The latest poster said *A Moorland Christmas*, and advertised the Christmas dinner that her family and Sandro were hosting down at the Tapas Hut.

Harrison Brimble and his wife were still running the same village store, which was strung now with Christmas lights. She could see Mrs Brimble through the window, behind the counter, her set of needles and yarn to the side while she helped a customer; Emma knew it would be picked up again as soon as she was finished. With winter settling its slithery fingers around Whistling's neck, she'd be knitting from sunup till sundown, getting as many blanket squares down as she could for those in need, only putting them aside when there was no one at the till.

The Whistle Bakery with its display of festive cakes, biscuits and gingerbread houses in the window, which had been painted with frost, was still going strong; people were queueing for their cobs and their cinnamon rolls while Joseph Clarke spoke a mile a minute, telling his customers all about his specials for the day, and to please sign the petition against the extension of Patience Cottage on your way out. For as long as she could remember the Clarkes had had an ongoing war with their neighbours over their many extensions to their home, which encroached on the Clarkes' views of the hills.

At the butcher's next door, she could see Alfred Bright, who doled out a daily giggle along with his wares, and didn't bother with a hello; instead he greeted you with, 'Did you hear about the chicken who found himself drunk in a pub in Sheffield?'

There were some changes too though, like the neon sign that flashed on the new supermarket at the edge of the village; the pizza bar had been replaced by a plastics store that sold all manner of things to help organise the home, and there was now an Indian takeaway next to the hardware store, where the eighty-year-old Mr Grigson – who'd finally plucked up the nerve to come to the cottage – was serving a customer, a grin on his usually crotchety face.

She stopped at Sue Redmond's bridal shop, which hadn't changed much either. There was still the same blue awning but the dresses in the window display had changed, along with the times; they were less poufy, and very few had sleeves. She looked at them, thinking how once, long ago, this shop had made her, Maggie, Jenny and Gretchen pause for hours picturing their own.

'Would it still be the pink dress and my old troll ring for you?' said a voice.

Emma whipped round. 'Gretchen!' she exclaimed. It had been ages since she'd seen her last.

'In the flesh,' she agreed, giving Emma a hug. Gretchen's hair was still as straight and as sleek as ever, in a neat bob, beneath a pale blue bobble hat. Her dark eyes had circles underneath them, no doubt from staying up all hours solving major tax crises for a major firm in Scotland.

'God, that's wonderful,' said Emma, holding her close. It had been over two years since she'd seen her; they kept in touch as much as they could, thanks to technology, but it wasn't the same.

'I got here last night, took the night train from Edinburgh – I'm here for the weekend to visit me mam, but I was just heading over to Hope Cottage right now to see you!'

Emma grinned. 'Saved you a trip then.'

'You got time for a cuppa, maybe some cake? The teashop still has the best chocolate fudge cake in town.'

'Emma sighed. 'I'd give anything to be able to taste that.'

'Well, come on then,' said Gretchen, linking her arm through hers, and Emma didn't have the heart to tell her she'd meant she couldn't actually taste it.

They sat on a crescent-shaped seat in the Harris sisters' teashop. Soft Christmas tunes were playing in the background, and strung up all along the walls were flashing twinkly lights. It was a small, genuinely vintage place that featured pale blue walls and floral print cushions that dated back to the fifties. It hadn't changed much in the years since. There were framed portraits on the walls of women in old-fashioned bathing suits and poodle-skirts and men with cigars and Cadillacs. Though many of the pictures now sported Christmas hats.

'Are you sure you don't want a bite?' asked Gretchen, after they'd caught up on most things. Emma hadn't explained in detail what had happened to her senses, just yet.

'I'd love to but I can't taste anything.'

Gretchen set her fork down. 'You're kidding?'

She shook her head. 'No, unfortunately not, but it's okay – I mean, just yesterday things were a little fuzzy, and unfocused, it was like that for weeks, and today my vision is perfect. I can honestly say that I don't think I will ever think of sight the same way again.'

'It's sort of a gift then when you think of it that way.'

Emma stared.

Gretchen coloured. 'I mean it's hell, I'm sure but…'

Emma shook her head. 'No, you're right – I never used to look at things properly, you know, I was busy…'

'Well, we're all busy, it's understandable, isn't it?' asked Gretchen, whose job was less nine to five and more nine to nine.

'I suppose so, but then, there's so much we miss,' Emma said, looking out onto the street. She blinked, and then gasped.

Jack Allen was standing right outside. When he saw her, he stopped, his eyes widening, then made to come in.

Emma drew in a breath. Gretchen gasped. 'Bloody hell – Jack Allen is coming in here.'

They shared a look. Emma tried to smooth back her hair, quickly.

'I was going to come past today – ask if you wanted to grab dinner or something,' said Jack, reaching their table.

Emma could see Gretchen's eyes widening.

'Um, that would be great.'

'Pull up a chair,' invited Gretchen.

'Okay,' he said with a smile.

Emma and Gretchen shared bemused stares. Jack had always been a bit wary of being seen with her in public; it had been one of the biggest issues between them – till now, seemingly.

A young waitress with long brown hair came over and took his order, and while he was busy talking to her the door opened with a tinkling chime; Emma looked up and saw Sandro come in. He gave a low whistle when he saw her, his eyes lighting up, that familiar dimple appearing in his cheek, as he came over. 'Look at you out in the world, Pajarita. Beautiful today, eh?'

She swallowed a laugh, remembering her blunder earlier. 'Yeah, it is.'

He winked at her. 'Todo bien,' he said, with a wink. 'Getting some tea for the Hut – there's a few people who want something other than Yorkshire Tea. Barmy lot, eh?'

'Really barmy,' she agreed.

He grinned, then departed with a mellow 'Adios.'

'Who was that?' breathed Gretchen, watching him go, her eyes popping. 'He's gorgeous.'

There were a few girls whispering in a booth nearby, who, from the looks they were shooting at Sandro's back, no doubt agreed.

'That's Sandro,' said Emma, for Gretchen's benefit. Jack had already met him, the first day she had, when he'd simply strolled into her house. 'He lives with us.'

Seeing Jack's frown – she hadn't actually told him that before – she explained, 'He's renting the annexe from Evie – he's renovating a house, so she offered it to him. He runs the Tapas Hut.'

'You're kidding! I've heard of that,' breathed Gretchen. 'Maggie was raving about it the other day, says it's gorgeous – got these views over the moors, and the owner… ah.'

'The owner what?' asked Emma.

Gretchen laughed. 'That he's this gorgeous Spaniard…'

'Oh,' said Emma, biting her lip.

'Gets a bit a rowdy though, so I've heard,' said Jack.

Emma shrugged. 'Can't say. I haven't been yet.'

'Sounds fun,' said Gretchen, eyeing Sandro at the till. She seemed to really like what she saw.

Jack pulled a face. 'I don't know, apparently it gets a bit out of hand, wild parties, cops been called out there because of the noise.'

'The noise I can believe,' said Emma, who'd been driven mildly crazy by Sandro's constant whistling and humming in her first few weeks at the cottage.

Gretchen's phone started to ring, and her face blanched. She smacked a hand to her forehead. 'Ah, Ems, that's me mam, I said I'd take her into town, I completely lost track of time.'

'Oh shame. We've been chatting for ages – no wonder! You go. It's been lovely. I'll give you a ring later.'

'Perfect, thanks love, bye Jack, nice seeing you again,' Gretchen said, giving Emma an incredulous look behind his back and leaving some money on the table to settle her bill, before legging it home.

The waitress brought over Jack's coffee and he took a sip. 'Alone at last,' he said.

She half-laughed, half-swallowed. Why did he make her feel as if she were still sixteen?

'You know I read your column,' he said.

'You get the *Mail & Ledger*?' she asked, surprised.

'I read it online. It's really great – fascinating, considering your family history with food. It kind of explains a lot actually.'

She heard a noise, and looked up. Sandro had dropped his wallet on the floor. She turned back to Jack. 'Like?'

'Just some things I used to wonder about…'

'How did you come to read it?' she asked.

'Can't remember. Think Stella mentioned it.'

'Ah,' said Emma. Though it didn't explain much; it was hardly the sort of thing she'd expect Stella to read.

He frowned. 'I heard that you were seeing someone up in London?'

She nodded. 'I was,' she sighed. 'We broke up.'

'After your accident?' He looked shocked.

She shook her head. 'It was just a bit before, actually.' Not wanting to go into how soon before.

'He was a good guy actually.'

Jack made a noise.

She grinned. 'Jealous?'

He looked at her. 'What do you think?'

She felt her stomach flip, but she couldn't help her smile.

'And – Sandro?'

She looked up.

'What about him?'

'Are you – and he…?'

She shook her head. 'He's just a friend.'

There was a noise, like glass breaking. She turned to see a waitress picking up a broken cup near Sandro. He had his back to her.

'Oh, okay, well that changes things,' said Jack, touching her hand.

'Does it?'

'Yeah, I think so – or at least I hope so. Can I see you again?'

She blinked. 'What do you mean?'

'Like maybe a date?'

'You want to go on a date with me?'

'Yes, I do.'

She blinked. 'Why now?'

'Because we should have just done it ages ago.'

She looked at him, her heart in her mouth.

'Okay.'

She didn't dare hope that her skin had gone back to normal, but then again, there hadn't been any new episodes like the shower incident for a while, so perhaps it was time to hope.

When she switched on the tap that night and put her hand under the spray, testing it for a full minute, it felt the way the spray should: warm, invigorating, but nothing more. After a while, she took a deep breath and then stepped in. When she was finished, and changed into a clean pair of joggers, a T-shirt and a jumper, she couldn't help smiling. She couldn't remember who'd said that happiness came in the little things, but she knew they were right.

It felt good to get into bed feeling so clean and fresh. Though after a while, when she checked the time, she couldn't help but frown. It was ten after midnight. Sandro was usually home at around this time, making her throw things at him for keeping her awake and waiting, before they settled down to listen to *Midnight in Prague*. At quarter past, she decided to just listen without him, though it felt a little flat without him there.

A noise startled her a few minutes later, and she pressed pause on the CD player.

'Hey, Pajarita.'

'Hey,' she called, feeling her face split into a wide grin. 'I didn't know if you were coming home tonight.'

'Course – just got stuck with a customer. Were you waiting?'

'Er, no, just wondering.'

'Coffee?'

'Please.'

He came in and took a seat on the bed, getting himself comfy, always so sure of his welcome.

'I cannot believe you started without me,' he said in mock outrage, his brown eyes narrowed as he plumped up a pillow. Pennywort wiggled himself into the crook of his arm.

'So where are they now?' he asked, crossing his feet and looking at her with a grin, the familiar dimple appearing in his cheek. 'Don't tell me I missed it?'

'When they finally kiss?' asked Emma, eyes dancing.

'Oh that?' he said, his voice airy, 'a macho sort of guy like me would hardly be bothered about that, eh? No I meant, when they finally rob the bank.'

'Oh that! No that hasn't happened yet, so I won't rewind then.'

His eyes popped. 'Well, maybe just to catch up, just a little,' he said, leaning over her to rewind it to where they'd left it off the night before.

She laughed. It was definitely the little things, she decided, trying not to think what it meant that she couldn't really get to sleep unless Sandro was home.

After Sandro went to bed, she thought of Jack, and their date. She couldn't believe it was finally happening for them.

TWENTY-TWO

The oval-shaped van was parked in the centre of the high street, across from the village green, topped with a sprinkling of snow. It was a cheerful-looking van, strung with red and green Christmas lights and painted bright yellow with a blue awning. It displayed its name in fine-brush lettering: *The Whistle Stop Library.*

Here you could get your books along with a cappuccino and a slice of cake, and take a seat next to a blazing heater, which was exactly what Emma was doing, though mostly she'd come to see her friend.

The library was run by her old, dear friend Jenny Hughes, and Emma was enjoying visiting it for the first time since its opening the year before. She'd chosen a stack of books – a mix of mysteries, epic romances and autobiographies – and was charmed to discover that this was where Sandro had headed for her audiobooks. She was sitting at a little table inside while she waited for Jenny, who was finishing up with her customers.

After Jenny finished, she put a 'Back in Five Minutes' sign on the counter and joined Emma, with two cappuccinos.

'You're spoiling me, thanks,' said Emma, taking her cup. 'I'm so sad I missed your opening. I missed a lot,' she went on sadly.

'Don't worry,' said Jen, 'you were busy, I understood.'

Jenny had been round to visit her at the cottage a few weeks before when Emma first got back, but it was nice to be able to see the little library van for herself at last.

Emma nodded. Still, she didn't like that she had used it as an excuse. 'So why did you decide to start it?'

'Why leave my high-paying accountancy job you mean?' asked Jenny, who'd shocked quite a few friends and family when she gave up her job in Manchester and moved back home to open this small independent library.

Many people had been grateful; the old library had closed down several years before, and it was quite a schlepp to get to the big one in town.

Emma nodded. 'You never said – just next thing we all knew, you were doing this,' she said, with a smile. 'I mean, it's fantastic, I just wondered what inspired it?'

'I think I just got to a stage when I realised – this is what I want to do, you know? Something I truly loved. For a long time, I was miserable, and I didn't even know it. I had a well-paid job, but I rented a flat in the week and only came home at weekends. I wanted to be here, back in Whistling. I know some people just want to get out when they grow up but I love it here.'

She blushed, seeing Emma's face. But Emma nodded. She could understand that. And in any case it was different for Jenny; she wasn't so involved with the village and all of its old rumours like she herself was, as her family had only moved here when she was a baby.

Jenny continued, 'I lived for the weekend. I mean, that's normal, I guess, but I was *really* living for it. It got so that I was sitting in the car park one day and crying before I went in to work. I didn't even know why I was crying. All I knew was that I was miserable. Everyone tells you "follow your passion", and I thought I had. I mean, I'm good at numbers, I like them, but I guess maybe I wasn't passionate about them. I didn't know what to do at first, so I got all these self-help books out the library, and one day I was listening to this podcast on happiness, and someone asked the host the question – how do you know what makes you happy? It was the question I kept asking myself. Like, I should know, no? But I didn't any more. So anyway, the host's answer was: think of the thing that made you happy when you were ten.'

'I didn't hear anything else after that. I just sat there thinking, and then it came to me – books. It's always been books. I've never been happier than with them. It was so simple and so obvious, and it was like a light bulb came on in my head, you know? Next thing you know I'd set up this business. I started as cheap as I could, found the van – it was going for a song – and started running it at the weekends. It was, what do they call it in the States, a side hustle, I suppose?'

Emma laughed. 'I love that.'

'Me too,' said Jenny. 'Well, it started doing quite well – most of the village is a member, and I get money from the coffees and sandwiches and cakes and stuff. It's not crazy money but it's enough for what I need, and I've just never been happier.'

Emma looked at her. 'That's incredible, so brave, Jen. I'm so proud of you – and this place, it's wonderful,' she said sincerely.

'Well when you write a best-selling book with your columns or the history of food one day, maybe you can do a book signing here,' Jen joked.

'You'll be my first call, I promise,' Emma said.

While she walked home, with her bag of books swinging companionably in her grandmother's string bag, her crutch digging slightly into her armpit, the cold air billowing out of her mouth in white plumes, she thought of what Jenny had said: 'What made you happy when you were ten?'

Like Jenny, it was an easy answer. When she was that age, she'd liked nothing better than being in the kitchen in Hope Cottage, figuring out what someone needed, then looking in The Book and trying to make something that might help. When she opened the door, she felt her cheeks, surprised to find that she'd been crying. The trouble was, loving what she did came with a price, one she'd never been prepared to pay.

That night, a message pinged on her mobile.

Can't stop thinking of you. Jack.

She closed her eyes. Felt her cheeks flush, then replied:

Didn't know you had my number? How did you get it?

He texted back.

Oh, I have my ways…

Maggie?

Maggie

She laughed.

So what you up to?

She blinked. Currently she was lying in bed, with Pennywort snoring beside her, waiting for Sandro to come home so that he could join them and listen to the audiobook and she could hear about his night at the Tapas Hut. Somehow, telling Jack this didn't seem like the best idea.

Just lying in bed with Pennywort.

Lucky Pennywort.

She laughed. *Do you want to get together tomorrow, maybe do a breakfast?*

Where, your place? Not sure Evie would want me there again.

Don't worry about Evie.

Easy for you to say.

She sighed. Was about to type a reply but he got there first.

Can't anyway sorry, got an early meeting. How about a coffee in town in the afternoon?

She touched Pennywort's fur, shook her head, muttering, 'Okay Jack, not the cottage, I get it.'

Still, she typed back. *Okay.*

It was after one in the morning when she gave up on waiting for Sandro. She sighed and switched off the light, feeling flat, and a little sad. 'I'm just tired,' she thought, snuggling up to Pennywort; but she felt wide awake, and spent a long time wondering where Sandro was, and why he hadn't come home.

The next morning, she felt tired, and still badly in need of a good night's sleep. Pennywort was asleep on her lap and she had her arm resting on his soft fur, but despite this she felt a bit out of sorts. Sandro still wasn't home.

She looked at the three-legged stool and frowned. She'd never been much of a coffee drinker before, but since Sandro had been bringing her a cup every morning for the past several weeks, she'd come to rely on it.

She got out of bed and went into the kitchen to put on a pot.

Evie came down not long after. 'Sandro must have slept at the Hut last night,' she said, watching Emma.

'Does he do that?'

'Sometimes,' said Evie. 'Usually when there's a new girl on the scene. Or he's feeling a bit down about something.'

Emma put down her cup. 'Are there a lot of girls?' she asked.

Evie shrugged. 'Hard to say, it's been a while since the last. Well, can you blame him? The girls around here are a bit wild for him.'

Emma looked down, suddenly sick of the sight of the coffee.

'So,' said Evie. 'Well…'

'Well?' asked Emma with a frown.

'Well, everyone is talking about it.'

She blinked. 'What?'

'Your impromptu date with Jack Allen.'

'Oh!' said Emma, but couldn't help grinning. 'Oh, yes. It just sort of happened.'

Evie raised a brow. 'Okay?'

Emma narrowed her eyes. 'What?'

'Nothing, I'm staying out of it.'

Emma stared.

'I promise.'

Emma's phone pinged and she looked at the screen. Jack.

Hope you slept well?

Her heart started to thud, all thoughts of Sandro's mysterious whereabouts forgotten.

'You all right there, love?' asked Evie.

Emma blinked, her mouth curving into a slow smile.

'That was him, I take it?'

'I thought you were staying out of this?'

Evie rolled her eyes. 'So did I,' she harrumphed.

Later that morning she made her way into the greenhouse, bundled in a thick coat and wearing her bright pink bobble hat, and took a seat at the bench, wondering if Sandro was going to be coming home at all today.

The sky was the colour of an old bruise, and it looked like it might rain. She put on the lamp, trying to banish the gloom. She still couldn't type just yet with her injured hand, but she was sure that at a push she could use her right hand if she needed to. Just then, a noise roused her.

'Sorry I'm late, Pajarita – I fell asleep at the Hut. Was a rough night.'

In the grey light, his face looked wan and tired. There were circles round his eyes and, when he took off his dark knitted beanie, his curly hair was even messier than usual. There was stubble on his jawline and his usual carefree smile was gone.

'Looks it,' she said with a grin. 'If you want to crash, I could probably type for myself – now that my vision's improved, it should be a lot easier, even if I just use the one hand.' She held up her right hand.

He gave a short laugh. 'That will take you all day. I don't mind; I just need some coffee.' He held up a cafetière and put the kettle on.

'Got a hangover?' she guessed.

'From hell,' he agreed. He looked fairly green. She shook her head, and then took him by his arm. 'C'mon, forget that. I'll make you a cure,' she said, leading him into the garden, where they made their way precariously towards the house, due to the slippery ground.

He gave her an amazed, slightly hopeful sort of look when they were in the kitchen.

She rolled her eyes. 'It's not magic… well, maybe a little.' She laughed.

A few minutes later she gave him a red-tinged drink with copious amounts of Tabasco in it, as well as a few Halloway secrets, like freshly grated ginger and honey. He sniffed it and his dark eyes watered. He gave a small, delicate cough and wrinkled his nose. 'What is it?'

'Hair of the dog.'

'What?' His eyes bulged.

She laughed. 'That's an expression – it just means that after a night of alcoholic drinks you need to drink another to feel a bit better. Drink up.'

'That makes absolutely no sense, why call it "hair of the dog" then?' he said, shaking his head.

'Oh! Well, the full expression is hair of the dog that bit you.'

He laughed. 'Ah, that makes sense. I thought it was going to be like "have your cake and eat it" – what else are you going to do with it, pave your driveway, eh?'

She chuckled.

'Okay,' he said, taking a deep breath, pinching his nose, then downing the mixture in one. His face twisted into a grimace. 'Oh God, Pajarita, that's horrible.'

'I know, sorry.'

When they got back to the greenhouse, though, he had more colour in his face.

'Where did you learn that?' he asked.

She snorted, 'Not the Halloway Recipe Book, if that's what you mean. That's just something I learned the hard way during my wild student years.'

He looked at her. 'You? Wild student years?'

'Yes,' she said, then laughed. 'Well, only for a little while. Pete sorted me out.'

'Pete?'

'My ex.'

'Ah. The one who wore lots of beige?'

She rolled her eyes, 'You've been speaking to my aunts.'

'Just Dot.'

'She exaggerated.'

'Oh?'

'Well, a little.'

He grinned. 'You liked him – that's all that matters.'

She nodded. 'True. Thanks.'

She looked away, thinking of Pete, feeling that familiar stab of guilt when she did. It had taken her a long time even just to admit to herself that he'd been right, that she hadn't felt about him the way he needed her to. She wished though that they had ended it differently; she hoped that wherever he was, he was happy. She'd respected his wishes though, not contacting him, even though it had been hard.

He grinned. 'Okay. Remind me though to be careful about taking any food or drink from you again – I can handle hot things, trust me, but I think you used most of the bottle.'

She laughed. 'Sorry, I usually taste it! Anyway, you should know by now that all Halloways come with a ready-made warning label – especially when it comes to food.'

He frowned. 'I wouldn't say a warning label.'

'You just haven't been here long enough.'

'Well, people can be stupid.'

She folded her lips, but didn't disagree. 'Well, maybe things are changing,' she said, thinking of Jack.

'You mean – with that guy I saw you with?'

She shrugged, couldn't help the small grin that formed.

A shadow passed over Sandro's eyes. 'I heard what he said.'

She frowned. 'What do you mean?'

'What he said about your column explaining things about your family.'

'Oh,' said Emma. 'Well, I suppose it does, in a way.'

He gave her a sceptical look. 'I like your column, I do – but Pajarita, come on,'

'What?'

'Well, it's very matter-of-fact at times, you know?'

'So?'

'Well, I would have thought, I don't know, that it would show the other side too – the inexplicable. I mean you can't just sweep all of this under a rug, pretend it doesn't exist. The things they make, they change people. I hear things, see them.'

'And you think it's real?'

'Don't you?'

'I don't know what to believe any more.'

'I wonder.'

'Wonder what?'

'If there isn't another reason.'

'Like what?'

'Like maybe you're just holding yourself back, trying to be like everyone else.'

'Maybe I am like everyone else.'

'No, you're not.'

'Oh, and you know this how?'

'I just do.'

She shook her head. 'You've lived here a couple of months, known me for a few weeks and you think that, what? Now you know me? Know what I feel?'

'You think it's not hard to see what's happened? How you've tried so very hard to make sense of all of this,' he said, indicating the cottage and everything else, 'with your column? But it's just a substitute, isn't it? It's the same as what you were saying about the "mock chocolate tarts" the other day, that's what your column is.'

Emma's eyes bulged. 'No, it's not.'

He shrugged. 'I think it is – and to me, I can honestly tell you, I don't think anyone is worth that. You shouldn't have to give up who you are just to be loved, you should find someone who will love for who you are, not who you're not. You deserve so much more than that.'

'You don't know what you're talking about.'

He shook his head. 'Actually, I think I do.'

'I love my job.'

'You *like* it, and you're good at it, but you know what I think?'

'What?'

He jerked his head towards the door of Hope Cottage. 'You *love* that.'

She shook her head. 'You're wrong, I've hated that for years.'

He shook his head. 'I've seen your notebooks – your recipes. Evie showed them to me; they're so full of life, and hope… and passion.'

'She had no right to do that.'

He shrugged. 'Of course she did, she loves you, they worry about you, about what's happened to you. You can't tell me that the way you feel about something like that is something you can just switch off?'

'I was a child, I didn't know any better.'

He shook his head, eyes wide with disbelief. 'But now you do?'

'Yes,' she spat, 'I do.'

He stared at her. 'You keep telling yourself that, maybe one day, eh, it'll really come true.'

She felt her blood boiling as she set her jaw. 'Thanks for your help today. But I'm better now. So, we can leave it at that – I can manage.'

'Fine,' he said, getting up fast, fists balled at his sides. 'Well, good luck with that, you do it so well.'

TWENTY-THREE

'Did you hear about Alfred Bright?' asked Dot, who was glazing the Christmas ham.

'The butcher?' said Aggie.

'No, the MI6 agent from Istanbul. Of course, the butcher, what other Alfred Bright do you know?'

Aggie rolled her eyes. 'Fine. Tell us.'

'Don't tell me he's leaving Whistling?' asked Emma, sadly. She really liked him, but she knew that times were tough now with the new supermarket, the Co-Mart, driving down business.

Evie shot her a look. Emma knew she was wondering if she hadn't, somehow, bungled the recipe that Evie had asked her to watch over while she nipped out to get the cream.

For a second, Emma found herself wondering the same thing, until she reminded herself that it was all nonsense anyway.

'No – the opposite, actually,' said Dot. 'Well, it seems that something went wrong with the new Co-Mart. Seems they didn't actually have the right permissions for a store that big – some stray piece of damning paperwork has come to light and, well, looks like they're going to have to relocate somewhere else, which is great news for the Brimbles, but especially poor Alfie.'

'I must have missed that recipe, Evie – what did you do?' asked Aggie.

Evie smiled. 'The Stand By Me Soufflé.'

'Really? That wasn't one of our best – a trickster, for sure. I'm surprised.'

Trickster was the name her aunts used for recipes that needed a bit of coaxing.

Evie frowned, pouring wine over the caramelised plums for a funny recipe called Plum up The Jam that Emma had created when she was about eleven. It was an effective treatment for anyone, like poor Gemma Harris, one of the sisters who ran the teashop in Whistling, who was prone to bouts of melancholy during the Christmas period. 'Well, I had a little help.'

'From who?' asked Dot in surprise. Slowly they all turned to look at Emma, mouths slightly ajar.

Emma took a sip of water. 'I just kept it from burning, that's all.'

Dot and Aggie stared at her with their big round Halloway eyes.

Emma rolled her eyes, and Dot went back to tending the ham.

'The funniest thing happened though,' she said. 'You know he's always been such a confirmed bachelor, old Alfie?'

They all nodded. A lot of people had tried to set him up over the years, but he always maintained he was happiest with a cup of tea, his comfy slippers and his old cat, Michael.

'Well, I was standing there in the queue, and you know he's always greeting his customers with a joke, well, he saw, Sandra Pike – you know, the nursery school teacher – and all of sudden, out of nowhere, he comes over all strange, gawking at her like she's Kate Middleton or something, and telling her that she's got the most soulful Spanish eyes he's ever seen. Can you believe it?'

Emma choked on her water.

'I mean, she's not even a bit Spanish – and she's got those cataracts. It was so *odd.*'

Aggie came over and pounded her back. 'You all right there, love?'

'Fine,' Emma choked.

The scent wakes her up, one day in the second week of December. It's warm, and rich, and thick, and hinting of spice, like cinnamon, and of roasted hazelnuts and chocolate. It whispers in her ear, making her toes curl in pleasure, before it leaves like a lover departing with a lingering kiss.

It's 2 a.m. when she creeps into the kitchen, heart thrumming in her chest, to search for it, wanting more.

She steps forward slowly, almost reverentially, in the dark, feeling a bit like she is on the precipice, between dreaming and being awake, between something old and something new. The herbs and spices that the Halloways have collected over the years all line up along the shelves on the old dresser in small bottles with little blue and white striped lids made of tin. It's these she seeks out in the dark. There are no labels to guide; that's not how it's ever worked, not how it ever would.

She unscrews the lid of the first one, and brings it to her nose. It's warm, spicy and slightly woody. Her head swims and she pictures crisp dark-gold biscuits, hot from the oven, that snap as you break them in two, yet dissolve in the mouth. She closes her eyes, breathes in the fragrance, like a drug, making her head swim. *Nutmeg.*

She puts it back, unscrews the next. It's something sweet, and lingering like liquorice. She remembers lazy afternoons in Provence, old men in flat caps drowsing in the sun as they sip thimblefuls of pastis, after a game of pétanque.

Aniseed.

She puts it back. It's not that.

Her fingers find a small jar. There are dried leaves inside, with sharp pointed edges, and she knows what it is by that alone, though she lifts it to her nose anyway. Mellow and deep and warming. She pictures cold winter days, long walks on the frosted moors, her every move followed by a short-eared owl, and suddenly the warmth of the cottage, and a hearty stew that warms the bones. *Bay.*

Not that either.

The next jar makes her rock on her heels. It's sweet, and slightly sharp, and when she closes her eyes, she sees hot baked earth, golden-coloured grass and sunshine flickering through a canopy of leaves, fruit bursting with juice. *Orange peel.*

She breaks off a piece to taste, but there's nothing yet. That's okay, she thinks. This is enough for now. More than enough.

She unscrews the lid of another. It's warm, and inviting, telling a hundred stories of sultry summers and monsoon weddings. *Turmeric.*

She breathes them all in for a moment, standing barefoot in the cold, then takes one up to her nose and sniffs. It's sharp, slightly bitter, and suddenly she's six years old again, and it's not long after she first arrived at Hope Cottage.

The shop bell tinkles as she enters. Emma's eyes trace over the name of the store, etched into the glass: Whistle-In Store.

An old man with long grey hair is seated at the counter. He has silvery eyes that glow in the dark, like slits of moonshine.

He stands up. 'Well, I'll be,' he says in greeting. 'Is this our lass?'

'Aye,' Evie nods. 'This is Emma.'

'Ee-by-gum,' he says. 'Now that's summat, she looks nowt like Margaret, 'cept for t'eyes. Red?'

It amazes Emma how there are so many people who sound like her mother, a whole village full of them. Though his is the heaviest accent she's heard since she arrived.

'Red,' Evie agrees, then goes on, 'How you doing there Harrison, feeling better?'

'Much,' he says. 'Ta for that soup.'

'Don't mention it,' says Evie.

'So, our lass, have yeh started at the school?'

Emma nods.

He looks at her. His silvery eyes are a bit strange, and they seem to look straight into her heart. 'People are always a little afraid of what they don't understand. Yeh job isn't ta make them – it's a fool's road trying ta make everyone like yeh. Some just won't. All yeh can do in this world, is be yerself, all right?'

Emma blinks.

Back in the kitchen, she frowned. It's strange what scent can do, how it can transport you back in time. She'd forgotten about that day. It wasn't long after Mrs Brimble had come for a recipe for Harrison. Strange; at the time, she was sure she hadn't known that, hadn't put the two together. It was only now that she realised he had been giving her good advice.

'Ours is an edible history,' Evie said once. It was true. There were memories in each bottle. Like this one, she thought, lifting up the one that always reminded her of home, and of Christmas. Warm and rich. *Cinnamon.*

Her eye fell on The Book. It was open to a recipe that spoke of new horizons, new beginnings too.

She bit her lip, and mused, 'I could just go back to bed.'

She could. It would be hard, but she could. But she knew she wasn't going to do that. Not until she tried to make whatever it was that had woken her up. It had been years since she'd baked. But her fingers knew what to do, how to light the range and coax the old behemoth into life. She gave it a pat, like all Halloway women did, like it was a slightly grouchy pet. 'I'm just trying something, okay,' she told it. 'Just a little trial, is all.'

It made a noise, as if, perhaps, it knew she was lying, that soon enough she'd be back for more.

By the time dawn had crested the horizon she'd made *pain au chocolat* and cinnamon buns, and sweet orange polenta cake.

She couldn't taste them but she breathed in their scent anyway.

When Evie came down, she stopped at the door, her hand on her heart. 'You did this?' she asked.

Emma nodded, a small, tired smile ghosting her face.

Evie stepped forward, took up a cinnamon bun, then took a bite, and closed her eyes in sudden bliss.

'It's good?' asked Emma, suddenly nervous. Evie's eyes glazed. 'Better than good.'

Emma's grin was huge.

There were other scents too that day. Some a bit of a shock. The sheets were sharp and musty. Her clothes in desperate need of a wash. Even Pennywort reeked. She pressed her nose into his fur and laughed with delight. After that everything got a wash – the duvet, herself and Pennywort, to his utter disgust.

When the rich aroma that was wet dog filled her nostrils, she laughed again, hugging the old bulldog so close that he huffed in her ear, making a mild protest but too lazy to do anything about it.

She looked up at Evie in a sudden fit of giggles. 'He's so smelly.'

Evie looked at her. 'You've lost it.'

'Maybe.' She grinned.

She was walking back from town, where she'd just dropped off a batch of her cinnamon buns with Aggie, when she smelt it. At the same moment Dot greeted her in the street with her usual, 'Have you heard the latest? Apparently,' she went on, 'Steve Galway's been given the sack from that auto shop outside town – he was falling down drunk at two in the afternoon, seems he's got even worse since Mary left him—'

But Emma didn't hear. She grabbed Dot's arm. 'That – what is that?'

Dot shook her head, confused. 'What?'

Emma closed her eyes. It was the smell – the one that had woken her up this morning. Like chocolate and cinnamon and roasted hazelnuts; sheer bliss. 'Come on,' she said, pulling Dot gently but firmly down the hill, past the ribbon of butterscotch cottages, to the edge of the moors, going as fast as her crutch would allow. The mist was coming in and it was cold. Dusk was approaching. Clouds rose above the sweeping expanse of heathland with its carpet of snow.

She could hear birdsong in the distance. The scent wild, and fresh, with bracken and moisture, and somewhere there was that scent that had been whispering to her, just out of reach.

'This way,' she said, pulling Dot's arm.

'You go on, love – I'll see you later,' Dot said with a laugh. 'Say hello for me.'

Emma frowned, then shrugged, carried on alone.

The light was beginning to fade as she made her way into a clearing that overlooked a river. Amber-coloured bulbs were strung around a small outdoor restaurant in the middle of nowhere, under a Bedouin-styled tent. Inside this were long wooden benches and tables, overlooking the snow-covered moorland that stretched on for miles. The big, pale wooden tables were topped with miniature Christmas trees; the benches were strewn with cosy mohair blankets and next to each were rows of fire pits, keeping the customers warm and snug. In the centre of the tent was a small metal van, strung with fairy lights, displaying a tapas menu written in chalk.

The Tapas Hut

There was soft Spanish music and the low hum of people talking. The air was thick with the scent of fried potatoes, paella, chilli and tortilla, and when she turned she smelt it again, that scent.

'Pajarita,' said a mild, mellow voice.

She turned. Sandro was standing behind her. She blinked, confused.

'This is a surprise,' he said. His eyes were like dark ink, his smile warm, like the glow of a fire; she felt herself edging closer to it without realising.

She bit her lip, looked away. 'It's beautiful here,' she said, knowing though that the words didn't do it justice.

'I'm sorry about the other day,' she went on.

'Me too,' he said, almost in a whisper. The words were uttered close to her neck and she shivered.

'You're cold,' he noted. 'How about a hot chocolate?'

'Put it on my tab,' said another, familiar voice.

She turned, started in surprise.

'Jack?'

He grinned, ran a hand through his dark blond hair. 'I was going to call you later. I'll have another pint,' he told Sandro, clapping him on the arm.

Sandro nodded. For a second the light from the fire cast a shadow on his face, and she wondered if she saw his jaw clench, or if it was simply a trick of the light.

His phone started to ring, and just before he answered she saw a name flash on the screen. *Sarah.*

Emma thought of what Evie had said, that he's always out when he's got a new girl on the scene.

No wonder he got in so late sometimes. Busy guy.

She frowned, thinking of the scent that had led her here. It had disappeared now; why was her brain playing tricks on her? Jack led her to a table. 'You all right?' he asked, seeing her face.

'Fine. Just a strange day.' She looked at him now, remembering what he'd said about the Tapas Hut. 'It's funny, I thought… well, the way you spoke about this place, that perhaps you didn't like it.'

He frowned. 'Did I? No, it's cool. I just said that it could get a bit rowdy sometimes. Well, as it's a bit far out it can sometimes attract a bad crowd – a few weeks ago I was here when Steve Galway came around with his mates. I think Sandro had to call the cops.'

'Oh,' said Emma. 'That's not good. Steve Galway is getting a bit out of hand since his wife left, at least so I've heard.'

'Yeah,' said Jack. 'That was so strange, I mean, people are saying…' His voice trailed off.

'What?'

He laughed. 'Nothing, never mind, silly rumours that's all.'

Emma could guess. People were saying that after years of putting up with Steve, Mary Galway had come to Hope Cottage for a recipe at last. Well, thought Emma, looking out at the moors, so what?

Sandro brought over their drinks, giving her shoulder a squeeze before he left.

Jack raised a brow. 'Something I should know about?'

Emma shook her head. 'No, we're friends, I guess.'

'You have to guess? How does that work?'

Emma looked at him, couldn't help answering. 'Maybe the way we used to be friends, though sometimes it was mainly a guess, perhaps?'

'I should never have let you go that day, I was an idiot. I'll do better this time, okay?'

She blinked. It was what she'd wanted to hear for the longest time.

Her eye fell on the stream, meandering through the hills in the distance, the castle in the background and the village of Whistling with its rows of cottages like golden dominoes ribboning the cobblestones. She pulled a blanket over her knees and leaned in closer to the burner, saw Sandro walking past, laughing at something someone said, his limbs loose, like they were oiled with butter.

Jack picked up her hand, slipped his inside it. 'You know, I always wanted to do this,' he said. 'Out in public.'

Her heart started to pound. She felt her stomach fill with butterflies.

'So, why didn't you?' she asked.

'I was afraid.'

She blinked, watched as his gaze fell on a nearby table; a few people seemed to be staring.

Jack averted his eyes, looked back at Emma. 'There's something to be said for getting older,' he said. 'You're less concerned about what people will think.'

They sat talking for hours, and it was close to midnight when he walked her home, helping her with her crutch. It was only then that she saw that he must have had a little too much to drink; he was swaying ever so slightly.

'I think it all rushed to my head when I stood up,' he said. 'Forgot to eat, I think.'

Emma opened the door to the cottage, switched on the light. There were the telltale signs of a household at rest, the low hum that came over the house while it slumbered. 'Come in. I made some buns and things earlier – it'll help soak up the alcohol,' she said. 'Here.' She moved the basket of baked goods forward.

He helped himself to a bun, closed his eyes in bliss as his tongue hit upon the cinnamon and chocolate combination. 'Now that, I would have to agree, is magic,' he said.

His eyes took in the small alcove at the back of the room and he looked at her, his eyes warm. 'So that's where you sleep?' he asked.

She was suddenly shy. 'Yes.'

He nodded. Then leaned over, touching her face, tracing a faint scar on her forehead from her accident. He pulled her face forward. Her heart started to beat fast. Up close she could smell his aftershave, subtle and inviting, and for just a second she wondered about it, but then she lost herself in the kiss.

TWENTY-FOUR

Taste came next. As if she were a newborn, her brain learned flavours slowly at first, though it remembered them all the same. The tang of a slice of cake, sour and tart, took her back to the first sugary-lemon crêpe she'd tried, down a sunny street on her first trip to Paris. A spicy sausage from a market the next day down in the village took her back even further to a memory she'd all but forgotten, when her mother offered her a taste and her blue eyes danced with laughter at Emma's expression.

Salt came next. She dipped her fingers in the grains and popped them on her tongue. Was there any dish it didn't help improve, anything better?

Sugar, probably. The day she could detect that things were sweet, it felt a little as if she'd found her own pot of gold at the end of a rainbow. She licked teaspoons of honey and peanut butter and sat at the table smiling to herself, buzzing on a sugar high.

'That's an easy way to get fat,' Aggie said, getting a spoon and taking a seat to join her.

Emma looked up, laughed. 'Then I'll get fat.'

Aggie grinned. 'It's worth it for this,' she agreed.

'Did you know this was an accident?' Emma asked, pointing at the jar.

'Nutella?'

She nodded. 'Yeah. It was in Italy during the war – they crushed hazelnuts to make the chocolate go further.'

Aggie shook her head at the genius of the Italians. 'Meanwhile Britain had things like mock chocolate.'

'Some things just aren't fair,' Emma agreed.

With Christmas Day steadily approaching, Evie and her aunts were busier than ever, and Emma was happy to at least help keep them fed, though she hadn't quite crossed over to helping them with a recipe. She watched as they made the final layer of the Good Cheer Christmas Cake, where it would rest until at last it would be distributed in small boxes to each and every one of the hundred plus villagers who lived in Whistling.

Emma couldn't seem to stop baking. It was like a dam had burst; she was waking up in the middle of the night with new ideas. Perhaps it was because it was Christmas – it always put her in the mood to bake, to create new things, or at least it used to. She gave in to it again now, making lemony cinnamon buns with white chocolate shavings. Gingerbread biscuits. Caramel roulade with caramelised apple slices. Pumpkin spice muffins. She filled the house with what she made, sent them off into the world, happy to see a face light up when they tried one.

Evie was glad to see the change, but she worried too. 'You're being careful?' she asked.

Emma shrugged, nonchalant. Of course. She knew what Evie meant, but why worry? 'I'm not making our recipes – it's just a bit of baking,' she protested.

Evie wasn't so sure. She knew you couldn't switch it off and on, like a tap. When it came to food, it was never simple, never straightforward, not for a Halloway. They had to be mindful of whatever they made, the way an alcoholic would; every sip counted. But still she didn't want Emma to stop. Later she wondered if she shouldn't have insisted that she followed the old rituals, paid the cost, or that perhaps Evie herself should have done it on her behalf; but she was busy, she told herself, distracted by all that needed to be done before Christmas.

Because odd things started to happen to the people who tried Emma's baking. After eating two cinnamon buns, shy, bookish Jenny Hughes found herself slipping her number into a library book taken out by Jonathan Martin, who'd been a few years above her at school and who she'd always had a secret crush on.

After she tried a slice of Emma's apple-pie, the ever-practical Maggie found herself signing up for an after-hours course in floristry.

When she made ginger snaps, Aggie got in touch with her old agent, and painted until midnight; and lazy-stay-in-her-pyjamas-till-noon Dot decided to become a rambler after she tried one of Emma's mince pies.

Evie found herself thinking about lost love too. Emma found her in the sitting room one day with an album on her lap, looking at a photograph from the fifties, showing a handsome man with black hair leaning casually against the wall of the teashop in town.

'Who's that?' she asked, curious.

'Your grandfather.'

Emma blinked. 'My grandfather?' Evie never mentioned him. She crept forward to get a better look. Saw the way he had a slight dimple in his chin, like her. He'd only ever been a subject that resulted in sad eyes and changed subjects, till now. Emma wondered at the change.

'What happened to him?' she asked now. There seemed to be a pattern to the men who were involved with the Halloway women – there were men like her Uncle Joe, who stood at Dot's side come what may; there were ones like her father, who'd whisked her mother away and tried in his own way to get her to be someone else, and then there were the ones who walked away. She'd always assumed he was one of them.

'He died.'

'I'm sorry,' she said, surprised. 'Why don't you ever talk about him?'

Evie took a shuddery breath. 'Because it's hard to talk about it – we didn't have an easy relationship, he didn't really accept this, our way of life here. He wanted us to get married, but when I told him that if we had a girl it meant that she would have to keep my surname – well, he just couldn't understand.

'I fell pregnant, and of course, he was a good man, wanted to do the "right thing" by getting married, but I wasn't going to change my mind – I wasn't going to be the one to break up Hope Cottage, and he wasn't going to let a child of his walk around with his wife's surname. It was the fifties, back then it was unheard of, so we never did. It's silly now when you think of it. Still, he was a good father in his way, though he became resentful that I'd put the cottage before him, and that started to influence what he said to Margaret, I think. It's hard when your parents have two such different views.

'He died, when she was about twelve. It affected her, changed her I think. She grew up fast after that – maybe too fast. There were other things too, but perhaps that laid the groundwork.'

'Why are you telling me this now?'

Evie shrugged, looked out the window, watched the snow falling on the cobbled street, saw a couple walking past bundled in coats, wearing thick gloves and scarves. 'I don't know, I just couldn't stop thinking about him today.' She set her coffee cup down, frowned and then looked at Emma. 'What were you thinking about when you made those buns yesterday?'

'Nothing really. There was this scent I was trying to capture… I suppose it reminded me a little of first love.' She blinked. 'You don't think…?'

Evie laughed. 'I do. Who else tried them?'

Emma folded her lips in thought. 'Jenny.'

'Jenny! Shy Jenny Hughes, who gave her number to Jonathan Martin....'

Emma's eyes widened in realisation.

'What were you thinking when you made those ginger biscuits Dot and Aggie tried?'

She thought. 'Nothing, I don't remember thinking anything strange. I was happy that I could taste things again, and it made me feel...' She trailed off.

Evie grinned. 'Like you could do anything, perhaps?'

Emma nodded, and sat down with a frown.

Evie shook her head, amazed. 'I gave one of those cinnamon buns to Sue Redmond when she came past for a moan, saying that she was struggling to find a way to come up with an amicable solution for dealing with her husband's half of the bridal shop in the divorce. She wasn't sure if she should ask for a recipe or not, so I told her to go home and think about it.

'The next day I saw her on the high street holding hands with him. Completely nonchalant when she saw me, as if she hadn't, just the day before, been looking for a way to cut him smoothly out of her life.'

Emma frowned. 'But I mean, that's love, isn't it? That doesn't necessarily mean that the buns did it – I mean, one day you hate someone's guts, the next—'

'They've been separated for three years.'

Emma blinked. 'Oh.'

Evie looked at her. 'I asked you if you'd been careful. You know that there's a cost.'

Emma closed her eyes. 'But they're not the recipes. I didn't think it would apply to a bit of baking. How can there be a cost even to that?'

Evie patted her shoulder. 'Because there is one, there always is – yours is recognising how much of what you feel goes into what you make.' She smiled, with a trace of pride and sadness. 'You are your mother's daughter, that's for sure.'

Emma half laughed, half gasped, sinking into a nearby chair.

'So, you've been baking?'

Emma jumped as if it were an accusation.

Dr Norton looked at her from the edge of the medical bed, his foot in her hands as he cut off the cast.

'Easy!' he admonished.

'Oh – um, just a little,' she said, reddening slightly.

'Great. It's like I said, it feeds the soul, quite magical really.'

She blinked. 'You have no idea,' she said truthfully.

Then she stared at her foot, free of its cast, and beamed at him. 'I can't believe it.'

He winked at her. 'Believe it.'

A text pinged on her mobile later that afternoon.

> *Dinner to celebrate your cast being off? What do you, think?*
> *Jack.*

Love to she replied. Then grinned like an idiot. She still couldn't believe this was finally happening. It was everything she'd wanted for years. She put down the tea towel she'd had in her hand, and looked for something to wear that didn't look like workout gear. It would be so wonderful to wear something nice and not have the cast on her leg.

There wasn't much in her suitcase, just a pair of black jeans and a soft cashmere jumper. It would have to do – she'd left all her best things behind in her flat in London; it hadn't occurred to her that she might need them here.

Her hair was in need of a wash and it was hard to do it in the shower with her hand still injured and in the sling. She reasoned washing her hair in the sink would probably be easier – it was what Evie usually did, but today she wasn't home to help.

She cursed as she got soap in her eyes. It wasn't really any easier this way, she realised. She wished she'd waited for Evie. 'For Christ's sake!' she exhaled, waking up Pennywort, who snorted at her and then climbed down from the table and made for the bed, apparently not eager to witness her meltdown.

'Pajarita? You okay?' came a soft, melodic voice from behind her.

Emma looked up through one eye. The other was stinging and squeezed shut. 'Um? I'm fine, thanks.'

Sandro snorted. 'You don't look fine,' he said, putting down a blue sports bag on the table.

He took a clean tea towel from a drawer and ran it under the water, then placed it over her eyes. Then he pulled a chair next to the sink, and said, 'Sit. Now lean back.'

She did as instructed. His fingers were firm, yet gentle, as they worked the shampoo into her scalp, massaging the skin near her neck.

His fingers sent shivers down her spine and she felt her toes curl in response. 'Your hair is really long,' he said, his fingers working the shampoo into the ends, and she felt herself sink back, melting into the pressure of his hands, the gentle weight of his arm against her neck.

He stopped and she felt her eyes snap open in surprise as he moved away and the cool air replaced his touch. Then the tap was being turned on and he was telling her to lean her head back against the sink as he rinsed her hair under the spray, the water warm, blocking out all sound, his fingers sluicing the shampoo out of her hair.

When he was done, he picked up the towel that she'd left on the back of the chair and wrapped it round her head. 'Do you need help to dry it?' he asked.

She was about to say yes, just so that he would keep touching her, when her phone flashed. A text came through. They both glanced at it.

Looking forward to tonight. Jack xx

Emma blinked. A shadow seemed to fall across Sandro's eyes. He stared at her for a moment, like he wanted to say something, and then picked up his bag. 'Enjoy your date,' he said, and then left.

She held her hands up to her flushed skin, staring after him, feeling utterly confused. Fighting the impulse to call him back. She frowned, looking at her phone, lost in thought.

Jack arrived early for their date. 'You look nice,' he said taking in her long, shining hair, her smart clothes.

'Thanks,' she said, smiling and smoothing down her jeans.

'I thought we could go to Martels,' he said, coming closer, giving her a kiss. Martels was one of the oldest restaurants in town. A part of her was a little disappointed that he didn't want to go to the Tapas Hut – Martels was nice, but a little shabby – but she didn't say anything, telling herself it didn't matter. Besides, after what had happened with Sandro, perhaps it was better. She felt her cheeks flush as she thought of it, and told herself she'd read too much into it.

Jack helped himself to a biscuit from the rack before they went. 'I haven't been able to stop thinking about those buns since you made them. They're heavenly – any chance of some more?'

She laughed. 'I'll make some just for you.'

He seemed pleased at the idea.

'I'll probably get fat, dating you,' he said.

She grinned. 'I don't really do low-cal, sorry. Not now, anyway.'

'Now?' he asked as they climbed into his car, the heaters slow to warm the interior so that she shivered. As she put on her seatbelt, she saw a couple walking on the hill. She frowned when she realised it was Sandro, talking to some woman, who was wearing a dark green coat and had long blonde hair beneath a green bobble hat. She had a mittened hand on his arm. They seemed to be having a rather animated conversation.

Was this one of the many girls who were always calling? *Holly? Sarah?*

She felt herself deflate slightly, like she had a slow puncture.

'Earth to Emma?' asked Jack.

'Sorry?' she said, tearing her gaze away, looking into Jack's somewhat confused eyes. She blinked, then forced a smile.

'You said now you don't do low-cal?'

'Oh?' She looked back at the figures in the street, walking towards the snow-covered heathland and out of sight, trying to remember what they had been talking about earlier, giving herself a mental shake. Enough of this, she told herself.

'Um… Oh, it's just that I've just spent the last few months not being able to taste or smell a thing, and now that I can, well, I don't want to waste it, you know? I'm not interested in being a glutton – but I'm just done with deprivation, life's too short, you know?' she said with a grin.

He nodded, put his hand on her knee and gave it a squeeze. 'I know,' he said.

She enjoyed their date. Martels was crowded, but cosy and warm; there were bands of green and gold tinsel strewn on the ceiling, like Christmas bunting, and in the corner was a very festive tree, twinkling with multicoloured lights, while soft Christmas tunes crooned by Etta James played in the background. They had been shown into a small, private booth by a waiter who was wearing a Christmas hat; the booth blocked their view of the rest of the restaurant, creating a private candlelit sanctuary, which lent the peeling paint charm and, along with the wine, helped the conversation flow all night.

It had been months since she wore anything that didn't come with a drawstring, and it felt good. The food had been wonderful, pasta in cream with wine and garlic, and she'd found herself groaning in pleasure, deciding then and there to never diet again.

'It's funny how life works, isn't it?' he asked. 'I mean, I never thought we'd be given another chance, that one day I'd be brave enough to go on a date in public with you. If my mammy could see me now.' He laughed.

She grinned, though a small part of her didn't like the fact that he'd had to summon his courage just to go on a date in public with her. For a second Sandro's words from the other morning echoed in her head. '*You shouldn't have to give up who you are to just to be loved, you should find someone who will love for who you are, not who you're not. You deserve so much more than that.*'

She blocked them out. Wasn't that what Jack was trying to do now, wasn't that what he'd said the other night?

She turned to him and smiled. The truth was she didn't relish the idea of running into Mrs Allen either; there were some people who did nor mellow with age, and she suspected Janet Allen was one of them. For now, she was quite happy to keep the fact she and Jack were together between them.

Unfortunately, years of living in London had made her forget that coming to one of the oldest restaurants in town with Jack Allen, where everyone knew her name, was about as subtle as announcing their status via loudspeaker.

Especially considering that, unbeknownst to them, a table full of Leas had sat and watched them all night, looks of horror twisting their faces. But no one's expression was worse than Stella's; by the end of that night she had decided upon a course of revenge so cold, many would have been hard pressed to remember that she was the vicar's daughter.

TWENTY-FIVE

By the next day, the rumours had spread like wildfire. There wasn't a person in Whistling who hadn't heard the news. Emma Halloway had got her hands on Jack Allen at last.

People's eyes followed her everywhere she went. Some gave her an encouraging sort of grin, and Harrison Brimble offered some good-natured ribbing when she popped in for that week's groceries, but others weren't so accepting.

Sue Redmond – the woman who'd recently got back together with her about-to-divorce husband – crossed the street quickly when she saw Emma approach, shooting her a look of fear laced with something else, like disapproval.

Steve Galway, leaning drunkenly outside the post office, wearing only his dirty grey vest despite the blistering cold, spat on the floor, and she heard him hiss, 'Witch', as she hurried past, bundled in her coat and thick woollen scarf.

There was an angry letter dropped through the letter box that accused her of the same.

'People can be idiots,' were Aggie's words of comfort. 'You and Jack have been fighting this thing for years, it's good to see you finally get together.

'Don't let it spoil it for you,' was her advice.

She tried as best as she could; she burned the letter, avoided the square. Tried not to think of it any more.

What did it matter if people stared and whispered? She'd been through it all before. Surely it was all worth it now that she had Jack by her side?

It was later that week and she'd just given her first radio presentation down at The Whistle Blower, a fun interview about the history of holiday food. Sandro had come along to offer a taste of what Christmas was like in Spain.

Now that she was mostly recovered, she knew that the time had come to make a decision about her flat in London. As a freelancer she didn't have to be based in London; she could travel there whenever she needed to, and with the money she'd save on rent, she could make things much more comfortable at Hope Cottage – including getting it painted, doing some roof repairs and fixing the old range.

The truth was she was happier at Hope Cottage than she'd been in years. Despite the rumours and the dark looks that had escalated since she'd started dating Jack Allen, there wasn't anywhere else she wanted to be. Still, giving up her flat wasn't an easy decision. It had represented something important in her life – an escape from everything she was going through now. Yet, in her heart she knew that really it had been the equivalent of burying your head in the sand like an ostrich – the biggest, loudest part of you was still there for all the world to see.

She travelled to London with Evie, Dot and Aggie, who'd offered to help pack up her things. It was a small flat and there wasn't that much to take in the end, as she'd rented it furnished. Just her books and clothes and a few odds and ends.

It was a surprise to her how little she'd accumulated in the past four years. Little more than three boxes full of things. 'This is it?' asked Dot in surprise.

She nodded. 'I suppose, looking at it now, I see how temporary this all was,' she said, looking around the small flat. 'It's funny what you don't see sometimes.'

'That's true,' said Evie.

The boxes were driven back in Aggie's van, which she used to cart around all her large paintings, and were placed in a corner of the Hope Cottage kitchen.

'Sandro said he's probably moving out soon,' Evie said.

Emma's mouth opened in surprise. 'He is?'

'Yes, well, they're mostly done with the renovations – it still needs work but now that there's a kitchen and a bathroom he says he can live in it while the rest is being done.'

'When is he moving?' she asked.

'Next few days, I should imagine.'

Emma frowned. 'But that's such short notice – I mean, surely it should be at least a month's notice, shouldn't it?'

Evie laughed. 'Not between friends. Anyway he's already paid me far too much as it is – he's so generous.'

'But, he *can't* leave.'

Evie touched her hand. 'We'll still see him, don't worry.'

Emma blinked. What was she going to do at Hope Cottage without Sandro? 'Maybe I can convince him to stay... I mean, if the farmhouse isn't completely ready, why move? It's like you said, we don't need the money.'

Evie and Aggie shared a look. 'Love,' Evie started, 'I think with you dating Jack now, well—'

'What's that got to do with anything? Sandro doesn't need to leave just because of that.'

Aggie touched her arm. 'I think Sandro feels differently.'

She frowned. What did that mean? He'd had enough of them – of her – perhaps? Maybe he was sick of feeling so needed. God knows, she'd relied upon him enough in the past, but she didn't think he'd minded… unless she'd been cramping his style. All those nights when he was at home with her making her laugh, Pennywort snoring in his lap while they listened to that silly, funny book, maybe he'd just been trying to be nice when he really wanted to be out with Holly, or Sarah, or whichever one it was that week.

By the third week in December, Emma could be found spending her mornings in the greenhouse working on her column and the afternoons working on her weekly show for the Whistling radio station. She'd got better at typing with her injured hand, though it played up in the cold. She'd got in contact with some of her old freelance clients and was starting to take on some more work there as well.

The greenhouse was quiet, filled with the scent of soil and rosemary and the aroma of fresh coffee. She swivelled her mouse and opened up a blank page, took a sip, and for a second she thought of a pair of dark eyes, waiting for her to announce her topic.

She bit her lip, tried to shake the image out of her mind; perhaps he'd find it amusing that whenever she wrote a column now, she imagined what he'd say, though she wondered if he even read them. He'd been busy of late, and she'd barely seen him. The last time he'd come past, Jack had been sitting at the table and he'd popped in for less than the time it took for him to change his shirt and leave again, with a slightly terse, 'Adios', no dimpled grin; no 'Hola, Pajarita' either. Even Pennywort looked despondent.

Now he had officially moved out, the house was so much emptier.

When she finished for the day, she flexed the muscles in her hand. They were tight and sore. She didn't mind the pain, not really; it was a reminder of how far she'd come.

An early night was just about the only thing on her mind when she closed her laptop and made for the warmth of the cottage, thinking of a nice warm bath as her feet sank into the snow-covered grass.

When she neared the back door however, she saw Jack waiting for her outside.

He looked slightly frazzled, his hazel eyes haunted, beneath an olive-green beanie.

'You okay?' she asked, opening the door.

'Yeah, no, fine,' he said, running a hand through his hair and giving her a kiss.

He took a seat at the table, not bothering to take off his coat. His eyes fell upon The Book, and for a second she saw a scowl darken his eyes.

'Jack?' she asked.

His eyes snapped to hers. He didn't say anything for a while, then he frowned, then half-jokingly he asked, 'I'd know if I were bewitched – right?'

Emma blinked. 'What?'

He puffed out his cheeks. 'It was Stella, she came past my place earlier…' His eye fell on The Book again and he gave a short laugh, though she could tell he wasn't really joking. 'It's not like you made one for me, did you?'

'Of course not,' she said, taken aback.

He nodded. 'Yeah, yeah, of course,' he said, with a shaky kind of grin. 'I mean it's not like they really work… that's what I told her – I told her you don't believe in any of this.' He pulled a slightly mocking face as he waved a hand around the cottage.

Emma frowned.

He looked up at her, his eyes widening with disbelief. 'You don't, do you?'

She stared at him for a while, and then frowned. 'And if I do?'

He gave a half-grin. 'What are you saying?'

She sighed. 'I'm saying that I've seen too much to *not* believe, you know?'

He blinked, his face blanching a little. 'So, the things you gave me… the strange things people have said that have happened to people who have eaten the things you made, like people getting back together with their exes—'

'And you think that's what happened to you, do you?' she asked, folding her arms.

He looked at her. She could see the circles under his eyes. He looked tired, and unsure.

'Well, Jack. You know what I remember?'

He shook his head.

'That you were the one knocking on my door the first week I got back, and how in the weeks since then you've been here, bringing me things to eat, coming to see how I was, coming to sit next to me in that teashop with Gretchen, getting my number from Maggie… running into me, texting me, oh, and then – yes – you walked me home one night from the Tapas Hut, and we sat right here, in this kitchen and you kissed me. And yes, somewhere between the time you brought me home and the time you decided to kiss me you had one of the buns I'd made. So yeah, I guess it must all fucking be because of that.'

'Emma—'

'Goodnight Jack,' she said, standing up and opening the door.

'I'm sorry.'

'Yeah, so am I,' she said, closing the door behind him.

TWENTY-SIX

For the first time in their lives, it was Emma telling Jack that she wouldn't be seeing him for a while.

The truth was, she didn't know what she felt any more. She'd thought for so long that their biggest problem had always been that he hadn't fought for her, not the way she wished he would; but she realised now that perhaps it was deeper than that. Perhaps he'd never really accepted her, and so, in many ways, she'd never really accepted herself. The trouble was, she was beginning to. She was starting to like the parts of herself that were odd, and different and perhaps a little inexplicable, and she didn't know if she could be with someone who couldn't accept who she was.

She spent a lot of time walking, often finding herself at the Tapas Hut. With the cold deepening and icy-cold winds blowing across the moorland, the clear plastic of the Bedouin tent protected Sandro's customers from the worst of the inclement weather, along with the gas heaters and blankets. From inside this warm, festive bubble, which was full of the scent of ginger, and nutmeg, and soft Christmas music, she could still see the snow-covered moors stretching down the valley and the castle down the hill.

The hut was a haven away from the rumours and stares, though most of them had died down anyway once people stopped seeing the two of them together.

Jack didn't want to accept that it was over.

'I was an idiot,' he said, the week before Christmas, catching up with her on the high street. She'd been having a cuppa and a chat with Maggie after she finished work.

'Come on Ems, are you going to punish me for ever, just because I gave in for a second to the stupid rumours? I mean, can you blame me?'

She sighed. 'No, I can't.'

He looked relieved. His face split into a grin.

'But Jack – even so, I can't be with someone who is always going to want me to be someone else, someone he can change.'

His eyes widened. 'I don't want you to change!'

'You don't wish I didn't have the family I do?'

He frowned. 'Yeah, but no one's family is perfect, and I mean it's not personal, it's just all that crap they believe in and how this place can get a bit nuts about it. C'mon, the mumbo-jumbo that comes with your grandmother and her sisters, that silly book of theirs, I mean… that's them, it's not you.'

Emma shook her head, wondering if he'd ever really seen her properly. 'It *is* me, Jack.'

She was sitting with Aggie, having a glass of mulled wine, the first time she heard Sandro play the guitar. It was a few nights later. The Tapas Hut was bathed in warm firelight, and it was warm in the tent despite the snow falling softly outside. The tables had small live miniature Christmas trees with silver bells on them and the air was scented with cinnamon and ginger.

There was a rowdy group near the front, who started calling for him to play.

Emma saw him from across the room. His dark eyes crinkled at the corners as he grinned, bowed to the pressure and took a seat by the fire with his guitar, the flames casting reddish lights in his dark hair.

The sound was mellow and rhythmic, slightly hypnotic. While he played, his face was solemn, deep in concentration.

'He's really beautiful.'

Aggie raised a brow.

'I mean, his playing is beautiful.'

Though he was too.

Afterwards he came and sat next to her. 'Pajarita,' he said, touching her hand. 'There's something I have to—'

He was interrupted by a woman with long blonde hair and a pretty smile, 'Sandy, oh my goodness, you're just so talented. I could listen to you all day.'

'Thanks, Holly.'

Emma looked away. So that was *Holly*. When she looked up she saw him staring at her. 'I think, you know, I'm going to call it a night. Bye, *Sandy.*'

'Hey, Pajarita, wait up.'

She stopped, turned in surprise to see Sandro behind her.

'Thought I'd walk you home.'

'Why?'

'Why not?'

'Well, I don't want to drag you away from anyone, *Sandy.*'

He snorted. 'Holly is just a friend.'

She frowned. 'Okay,' she said, slightly sarcastically.

He cocked his head to the side, staring at her as they walked. 'What does that mean?'

'Nothing,' she said.

He was still staring at her, so she shrugged. 'Just that, well, you seem to have a lot of friends, you know?'

'So?'

She scoffed. 'Well, I suppose it is a free country – and you are the good-looking foreigner, why not take advantage?'

'Is that what you think?'

She looked at him. 'Sorry – I mean, it's just I've seen some of the people who call, all the Hollys and Sarahs, and well, Dot's told me some stories.'

He shook his head. 'Dot – despite popular opinion – is not an authority on everything, eh, Pajarita.'

'What is that supposed to mean?'

'Well, that sometimes she misses things that are fairly obvious to just about everyone else.'

She frowned. 'Like what?'

His face looked suddenly angry. 'Like that Jack Allen doesn't deserve you – and he never has. Maybe that's a rumour she should have thought to spread around.'

'What?' said Emma. His face was inches from hers. She felt her heart start to pound. 'Emma—' he started.

'So that's how it is,' said a voice from behind.

She turned, sharply. 'Jack?'

His face was screwed up in anger. His gaze glassy in the streetlight. A strong scent of beer was coming off him, and he looked slightly scruffy, his blond head uncovered and messy, his dark coat open, as if he couldn't feel the biting cold.

'Just be careful mate – she pretends to give a shit, like you're the most important thing in her life, then one day, poof, like magic – you're out and Spanish boy is in.'

Emma's eyes widened. 'It's not like that, Jack.'

Sandro took a step away from her, a frown between his eyes. 'Right. I think I'd better go,' he said, his face tightening.

'Yeah, I think you should,' spat Jack.

'Oh really?' said Sandro, his eyes going suddenly cold.

'Stop it!' said Emma. 'Jack, the only one who should go is you, you're drunk. We'll talk when you're sober, all right?'

TWENTY-SEVEN

Evie's face looked sad and anxious when she woke Emma the next morning with the news.

'What is it?' asked Emma, feeling her heart lurch in sudden fear at the look in her eyes.

'It's Jack. I'm so sorry, love, but there's been an accident.'

Emma felt the air leave her lungs. There were tears in Evie's eyes. 'Seems he got hit by a drink driver last night, Stevie Galway, apparently he didn't see Jack on the road, and…'

Emma gasped. 'Is-is he…' She couldn't find the words.

'He's alive, but they're not sure if he's going to make it.'

Tears streamed down Emma's face, into her neck. 'Oh my God.'

After he'd confronted her and Sandro, the two had looked ready to kill each other. So she'd pushed Sandro back towards the Hut, and Jack in the opposite direction, and only when she was sure that they'd both walked away had she gone home. She only wished now that she'd seen Jack safely home.

Mrs Allen didn't tell her to leave the hospital; she watched her approach with sad, lost eyes.

Stella Lea was sitting a little back from her, like she was an island, an island of grief and despair. Her eyes were sad, like something inside her had broken.

Emma swallowed. A tear slipped down her cheek as she neared them. 'Mrs Allen…' She hesitated. 'I know we have our differences, but I care about Jack – and I just need to know how he's—' She took a shuddery breath. 'How he's doing,' she finished.

Janet Allen's face crumpled. For a second, Emma thought she wouldn't speak to her, but then she took a deep breath and looked at her. Perhaps it was the first time she'd ever really looked.

'H-he's in a critical condition,' she said, her eyes pooling with tears.

Behind them Stella was quietly sobbing.

Emma felt her knees wobble as she lowered herself into the seat in the waiting room next to Mrs Allen.

Her hands started to shake. 'Is there anything I can do?' she asked. 'Donate blood, get you something – tea, maybe?'

Mrs Allen blinked. 'N-no.' A second passed, then she said, 'But thank you, Emma.'

She closed her eyes. 'You know you look like him, a little – your dad. Liam… he was my brother's best friend, I didn't know if you knew that. He was a wonderful man.'

Emma eyes filled with tears. 'Thank you,' she said.

'The doctors have told us to prepare ourselves,' said Mrs Allen, dissolving into tears.

Emma felt herself go into shock. Sitting in that hard plastic chair, she watched as Mrs Allen left to be at Jack's side, where she, as a non-family member, wasn't allowed to be.

Sitting staring at the speckled blue and white tiles, she realised that this wasn't helping anyone, but that there was something she could do.

Back at the cottage, she felt numb and worn out, but determined. She switched on the light and went to the dresser, scanning the shelves until she found it. An old black notebook that had once belonged to her mother.

Perhaps, deep down, somehow, she had known it was there all along. At last she found it, near the back of the notebook and folded in half, a two-hundred-year-old recipe about changing fortunes called Fortune's Promise. She'd guessed that if Margaret had been anything like her she couldn't have burned it.

Emma closed her eyes, prayed that it would work, then she took the notebook, one of the only things she had from her mother – her only real connection with her – and buried it beneath the frozen ground in the vegetable garden.

She'd just lit the old range and coaxed it into life when there was an insistent knock on the door. When she opened it, her mouth fell open in surprise. Janet Allen and Stella Lea were standing outside; they both shared the same, desperate, look.

Emma motioned them in, her eyes wide.

She told them to take a seat, frowning in disbelief at the same time. She knew why they were here, but still, she couldn't believe it somehow. 'I-well…' began Janet, taking a deep breath. 'You told me earlier, if there was anything I needed…' her mouth wobbled. 'There's only one thing, really, and I'm at my wits' end now, I'd do just about anything, even—' She broke off, then looked at the floor.

'Come to us?'

She nodded. A big fat tear rolled off the end of Stella's nose. She didn't have to say anything. Emma guessed she felt the same way.

'I'm going to try something,' she said. 'Something that will hopefully put things right – as far as it can.'

Janet breathed out. She hadn't asked if Emma would help; she knew, no matter their differences, Emma would do anything to help Jack.

'S-so, um, I give up something of value, is that right?' asked Janet.

Emma nodded.

They both handed her their tokens, a prized necklace and an heirloom watch, which Emma knew meant that they knew, that somehow the rumours of what happened here had reached them.

'I'm going to do it with you – pay a cost too.' She touched their hands, and her lips trembled. 'I have to say the old words – it's the tradition.'

Perhaps they'd heard of that too, but it still caused Janet Allen's tears to splash onto the table as Emma said, 'I make no promises…', though she added one of her own in any case. 'But I promise that I will try' – she took a breath – 'with everything that I have.'

'We'll help you make it, if you like.'

Emma nodded. 'I think, yes, that would be best.'

Emma set them to work, peeling and chopping and folding the mixture together. As the afternoon wore on, she stirred it together as she said the words, keeping her intentions clear and firm; hoping with every last bit of hope she had that it would work.

When it was done, they ate it there, as night approached the wintry kitchen, bite by bite.

Janet and Stella left not long before dawn broke. 'I have to go,' said Janet. 'Got to get back to the hospital – but Emma, even if …' She couldn't finish her sentence, but Emma understood.

Stella took a breath. 'We'll know you tried. Thank you.'

Emma nodded, and thought, it had to work, it just had to.

She woke up to the sound of the phone ringing. It was Christmas morning.

She dashed across the room and pressed the receiver to her ear, only to hear Janet Allen, through happy tears: 'He's going to be okay, he's pulled through!'

When she went into Jack's room in the hospital, not long after, she saw that his face was full of dark criss-crossing gashes, traced with dried blood. His leg was in a cast.

'Oh Jack,' she said, hand on her heart.

His eyes opened. 'Emma.'

'Hi.' She took a seat next to him. 'You gave us such a fright.'

'I know. I'm sorry.'

He looked at her, his face amazed. 'They came to you – my mum, and Stella, to Hope Cottage?'

Emma nodded.

'I can't believe it.'

'Neither can I, really.'

He looked at her. 'Emma, I'm so sorry about what happened. I should have fought for you, tried harder – I'm so sorry.'

She squeezed his hand. 'It's okay, Jack. You know, you were my first love, and I'll never regret it, I could never regret you,' she said truthfully.

He looked down. 'So, I *am* too late.' His eyes were sad.

She bit her lip, touched his arm. 'I just think we're both about ten years too late, Jack.'

TWENTY-EIGHT

Elvis was singing carols on the old wireless, which was tuned in to The Old Whistle station. Pennywort was dozing at the table watching as Emma, Dot and Aggie loaded the small boxes of Good Cheer Christmas Cake, trays and assorted pots and pans into Aggie's van so that she could take it down to the Tapas Hut, where Christmas was in full swing.

Deciding to walk instead, Emma and Evie linked arms, their wellington-clad feet sinking into the snow.

When they got to the hut, Emma saw that Sandro was busy, carrying plates and platters. She smiled at him, feeling suddenly shy; he only gave her a small nod before his attention was pulled away by Nico.

There were fairy lights and lanterns making an amber string of light around the tent, creating an almost enchanted feel in the darkening sun, as they took a seat next to old friends and neighbours: the Brimbles, the butcher Alfred Bright, and her old friends, Maggie, her husband Jase and Mikey, who was running around all the tables and giggling. There was Jenny with her new boyfriend, and Gretchen, next to her mum, her hair sleek, dark eyes alight. All the tables were filled with people, laughing and stuffing their mouths with Dot's glazed ham and Aggie's Yorkshire pudding, unbuttoning their trousers and sharing a cracker with a neighbour.

She saw Evie having a word with Sandro, but looked away when Maggie said, 'Share a cracker, cracker', and she pulled till there was a little bang and a small toy car fell into her lap.

Afterwards everyone had a slice of the Halloways' Christmas Cake. She heard Dot tell Ann Brimble, 'Rumour has it that even the Allens and the Leas took a piece this year, down at the hospital. Wonders never cease!'

Emma grinned, but didn't say anything. She was sure Dot would hear about what had happened soon enough. Mostly, despite enjoying her dinner and the company of old friends, she spent most of the afternoon wondering where Sandro was, cricking her neck any time someone came out of the Hut. Finally she turned to Evie, who she'd seen chatting with him earlier. 'Where's Sandro? I can't see him anywhere.'

Evie stared, her face blanching a little, as she looked at her. 'I thought you knew? Thought he'd told you…'

'Told me what?' said Emma, straightening, a small stab of fear unfurling in her chest.

'He said something about going home for a little while.'

She frowned. 'To the cottage… did he forget something?'

Evie blinked. 'No love, to *Spain*.'

Emma's eyes widened and her heart started to pound. 'What! When?'

'About a half-hour ago – he left Nico in charge. He's gone to the Whistling coach station – it's the only service running to the airport today. His decision to leave was a bit sudden,' Evie admitted.

'What! He can't leave – I mean, he never even said goodbye!'

Evie looked upset. 'Oh love, he was in terrible shape, he heard about everything you did for Jack. I think he wanted to be happy for you both, but you've got to understand… I mean, the way he feels about you—'

'The way *he* feels?'

'He's crazy about you – it's why he hardly ever comes around any more, why he wanted to move out.'

Emma shot up out of her seat. Her face was horror-struck. 'The stupid *arse*, he can't leave me now, not after what he's done!' she said throwing her napkin onto the table.

'What's he done?' asked Dot, looking from Aggie to Evie in shock, as Emma tore off towards the coach station, running at full tilt, the wind whipping her long red hair all around her face, her coat flying out behind her as she staggered through the thick snow.

'Well,' said Evie, a wide grin splitting her face. 'He's only gone and made her fall in love with him, hasn't he?'

'He never!' exclaimed Dot.

'Stranger things have happened,' said Evie.

'In Whistling? I doubt that.'

Emma ran and ran, skidding along patches of frosted heath and snow, her lungs on fire. She finally reached the Whistling coach station, just outside the village, and bent over, hands on her knees as she gasped for breath.

'Cancelled, love,' said a woman in a heavy tweed coat, a scarf looped around her face and a purple woollie hat on her dark hair. She nodded. 'Had family coming from London and everything for Christmas tea. Looks like it'll just be us now.' She sighed.

'Oh?' said Emma. 'Erm, sorry,' she added as a small shoot of hope made its way into her heart.

She whirled away, looking at all the disappointed faces, searching for Sandro's, but he wasn't there. 'H-have any of the coaches gone today?' she asked a tall man with a moustache who was walking past, his head down.

'Don't right know, love. Suspect not.'

She nodded. Bit her lip in thought, and then left the station. Dusk was beginning to settle, snow was falling ever faster and there was a bright glow over the moors. She realised, suddenly, just how cold she was. Her feet were frozen from their long dash across them. She walked slowly, back in the general direction of the Hut. And then she smelt it.

That scent again. The one that had once woken her up, made her toes curl in pleasure. It was like chocolate mixed with hazelnut and cinnamon.

Then suddenly, she whirled around, and she knew.

'It was you.'

She felt his hand touch her face, his fingers trail softly along her neck. When she opened her eyes, he was standing in front of her, his dark eyes staring into hers, that familiar dimple appearing in his cheek.

'What was me?'

'Everything, I think. What I've been feeling, how I've changed. It's like, since my accident, I've seen things differently, myself differently – and what I want too.'

He caressed her face. 'Which is?'

She swallowed. 'You.'

He kissed her then and she realised that it was love, real love that she felt and that Evie was right, it was still magic, even when you knew how it worked.

LETTER FROM LILY

Thank you so much for reading *Christmas at Hope Cottage*, I really hope you enjoyed it. In many ways the Halloways – particularly Dot, Aggie and Evie – are based on some of the wonderful, if a little eccentric, women in my own family. Growing up I semi-believed that my mother was capable of magic, and I think that belief inspired this story in many ways – the things we believe as children, then later question as adults. I had an aunt very much like Dot with her own 'secret library' in the pantry; getting a book from it was always a bit of an illicit treat, even if they always smelt a little like mothballs.

If you'd like to hear about my new releases, please join my newsletter at the link below:

www.bookouture.com/lily-graham

And if you liked the story, I'd so appreciate it if you could leave a review; it really helps to spread the word!

If you're wondering what's next – I'm busy working on my fifth novel set on an island in Spain, about a woman who inherits a villa only to discover the incredible story behind it during the years of the Inquisition. I think if you enjoyed *Summer at Seafall Cottage* (previously titled *The Cornish Escape*), you might enjoy this one as well.

Do get in touch on Facebook and Twitter, or pop on over to my website, where I'm often chatting about writing, announcing competitions and much more.

ACKNOWLEDGEMENTS

Thank you to my family for bearing with me during the writing of this book. I think each book presents its own challenges, but this was by far the biggest one to date, during a difficult period. The fact that it eventually became a book at all is thanks solely to the incredible team at Bookouture and their endless patience and support. Thanks especially to Natalie Butlin for putting up with me and all my doubts and fears, and for being so incredibly kind and supportive, when I was driving even myself mad (and probably her, though she was too kind to say), and to the gorgeous Lydia Vassar-Smith as ever for believing in me and my stories.

Thank you to the readers and bloggers who have been with me on this journey – you all make it the best job in the world; your tweets, comments and emails have meant the world to me. I couldn't do it without you.

Researching Emma's columns was really fascinating and my research is thanks to the book *English Food* by Jane Grigson, as well as documentaries by Clarissa Dickson Wright and articles from the BBC. While I've tried my best to be as accurate as possible, any mistakes are entirely my own, and with great apology.

Manufactured by Amazon.ca
Bolton, ON